THE
TURING
PROTOCOL

NICK CROYDON

THE TURING PROTOCOL

**SIMON &
SCHUSTER**

London · New York · Amsterdam/Antwerp · Sydney/Melbourne · Toronto · New Delhi

First published in Australia in 2025 by Affirm Press, a Simon & Schuster (Australia) Pty Limited company
First published in Great Britain by Simon & Schuster UK Ltd, 2025

1 3 5 7 9 10 8 6 4 2

Simon & Schuster UK Ltd, 1st Floor
222 Gray's Inn Road, London WC1X 8HB

Simon & Schuster Australia, Sydney
Simon & Schuster India, New Delhi

www.simonandschuster.co.uk
www.simonandschuster.com.au
www.simonandschuster.co.in

The authorised representative in the EEA is Simon & Schuster Netherlands BV, Herculesplein 96, 3584 AA Utrecht, Netherlands. info@simonandschuster.nl

A CIP catalogue record for this book is available from the British Library

Hardback ISBN: 978-1-3985-5215-9
eBook ISBN: 978-1-3985-5216-6
Audio ISBN: 978-1-3985-5217-3

Typeset in Garamond Premier Pro
Printed and Bound in the UK using 100% Renewable Electricity
at CPI Group (UK) Ltd

MIX
Paper | Supporting responsible forestry
FSC
www.fsc.org
FSC® C013604

For my wife, Esther,
who has followed me around the world and back again.
The sacrifice of leaving behind her family, friends and
country became even more prominent when I had to
write about them. Thank you for your love and
always being there for me.

PROLOGUE

London

March 1st, 2022

The bomb's massive explosion shook the ground, shattered electricity substations and destroyed apartment complexes and hospitals, killing hundreds of Kyiv civilians. The cries of women and children were punctuated by the sound of rapid gunfire as Ukrainian soldiers fought the Russians street by street, house by house, the fallen left dead in their own blood on the desolate streets.

Annabelle turned off her TV, unable to watch any more.

She sat in the kitchen of her father's apartment in Paddington, sipping a latte from Harrison's on Spring Street, her customary beverage, even if the rest of the day would be anything but customary. The war was intensifying by the hour.

How had life come to this?

She had no answer. But she did have access to power – to a singular, godlike technology, unknown to any other person alive – enabling her to alter this war, perhaps end it. But to use it was to break a solemn promise she had made to her father four years ago. The power was within Annabelle's reach at all times. But the use of it, even with good intentions, came with great risks and unforeseeable consequences.

It terrified Annabelle to possess this power and the secret of it, all alone, but to involve anyone else entailed monumental risk, both to her and her family, who'd guarded the secret since World War II.

She paced, thinking, weighing the dangers against her chances of using the device successfully.

Could it even be done?

It came down to belief. Belief in herself, belief in her own ability to use the power safely, responsibly, not just for her, not just for her family or even her country, but for all humankind.

PART 1

CHAPTER 1

London, Savoy Hotel

June 6th, 2018

Since she was twelve years old, Annabelle's father, David McIntosh, would take her for afternoon tea at the Savoy Hotel, where they enjoyed the mouth-watering delights of smoked salmon sandwiches, strawberry tarts, a pot of Earl Grey for her father and a hot chocolate for her. As she got older, these wonderful tea parties in the opulent lounge would give way to the American Bar, the hotel's Art Deco cocktail bar, where they would listen to the soulful tunes of the resident pianist while enjoying glasses of champagne.

She rarely wore a hat, but for her father and the location she made an extra effort. Her pink and yellow summer dress from Karen Millen was stylish but not overstated, perfect for the uncommon heat of the English summer. Entering the hotel lobby, she was hit by the cool air conditioning as she scanned the lounge for her father. He was obsessed with being on time for appointments and within seconds she saw him, wearing his 'posh cloths', as he called them: chinos, button-down Oxford shirt from Polo and a blazer. Despite being in his early seventies, David was handsome and would easily pass for someone ten years younger.

She walked steadily towards him, her high heels reverberating through the lobby as they connected with the marble floor. Her smile widened with her excitement. Every year was the same: the hotel, seeing him. She felt like a teenager all over again, basking in the company of someone who she loved.

But today she could tell there was something wrong.

He was nervous, preoccupied too. He barely touched his champagne following the toast. This was not like him. He was usually full of energy, eager to see and talk to his daughter. He started their conversation on safe and familiar ground. 'How are the boys?' he said. He knew how they were.

'They're fine,' she replied anyway. 'Alex is growing up so fast. Too fast. But Justin still likes me to cuddle him and kiss him like a little baby. It melts my heart every time.'

'And Edward? How's his law practice? Is he coping, being married to a government minister? It can't be easy for him.'

At the age of thirty-seven, she had been elected as Member of Parliament for Guildford in the 2015 general election and now, just three years later, had been invited to join Theresa May, the British prime minister, as a junior minister for health. Her husband, Edward, ran a successful law firm in London.

'He adores the boys, and the firm is doing well. For both of us, the pressure from work is sometimes overwhelming. I don't know what I'd do without him.'

'I'm so proud of you, Belle. It's not easy to juggle career and parenting, and you hardly had the best teacher in me.' David's guilt from being absent from his daughter's life could be seen in his eyes.

'Don't say that, Dad. You did your best, I know that, and anyway I haven't turned out so bad, have I?'

'No, Belle,' said David, staring at his untouched champagne.

He paused for a long moment. It worried her. Her father was not one to be at a loss for words. David looked at his daughter and there it was, a subtle change in his posture, his eyes alert, focused, back on mission.

'It's your fortieth birthday, Belle,' he said as if she might not know. 'I need to give you something very important. Something given to me by your grandma when I was a bit younger than you.'

'A present, from Grandma? From Scotland?' Annabelle said, perplexed. 'She's been gone so long. Why didn't she give it to me herself when she was alive? And why are you just giving it to me now? Why wait, Dad?'

'I'm not sure I would class this as a present,' he said. 'It's more of a ... legacy. This is something that goes back to World War II, and you have to believe me when I tell you this – what I'm going to give you, Belle ... it's important. And it needs to be protected at all costs.'

Annabelle, who was nervous now, stared at her father, his face so serious, and found herself unable to speak. She leant forward in her chair, holding her gaze, urging him to continue, confused and impatient.

'Okay. Tell me, Dad, where is this mysterious gift? Do you have it on you?'

'I think,' her father said, 'that maybe we should order a real drink first.'

CHAPTER 2

Princeton University

June 1938

Alan Turing received his PhD from Princeton University on the 21st of June 1938. His doctoral adviser was Alonzo Church, who had invited him for afternoon tea at Fine Hall, often the meeting point of Princeton's finest mathematicians. The decor was ancient: antique mahogany-lined walls and tables contrasted their golden browns with the lush green sofas and less comfortable chairs. Glass chandeliers shone a minimal light, adding to the reverence of the room and the masters of mathematics who frequented it. Alan knew it was considered an honour to be invited by the faculty as he took his seat. Even though he had worked with Church for a long time solving complex problems, he was nervous, and he thought he knew why.

'So, I hear you turned down my colleague von Neumann's offer of a job and to stay on at Princeton,' said Church.

'Yes, I'm afraid so. As tempting as the offer is, I feel I really must return to Cambridge,' replied Alan.

'That would be a pity, Alan,' said Church. 'You know that I admire your mind and we work well together, which is not always the case in a place like Princeton. Will you not reconsider? Have you considered the political landscape? It looks like Mr Hitler may have designs on the rest of Europe. Are you sure this is such a good time to be returning to the motherland?'

'I'm sure it is not,' Alan replied. 'But if there's going to be trouble, maybe I will be able to help in some way.'

'Surely you are not going to enlist.'

'No, nothing like that, but the government will need cryptographers, and the work that we've been doing here could be an enormous help.'

'You could perform that work here, in safety,' suggested Church, eager to retain Alan's brilliance and his friendship.

'Yes, I'm just not so sure that would be honourable, to let my countrymen suffer while I remain here. My mind is quite made up. In fact, I'm booked on the *Normandie* in July and will return to England.'

'I see,' said Church. 'All I can do then is to wish you safe travels. It has been my absolute pleasure working with you, and I hope we will see each other soon, in less troubling times.'

'Likewise, Alonzo. Thank you for your guidance and your friendship. I will never forget it.' The two men shook hands and wished each other well.

As Alan left the hall, other members of the faculty came to wish him well on his journey.

Alan felt excited to be going home but not without a little trepidation at leaving the university, its comfortable setting and brilliant minds.

~

Dr Alan Turing sailed from America in July 1938, returning to King's College at Cambridge University. Once settled into his rooms, he went for a walk around the college grounds. Alan sensed immediately that the normal peaceful courtyards and meeting places were gone. The heated discussions between students and colleagues about politics, economics and sport were replaced with concerns of war. Jewish students, even professors, kept to themselves, not wanting to attract the attention of the British Fascist party and its members, many of whom sat in the same lecture halls, sporting pins with the sign of the swastika, their elitist confidence on show.

Hitler and his Nazi party had risen to power in Germany. In March 1939, they invaded what remained of Czecho-Slovakia unopposed by European nations. They were determined to create a new super race, a third Reich. The German nation would control Europe, and the 'Untermensch' – the inferior, comprising Jews, Gypsies and impure bloods – would be wiped off the face of the earth.

The efforts of the prime minister, Neville Chamberlain, had bought some time but failed to prevent their plan, and on the 1st of September 1939, the German Army invaded Poland.

Three days later, on September 4th, the day after Britain declared war on Germany, Alan reported for duty at Bletchley Park, fifty miles north of London.

Bletchley was the home of the Government Code and Cypher School. Alan, being a mathematical genius, was attached to Hut 8, where he and the rest of the team were tasked with breaking the code used by the Germans in their Enigma machine.

Enigma looked like a typewriter. A series of wheels and light sockets lit up a character when a key was pressed. An 'A' might be translated into a 'Q'. But the code was changed every twenty-four hours at midnight, giving the team only a small window of time to glean meaningful information from the traffic intercepted by Communications. Without a fixed cypher, it was impossible to break the code.

At the start of the war, the team at Bletchley was pitifully small. Alan was joined by Gordon Welchman, who had studied mathematics at Cambridge, becoming Dean of Sussex College before the war. The pair were later joined by UK chess champion Hugh Alexander, an Irishman who, like his colleagues, had studied mathematics at Cambridge, obtaining a first class degree. At the outbreak of the war, Hugh, along with the rest of the British chess team, had been competing in Buenos Aires, Argentina. Abandoning the competition, they returned to London, where Hugh was recruited to Bletchley and ultimately appointed to Hut 8.

Alan and his meagre team used mathematical cyphers and algorithms to interpret the many messages that flooded in. Occasionally they had a lucky break, but nothing that could provide the key. He was convinced that no man was going to solve the problem of Enigma – there were just too many possible outcomes. He proceeded to build a machine consisting of hundreds of valves and rotors joined together by complex wiring that would test the millions of possible combinations from the encrypted signals being received. The task took months of failure and frustration. The machine was huge, seven feet tall and seven feet wide and two feet deep.

By 1940, the Battle of the Atlantic was raging. German U-boats were sinking 280,000 tons of shipping per month, killing thousands of young seamen. The human toll weighed heavy on the frustrated code breakers, and in particular Alan. With every loss, the pressure increased. The team gave Alan's machine a nickname, Victory, but as the days passed without any victories, he felt the name somewhat mocking.

Victory's rotors spun through the possible combinations in a monotony of cacophonous noise, only to be silenced by the bell that rang out signifying the retirement of that day's code and another failure. Alan's frustration turned into anger. He became critical, not only of himself but of his colleagues, lashing out at their stupidity and failures.

He needed help. The team was too small. He needed to recruit.

Much to the bemusement of his colleagues, Alan placed a crossword competition in *The Times*, asking anyone who solved it in less than ten minutes to ring a telephone number. To the team's amazement, this led to a small number of men and one woman attending a test, overseen by

Alan personally. Only one contestant passed his exacting exam: Joan Clarke.

She was a remarkable mathematician who had obtained a double first in mathematics at Cambridge, although this was in name only as Cambridge did not admit women to 'full' degrees until 1948. Joan had a quiet disposition and dressed plainly but had an extraordinary brain for solving analytical problems. Initially, she was placed in an administrative role with other women.

One week later, she joined her colleagues in Hut 8, although her papers referred to her as a clerk and she was paid accordingly. Joan was excited to be working alongside the most brilliant minds in the country, where she could make a difference, save lives. The prospect suddenly turned to fear and self-doubt – would she be good enough? Would she fit in? As she stared at the small wooden hut, her trepidation calmed. 'They're just mathematicians,' she told herself, 'no different to those at Cambridge, and they're men, no different to all the men you have encountered and bettered your whole life.'

Joan took a deep breath as she stepped into Hut 8 and the world of Alan Turing, unlike any other man she had encountered, anywhere.

CHAPTER 3

Bletchley

July 1940

Joan spent her first weeks at Bletchley trying to interpret German naval signals using different cyphers, anything that could give a location or a heading. She had been successful with only two transcripts, but nevertheless received praise from Alan and Hugh, made even sweeter when they told her that hers were the only successes of the day.

Taking a break, she stepped through the wooden door and lit a cigarette, breathing down the unfiltered tobacco smoke deep into her lungs, the rush coursing through her body as she took in her surroundings. She gazed at the beautiful grounds of Bletchley Park. The impressive Tudor-Baroque mansion sat on 58 acres of land and its lawns and flowerbeds were well attended. She took in the splendour of the beautiful roses and tulips, their bright yellow and red petals in sharp contrast to the bland wooden huts that housed the code breakers.

The smell of freshly cut grass hung in the damp still air as she lifted her head to the sky. Less than fifty miles away over London, RAF Spitfires and Hurricanes weaved through Luftwaffe bombers and their Messerschmitt escorts. The Battle of Britain had begun, and victory seemed an unlikely outcome. Joan, like everyone else, lived in a paradox, trying to get on with their lives calmly while in constant fear of the German bombs.

But this Friday evening Joan had been invited by the boys from Hut 8 to join them for a drink and dinner at their local pub, the Eight Belles. Joan went back inside to finish her work, before changing for her big night out. She had been at Bletchley for only a month, but working with Alan, Gordon and Hugh she had found acceptance, an appreciation for her mind, her opinions and her genius. Never had she experienced this freedom as a woman, to be held in esteem, to be valued as an equal. It was intoxicating. Alan had already changed her working hours to coincide with his, and as they worked more closely together, she found herself drawn to his brilliance despite his clumsy nature and famous bad temper.

The team were eager to leave for the night, but Alan, who was the Head of Hut 8, was still working in his office. Gordon looked at Hugh, who gave him a nod, and he stepped inside.

'Are you coming, Alan?' asked Gordon.

'Where – to the pub? I don't see anything to celebrate,' said Alan. 'Or are you simply drowning your sorrows, while our men perish because we're not good enough?'

Joan saw the anguish in Gordon's expression as he lowered his head to avoid eye contact with his stewing boss.

She went to his aid, placing her hand on Alan's arm.

'We all feel the pressure, Alan,' she said. 'We see the list of the dead from the admiralty. Don't think that we do not care – we do, terribly. Now you are their leader, you need to motivate them, so get your coat and cheer up.'

'I'm not sure that I know how, but I'll try,' said Alan, his anger and frustration dissipating as it always did in Joan's presence and with her delicate touch. Alan tidied his desk and picked up his coat and hat, running to catch up with Joan and the team.

The drinks and conversation flowed; air-raid sirens blared in the distance, but no one moved, such was the precarious nature of being alive in 1940. People got on with their lives, almost ambivalent towards the daily dangers they faced. Apart from a few locals, nearly everyone at the pub worked at Bletchley, which now boasted a staff of nearly 500 personnel and was growing every day.

The warm ale and Joan's gin and tonic helped in masking the blandness of their pie and veg dinner, the result of a nation starved by the German Wolf Pack submarines that hunted and sunk the supply ships, the very prey that the Bletchley team pursued across the Atlantic Ocean.

'Have you thought,' said Alan, trying to lighten the mood after his earlier outburst, 'that when we are successful in our work, the quality of our dinners may drastically improve?'

'Well, judging by what's on my plate, we should jolly well work harder or we may all starve to death,' Joan said.

'At least the beer is still good. I'll get another round,' said Hugh.

While he was at the bar, Hugh caught the eye of a rather striking brunette and invited her to join them at their table. Joan noticed the woman walk towards them: she was extremely pretty and had an athletic figure. *Only Hugh*, she thought. *Five minutes at the bar and he catches the most attractive woman in the joint.*

'Hello, I'm Esther,' the woman said as everyone made their introductions.

Esther worked in communications and started an animated discussion with the group about the German originator of the messages she had been assigned.

'I sometimes feel that we know each other,' she said. 'I'm certain he's a man. I can even tell when he's replaced, if he's sick or on leave.'

'How so?' Alan said.

'He always starts with a weather report, followed by instructions and coordinates. He wishes them good hunting and of course finishes with Heil Hitler,' said Esther.

'What do you mean, "of course Heil Hitler"?'

'Every report ends with Heil Hitler, sir.'

Joan stared at Hugh, Alan and Gordon. They looked as amazed as she felt.

'Excuse us,' Alan said, 'we have to go.'

Joan rose with the others, and they bolted for the door, knocking over glasses and chairs in their hurry, leaving a rather stunned Esther in their wake.

Back at Hut 8, the team discussed the revelation from their new friend.

'So,' said Alan, 'we now know, thanks to the lovely Esther, that every communication ends with Heil Hitler, which gives us six known unique characters, which we can substitute into the whole coded message – that's six out of twenty-six letters now understood. We've been trying to crack all the code, when all we needed was Heil bloody Hitler.'

Joan found two more letters from the alphabet that appeared with 99 per cent probability, increasing the known letters to eight, or 30 per cent of the alphabet. Joan and the rest of the team stood by as Alan and Hugh changed the settings on Victory and turned on the power.

Alan's machine whirled into its familiar pattern of noises and movements. Nothing. They waited. Alan stared nervously at Hugh, Gordon and Joan. Hugh shuffled his feet from side to side, puffing nervously on his pipe as Victory continued the calculations.

Clunk. The noise reverberated around the room, followed by another and another, and then the loudest silence they had ever heard as Victory became still.

Hugh scrambled for a pencil and paper. Joan picked up the latest report and read out the first set of letters, 'CKXT BHYHJ.'

Hugh wrote down the corresponding code letters. With the transcript finished, Hugh translated the German text.

From Naval Command
To U-36 commander

Proceed to area 1841 Atlantic.
Convoy spotted join Wolf Pack Zulu.
Good hunting
Heil Hitler

'Alan, you've bloody done it,' said Hugh.

Alan silently picked the paper from Hugh's hand and read the message.

'No, Hugh. We have bloody done it.'

The eyes of his three colleagues shone with pride. Alan chuckled and smiled with relief.

~

The Victory machine worked, allowing the team to accurately read and decipher messages sent from German High Command directly to the commanders in the field. The intelligence was codenamed Ultra.

More personnel were added to the team and set to work on the task. The group could now accurately interpret the orders being given to the German Navy, intercepting the U-boats where possible or directing Allied convoys away from the murderous Wolf Packs.

The Germans responded, increasing the numbers of active U-boats. But the success of Ultra reduced Allied losses to just 60,000 tons per month.

They could have reduced the losses even further, saving more lives, but such success would have tipped off the Germans that Enigma had been compromised.

Alan sat in his room holding a cypher that he had decided not to act on. He agonised every time he allowed an attack to go ahead, his justification being that the convoy was too close to the attacking U-boats, that a sudden deviation in their course would seem odd and could alert the German Navy that their intelligence was compromised. But who was he to decide?

He had no proof that the change in direction would be noticed to such a degree. How many would die tonight because of his decision?

He turned on the wireless, allowing the music of Mozart and Chopin to wash over his body, relaxing his mind and diverting his thoughts. But as sleep came, he knew the screams of the drowning sailors would visit him.

~

Alan entered Hut 8 the next morning, the black marks under his eyes clearly visible.

'Are you okay?' asked Joan.

'Just tired, and to be honest I'm struggling with the intel and some of the decisions I have to make. Last night, a convoy was attacked in the Atlantic and I let it happen, three ships went down with 256 souls. I could have saved them, Joan,' he said, his eyes pleading for forgiveness.

'Why didn't you?' she said, the abruptness of her reply adding to Alan's sorrow.

Alan was looking for sympathy and was taken aback by the question.

'Because we only got the intelligence when the Wolf Pack was within twenty miles of the convoy – it would have been noticed and the chances of escape were small. But I do wonder whether a small chance was better than none,' Alan said.

The additional explanation softened Joan's demeanour. 'There's your answer. You weighed up the probability of saving potential lives against the discovery by the Germans that we had broken their code and you came up short. You did the right thing, Alan, the painful and sad thing, but right all the same.'

'Thank you. I'm not sure their families would agree, Joan, but thank you for listening.'

The pain was still in his eyes as Joan examined the man standing in front of her. She considered the weight that he bore, making life and death decisions, continually driving the team for improved results, his bravery and vulnerability rarely on display, but seen by her. Alan was known for his awkwardness and snappy remarks but she was seeing another side, gentle, caring and sensitive. She found this side of him attractive and his brain exciting.

~

They were often seen taking walks together, having animated conversations, captivated by each other's company. Although the Hut 8 team would often go to the pub, it was now equally common for Joan and Alan to have dinner on their own, or to meet up on the weekend, when they could go and walk in the London parks. Their relationship grew stronger, but somehow remained relaxed. Unlike other couples, they were not worried about romance or what their friends would think. They had their work and they were both equally dedicated to it.

Alan realised that his admiration for Joan had grown beyond their professional relationship. He was immensely fond of her; she relaxed him unlike anyone from either sex had done before. He missed her when she was gone and looked forward to their time together, alone. Could this be love, he wondered.

During one of their long walks after work, Alan finally plucked up the courage to tell Joan exactly how he felt about her, and although it was completely unplanned, this culminated in an unexpected marriage proposal. He was so nervous that he forgot to give her the opportunity to reply.

'Look, Joan,' he said, 'before you answer me, I need to tell you something. About the way I am.'

Passing an empty park bench, Alan held both of Joan's hands and they sat. She gazed into his desperate eyes and squeezed his fingers, saying nothing but nodding as if to say, 'Go on.'

'You're the first woman that I've ever felt ... comfortable with, let alone happy with or ... able to love. I don't know how to be with a woman, even whether I'll be able to ...'

'Shhh,' whispered Joan. She stroked his cheek lightly with her fingers. 'I rather suspected as much, but as time has gone by, I thought, what difference does it make? We're so very happy together – surely this can be enough. Love is not absolutely defined, an equation with only one rule. So, yes. Yes.'

Alan kissed her cheek.

'There is one thing, though,' she said, 'and this will terrify you.'

'I know,' Alan interrupted, 'I'm going to have to meet your parents.'

'Quite so,' giggled Joan, but she shared Alan's nervousness in introducing her somewhat eccentric and introverted fiancé to her conservative traditional parents.

~

Joan and Alan returned to their hut holding hands. Alan stopped short, looking at Joan, his blue eyes shining as he smiled at his fiancée. Entering the hut, Alan separated from Joan and clapped his hands together. 'Sorry, everyone. Sorry to interrupt, but I – sorry – Joan and I would like to inform you that we're engaged,' he said, relieved not only with her answer but with it now being public knowledge.

'Congratulations,' said Hugh, the first to shake hands with Alan and embrace Joan. Gordon and the rest of the now enlarged team followed with their felicitations.

Spirits were high, but there were also a few conspiratorial looks between team members, who, working with Alan so closely, had made up their minds about his sexuality. Despite various thoughts about the announcement, though, no one was going to give up an excuse for a party. 'Let's go, chaps, off to the Eight Belles, and bring your wallet, Alan,' cried Hugh jubilantly.

The rest of the group fell into line, and they marched off to celebrate.

CHAPTER 4

London, Savoy Hotel

June 6th, 2018

The waiter brought two dirty martinis, one for David and one for Annabelle. She took a large gulp of the cool, smooth liquor, the acidic bite of the olive juice drying on her tongue. Her father was being unusually evasive and she was losing patience.

'What do you mean a present from Grandma that's not really a present? And it's dangerous? What the hell's going on?'

'This is going to be a lot to take in, Belle, and absolutely has to remain a secret,' her father replied quietly. 'Your grandma in Scotland is not my biological mother, as you know. In every other sense, she was my mother, and I loved her, as I know you did.' He took a long sip of his martini and paused to struggle with something internally. 'I'm not sure I should even tell you any of this.'

'You have to now. Explain yourself before I get even more angry than I am. You're talking in riddles – a present from the past, a legacy, danger. Can you just get on and explain yourself, Dad?' said Annabelle, exasperated.

'Okay, but please remain calm while I try and explain this, and let me finish before asking questions. I understand how you feel because I felt the same way when I found out. The difference for me was that the person telling the story was a total stranger. And she told me she was my real mother.'

'She said she was your mother? You're not making sense.' Annabelle finished off her martini and set the glass down, wanting another drink straightaway. She lifted a finger to the waiter and gestured for him to bring one more. 'Who was this woman? And why did you entertain her story?'

'Her married name was Joan Murray, but she became famous under her maiden name, Joan Clarke,' Annabelle's father said. 'She was a mathematical genius who helped win the war. She was a code breaker at Bletchley Park.'

'*That* Joan Clarke! The Enigma code, GCHQ and all that?'

Her father nodded.

'How did you meet?' she asked.

'She wrote to me and invited me here, to the Savoy, for tea,' explained David.

'And she told you that she was your mother?'

'Yes,' he replied.

'Did she have any proof? Did you believe her?'

'As you can imagine, I was completely shocked. I knew I was adopted, but they told me my birth mother had died having me, and then I was faced with this. All I wanted to do was run away and talk to Ma,' said David.

'What did you do?'

'Nothing. I sat drinking tea as she showed me letters, photographs of my childhood, which now was shown to be a lie. I felt betrayed, sick to my stomach. I was upset, Belle.'

'What did she tell you next – that Alan Turing was your father?' She laughed at how preposterous this all was.

The waiter placed a fresh martini in front of Annabelle and she took a sip.

'Unbelievable, really, unbelievable,' she said.

Her father's face took on a serious look as he stared at her.

'That's exactly what she told me. Your grandfather, my father, was Alan Turing.'

'That can't be true. Turing was gay. The bloody government chemically castrated the guy because he was a homosexual. How can he be your father, and how would you possibly believe Joan Clarke, if it was even the real Joan Clarke?'

'It was her.' Her father tapped the stem of his glass nervously, deep in thought. 'According to Joan, during their time at Bletchley Park, she and Turing got very close. There was a mutual respect for each other's intellect and dedication to their work. Turing proposed to Joan, and even though she knew of his sexuality, she accepted it, and was quite prepared to be his wife and live as a mathematical couple, problem-solving their way through life.'

'Is this why you took me to the museum at Bletchley Park when I was younger? I mean, it was interesting, Dad, but not exactly my chosen interest. If I remember correctly, didn't Turing break off their engagement? How could you possibly be their child? They were never married,' said Annabelle triumphantly.

'That's correct. In fact, according to Joan, it ended badly. Alan travelled to America at the end of 1942 to work with the US security services.'

'Doing what exactly?' asked Annabelle, trying to wrap her head around this enormous new story.

CHAPTER 5

London

October 1942

Alan was summoned to meet with Major General Stewart Menzies, the Chief of MI6, the Secret Intelligence Service. Although Alan reported to Commander Alastair Denniston, Bletchley was part of the Secret Intelligence Service, so Menzies had control. Alan had only met him once before, at the very start of the project. He was nervous and was sure nothing good was going to come from the meeting.

Alan entered St Ermin's Hotel, near the Secret Intelligence Service building at 54 Broadway. In the hotel's Caxton Bar, he found Menzies sitting in a high-backed green leather chair, warming his brandy glass between his hands, a half-smoked cigarette in the ashtray next to him. Alan was nervous in the company of such a powerful and dangerous man, and failed to make eye contact as he approached his chair.

'Drink? Or is it too early for you?' asked Menzies.

'I'll have whatever you're having,' Alan said. 'I'm assuming I might need it.'

'Quite so,' confirmed Menzies. He signalled the barman to refill his Hennessy and bring one for his guest. 'Look, Alan, the work that you and your team are doing is first-rate. Everyone is pleased, including Churchill.'

Churchill, Alan thought. That Churchill was pleased meant a great deal to Alan. He respected him, not just because he was prime minister but for the way he would not back down to the tyranny of Hitler, the ultimate bully. However, Alan sensed there was another reason for his being here, beyond mere congratulations.

'In fact, this request comes directly from Winston himself,' Menzies said. 'It seems that the Americans need some help with their cryptographers, and we thought you could go over to Washington as a liaison and see if you can lend a hand. But first you will travel to New York and work with Bell Laboratories on their encrypted telegraph scrambler, which is to operate between Washington and London, known as Project X. What do you say?'

America had joined the war after the Japanese Empire bombed their Pacific Fleet, based at Pearl Harbor near Honolulu, on the 7th of December 1941. More and more so-called Turing Machines were being built on both sides of the Atlantic, but American resources were vastly superior to those of Britain.

And there was a new scientific challenge, in America and Germany.

The race to build an atomic bomb.

'You want me to tell the Yanks what we're doing?' Alan said, puzzled.

'No. US intelligence is as leaky as a bombed dam. We want you to appear to help, give them some minor intel, solve a few problems, nothing important. There's a side mission we want you to undertake.'

Alan felt his face redden, hot with anger. Was he being recruited into MI6's dangerous games? If so, he wanted nothing to do with it. He wasn't built to spy on actual people, scientists and colleagues. He knew nothing about that world. Codes. Cyphers. Breaking them and creating them. That was his world. Not ... this.

The waiter arrived with their drinks.

'I'm a mathematician,' Turing said. 'I'll leave what you do best to you chaps.'

'This is a mathematical mission,' Menzies said. 'There is a group of US physicists working on what they call the Manhattan Project, code for building the atomic bomb. The team is led by Robert Oppenheimer.'

'I've heard of him. He was at Cambridge, but before my time,' said Alan.

Oppenheimer was a brilliant physicist and resident professor at the University of California at Berkeley. Now he was playing a more sinister game: the physics of separating uranium-235 from uranium-238. He understood the theory well; however, putting it into practice and building the bomb casing was proving immensely difficult.

'Apparently, they've encountered a few problems, and we thought that you could offer to help,' said Menzies. 'But at the same time, find out whether you think they can actually pull this thing off. If the Americans get the bomb, it will change not only the course of the war, but also the power balance of the world.'

'But they are our allies. Ending the war is what we all want,' stressed Alan.

'Agreed, but it would be most helpful if we know firstly that it can be done and secondly when. We have our own atomic program to think of, and this is why it is imperative that you accept this mission.'

'So let me summarise. You want me to go help the US security services without actually divulging anything of importance, and then worm my way into a top-secret group of scientists and discover whether they are wasting their time,' Alan scoffed.

'In a nutshell, old chap. You have this spy stuff down pat.' Menzies smiled. 'You leave on the 6th of November and will stay for four months. One of our agents from Washington will meet you in New York. He'll ensure that you don't get into too much trouble. I've booked tickets on the *Queen Elizabeth*, so you can tell your team to pay particular attention to your route – between your chaps and her 32 knots, you should be perfectly safe from the U-boats.'

'I don't suppose I have a choice in the matter?'

'Of course you do,' said Menzies with a smile. 'But we appreciate that you chose to volunteer, Alan. New York will be fun, no bombs, good food, you should be thanking me. Shall we have a toast? Bon voyage, perhaps?'

Alan and Menzies clinked glasses, and Alan downed his brandy, leaving the hotel with a feeling of dread. He walked off into the drizzling rain, the grey night turning blacker and blacker, reflecting his mood.

CHAPTER 6

New York

November 1942

Alan arrived in New York six days after leaving Southampton, unscathed except for a bout of seasickness and the tedium of listening to what passed as dinner conversation on board the ship. He was met by Charles Phillips, a British-born Canadian who worked out of the embassy in Washington.

Charles was young, well dressed and full of energy. Alan took an instant liking to him. But he knew, of course, that Charles worked for MI6, so he would be careful not to let him get too close.

Charles hailed a cab, and the two men were driven to the opulence that was the Waldorf Astoria hotel at 301 Park Avenue.

This was not Alan's first time to America or to New York, having studied at Princeton. But to be in such a vibrant city without the threat of bombs dropping from planes overhead was so relaxing – not exactly a word Alan would usually associate with central New York.

The streets were alive with people; lights were blazing on the streets and all around Times Square. Save for people in uniform, it would have been hard to tell that there was a war on at all.

Alan admired the grandeur of the lobby as they headed for the registration desk to check in. 'It's a lot to take in, Charles,' he said.

'You'll do swell,' Charles said. 'To get you started, I've arranged for you to meet someone on Monday as a surprise.'

'Who?' asked Alan.

'Monday! Use the weekend to get some rest, take a load off and enjoy yourself.'

Charles waved as Alan got the lift, accompanied by a bellboy, his luggage having already been transported to his room and unpacked.

When they got to his room, Alan tipped the boy, then collapsed onto his vast, comfortable bed and promptly fell asleep.

~

First thing Monday morning, Alan and Charles took breakfast at the hotel. Alan couldn't believe what was on offer. Clearly rationing didn't exist at the Waldorf. He ordered bacon, eggs, sausage and hash browns for himself, and pancakes covered in berries and delicious maple syrup for his companion.

'These are amazing,' said Charles through a mouthful. 'I think I should meet you here for breakfast every day. I'm going to put on five pounds just looking at this spread.'

When they were both finally full to bursting, they headed off on the short walk to Broadway for the surprise meeting.

The building was unremarkable, devoid of any sign of life. Alan knocked tentatively on the grey wooden door. Footsteps approached and the door opened inwards.

'Come in, come in. It's a pleasure to meet you, Mr Turing. I read your thesis at Princeton and could not miss this opportunity to meet you,' said the small, grey-haired gentleman who answered. Alan could hardly speak as he came face to face with the revered scientist, his idol since childhood.

'Please, call me Alan, and the honour is all mine, Mr Einstein,' said Alan.

'And this fine gentleman is Mr Oppenheimer.'

Oppenheimer was a tall man, gaunt in the face, who removed his pipe as everyone shook hands and took their seats at a round table in the corner of the small, nondescript office. Oppenheimer served coffee, eager to start the conversation.

Charles was excused, and the three boffins set to talking about their academic lives, their shared love of various universities on both sides of the pond and, of course, their mutual passion, physics. After several hours, the conversation turned to the project at hand.

'Where do you think you will encounter your biggest issues, the atom separation process or the casing design?' asked Alan.

'Both will be overcome,' said Oppenheimer confidently. 'We are putting together a sizeable team in New Mexico. You would be welcome, Alan, if you wanted to join us.'

'The work would be challenging, which is always a temptation for me,' said Alan, 'but I'm not sure I would want to create such destructive power and, even less, trust any government to control its use.'

'You and I agree,' said Einstein. 'As Mr Oppenheimer knows, and the State Department for that matter, I'm an active pacifist. And you raise a crucial dilemma.'

Oppenheimer interjected, defensively. 'I come at the issue from a different point of view. We must have this capability first. To fail could put the Germans, or even the Russians for that matter, in a position to threaten the United States. My job is to solve the problem. It is the job of government to determine its use.'

'You both raise interesting points,' said Alan. 'From my side, I like to think that the work that I do saves lives rather than destroys them. Imagine if that bomb were in the hands of Adolf Hitler now.'

'That's my point – that's why we need to have the capability first, to control the outcome,' said Oppenheimer.

'Assuming, of course, that we are the good guys,' said Alan.

'Well, there you have it,' said Einstein. 'Put three scientists in the same room and you will get three different opinions, the way it should be. It is time for me to leave you to your endeavours with my best wishes and this thought: "A person who never made a mistake never tried anything new." Good luck, gentlemen.'

Turing was sad to see his idol leave the group. Oppenheimer was clearly set on a course, whereas Einstein was willing to challenge those in power. He would never forget this meeting.

After Einstein left them, the two scientists continued their passionate discussion. At some point, it even took on a spiritual tone, leading the conversation through the philosophy of their work, to the morals of the intended outcome.

'Those of us who work for the government, designing weapons, building bombs, how do you think we'll be remembered, Alan?' enquired Oppenheimer. 'As scientists or murderers?'

'In times of war, it's not possible to be entirely innocent,' Alan said. 'Even though I know that death and mayhem are a direct result of my actions, I believe that I'm working towards a common good. If I can shorten the war, millions of lives might be saved on both sides. Surely that is a noble endeavour.'

'I could apply that logic to my project. If I am successful, it will shorten, if not finish the war. Thousands may die, but hundreds of thousands, even millions of people may live from the same outcome – would you consider that "noble", Alan?'

Alan nodded. 'However, once invented, it is impossible to uninvent it. When the atomic age is released from Pandora's box, warfare will never be the same again. You must know that the resources you are receiving are for a reason. Your government surely will use the weapon, not only, as you say, to shorten the war but to demonstrate to the world the power they possess. It will be inevitable that other countries will obtain nuclear capability, and proliferation will occur.'

'I understand, Alan, and agree with your conclusions, but I cannot stand by and let another power take the advantage. Even if, in the future, atomic weapons create a political stalemate where usage of the technology would result in mutual destruction, I find this to be a much better place than to be disadvantaged and threatened by communism or fascism. America must be the first country to embrace and control this power, and I will do everything I can to ensure that outcome,' said Oppenheimer, annoyed at having to justify his actions.

Thinking of his mission, Alan hoped he had not gone too far in upsetting Oppenheimer. He said, 'You have proved your point, Robert. We are at an intellectual stalemate over the subject, and perhaps that is a good place to be. I respect your opinion, and despite my misgivings I would like to stay on for a while and help you as far as I am able, if you will permit me.'

'Gladly,' said Oppenheimer.

The two academics spent the rest of the week wrestling with high maths, advanced physics and complex designs. More questions than answers were found, but progress was made and a lasting friendship between these like-minded gentlemen was kindled in chalk dust on a Manhattan blackboard.

CHAPTER 7

Bletchley

1943

By March 1943, the Germans had surrendered at Stalingrad and were in full retreat, while the British were finally having success against Rommel in Africa. The size of the campaigns and the intelligence that was gathered and distributed was on a gigantic scale.

But for Alan, life had become more mundane. After an extremely successful stint in the US, in both New York and Washington, he returned to Bletchley Park, his reputation greater than ever. There he found, though, that the intelligence teams could now be run by his staff, with little supervision required.

His time in the US had a profound effect on Alan. He was convinced that Oppenheimer would be successful with the bomb and that the world would change. Technology would make everything smaller, faster and more dangerous; countries would compete for their position in the world, and inevitably humanity would suffer. Information was key. Getting that information into the hands of the right people would save lives, maybe even prevent wars, and it would always be a race against time.

Receiving the messages, decrypting the messages and translating the messages could now be achieved in minutes. The problem was always time, or the lack of it. If a message could be sent back in time, the options available to the message reader would be limitless.

Imagine how many more lives could be saved during a war if we had more time, Alan thought. Building a machine that could send a message back in time would truly be a challenge, likely impossible, but if successful, the power would be unrivalled.

Alan knew that an electrical pulse travelled extremely fast, in fact at 90 per cent of the speed of light, or 270,000 kilometres per second. If he could somehow speed up a Morse code message and go beyond the speed of light, then theoretically a message could be sent back in time.

If he was to be successful, he would need the utmost secrecy. Such power would be dangerous, and highly sought after. To investigate this project, he'd need to build a new machine, away from prying eyes, and known only to himself.

Alan spent weeks drawing plans and running complex calculations, testing his theory. He thought he was close on paper, and now he wanted to start actual testing. It would take most of his savings to purchase the hardware, and he needed somewhere to build the machine.

His old school chum David Sanders was now a director of Harrods. David had told Alan about all the tunnels and storerooms underneath the famous store in Brompton Road. So he set off for Knightsbridge, deciding to pay him a visit.

~

When David greeted him at the office door, Alan was taken aback by the horrific scar tissue on his friend's hands and face, caused by the burns he'd sustained while bailing out of his Spitfire during the Battle of Britain in 1940.

'I'm sorry I didn't come to visit you earlier. Damn shoddy behaviour of me,' Alan said, looking his friend in the eye.

'The war has affected us all. I'm still alive, unlike so many of our schoolfriends,' replied David. 'I'm not going to ask what you are up to these days, I'm sure it's all very hush-hush with that brain of yours.'

'I'm here to take you to lunch, of course,' said Alan.

'And? I know you, my old friend, what else?'

Alan smiled. 'Okay, you got me. I remember that you once told me that underneath these streets there are secret tunnels and offices spread all over Knightsbridge.'

'It's no secret,' replied David. 'If there's an air raid, we often take customers down to the basement levels, as the Underground gets too crowded, especially for some of our more discerning clientele.'

'Would it be an imposition to show me around before lunch? I would be fascinated to see it,' said Alan.

'Not at all, dear boy, follow me,' said David, leading his friend through the glamorous store.

Alan and David walked down the sweeping staircase to the Banking Department. The decor was pure grandeur: marble flooring, Persian rugs and gold and green trappings. David showed his pass to the security guard – not that it was needed, as David was known and slightly feared by every member of staff. The two friends proceeded down less glamorous stairs to the basement levels.

'There are many entrances to the underground tunnels,' David said. 'Mostly we use them for storage and offices. We move product from the warehouse to the shop floor without the need to clutter the store with boxes, and of course the cash goes through here. You'd be amazed how much cash this place takes in a day, which is why we have our own bank. Do you still have an account with us?'

'Indeed, I do.'

'In that case, let's go through the bank entrance.'

Alan followed David. The tunnels were much wider than Alan had expected, well lit and surprisingly dry.

'So here we are under the bank. If we were to follow straight on, we'd pass underneath Brompton Road to the warehouse in Lancelot Place. To the right is Hans Crescent, and behind us Hans Place.'

Alan stared in amazement. There must have been one hundred men and women, moving carts around from one place to another.

'Come on, Alan, enough of the cloak and dagger. What's this all about?' asked David finally.

Alan knew that his friend was used to being obeyed, and that he had the intellect to spot a complete fabrication, so he chose his words carefully.

'I can't tell you what I do, or who I work for, but what I'm looking for is a room where I can store some equipment, enough space for a desk and a chair, and which will be secure. I know it's a lot to ask, and I'm afraid I can't really tell you much more, except that you'll be helping enormously. Of course, you can't tell anyone, not even your superiors.'

'Blimey, Alan, you don't ask for much,' he exclaimed. They continued to walk among the hustle and bustle while David pondered his friend's strange request. 'How often will you need to use it?' he asked.

'Initially, once or twice a week. But over time, less often. It'll become secure storage with occasional visits.'

'I may have the answer. We have safety deposit boxes. And attached to the room for the safety deposit boxes, which are already underground, is an entrance to our strongrooms, which are mostly used for the store, but we do have some rather interesting customers who need to store somewhat larger items, away from prying wives and the taxman. Anyway, we have some free that I think will suit your purpose. Let's look and complete the paperwork, all legit and above board.'

David took Alan down the stairs to the safety deposit room. The guard saw the two men approach in the large mirror attached to the door facing the stairs. He pressed the door release, and they entered the secure office.

'Hello, James,' David said. 'Just showing one of our customers around. He's in need of a strongroom, downstairs.'

'Very well, sir. Number seven is available,' said the uniformed James, handing David the key to the strongroom door. Further down they went until they were standing in front of a massive steel door. David opened the lock and switched on the light. The empty room was about ten feet by six feet and eight feet high and, most importantly, had electrical power.

It was perfect.

David and Alan returned to the secure office, where the guard produced the paperwork for the strongroom at a fee of £10 a year. The guard explained that there were guards on duty from 7am to 7pm except on Sundays, when they were closed.

Alan signed the paperwork, which included a password that had to be given to the guard each time Alan entered the safety deposit room.

The guard took the customer index card and wrote down the word, NAUTILUS, after Jules Verne's magical submarine.

Alan handed over the first year's rent. The two gentlemen left, going back up the stairs to the shop floor.

'Where do you want to go for lunch?' Alan said.

'Let's go upstairs to the staff restaurant. The director's private dining room has the finest cuisine in London, and the best part is it's only a shilling.'

The two men laughed and headed upstairs for their luxuriously economical lunch, Alan already considering how he would get his equipment into the room without alerting suspicion. Security was already a part of his life, but it was about to increase and reach another level.

CHAPTER 8

Bletchley

1943

Alan rubbed his temples but the headache remained. Secluded in his office, he was scribbling down ideas on how he could speed up the Morse process. Could the electrical pulse be broken down to smaller parts? Individual electrons? How could he break down the particles, break the speed of light and then reconstruct it all at the receiving end? Alan was stumped. Needing to clear his head, he went for a run.

As always, vigorous exercise restored him. There was something about the blood pumping through his veins that gave him clarity of thought. Oppenheimer had told him there were two methods to separate atoms from isotopes, the diffusion method and electromagnetism. He wondered whether electromagnets could be the answer. Alan had read about the early advances of magnetic accelerators by people like Ernest Lawrence and Stanley Livingston, who in 1934 had built a circular twenty-seven-inch cyclotron. This machine spun particles close to the speed of light, but they never exceeded it.

He wasn't going to find the answers in Bletchley. There was only one place that could help him: America.

On the pretext of improving the telephone scrambler technology,

Alan convinced Menzies that he could advance the distance over which messages could travel and at the same time reduce the size of the electronics required to support it. So once again, Alan went to New York to work at Bell Labs, where he had the space and all the current electronic technology at his disposal. He had White House credentials that allowed him to ship components to London, some destined for Churchill's war rooms and others that would end their journey in his strongroom.

Alan visited MIT in Massachusetts and UC Berkeley in California, seeking out the young and brilliant, picking the brains of the up-and-coming scientists and engineers. He gleaned snippets of an idea from one or a design improvement from another but at the same time protected the secrecy of the big idea, which was known only to him. He asked his White House liaison, Charles, whether it would be possible to visit Oppenheimer. The request was denied, the Americans saying that it was a crucial time for Oppenheimer and his project.

Alan split his time over the next few months, making improvements to the scrambler device, as he had promised Menzies, but at the same time solving problems and acquiring components for his own machine. As Christmas approached, he was nearly there; he even had a first concept of the machine design and engineering requirements. But it was too dangerous to build a prototype in the US. Taking advantage of the festive season, Alan shipped out the final components for his machine, which joined the thousands of parcels crossing the Atlantic.

He returned to London in January 1944 feeling extremely frustrated. How were the Germans holding on? The Russians were attacking from the north and the Americans had taken Italy. The Allies had unprecedented access to German intelligence; the war should have been won by now.

Back at Bletchley, he received a telegram from Menzies, this time ordering him to the office at Whitehall.

~

Alan showed his pass to the guard and was escorted by a soldier to an empty office. The decor was traditional: leather chairs, a large oak desk and a bookcase containing an array of books that looked as though they had never been read. The desktop was empty save for a telephone – no files, no papers, nothing to allude to the character of the man who occupied the office. Menzies entered from a side door.

'I read your report on the improvements to the scrambler system. Jolly good work,' Menzies said. 'I also see that the Americans denied you access to Oppenheimer, so he must be getting closer. Have you had any thoughts on their timetable? I take it that you continue to believe they will be successful in creating the device?'

'I do, but I still think it's impossible to come up with a meaningful timetable. Hopefully we'll be able to win the war before the use of such a weapon is needed.'

'In a way, that's why I have brought you here. What I'm about to tell you is top secret. You can't share this with any member of your team, on pain of death, understood?'

The seriousness of Menzies' tone unnerved Alan.

'Yes, sir, perfectly.'

'Good. As you know, the Russians are moving against the Germans from the north, and the Allies have secured Sicily and mainland Italy. The final push is going to come through France. An intensive naval bombardment with full air support will be followed by dropping paratroopers and US Rangers behind enemy lines. We're then going to land over one million troops on the French coast. It's going to be the largest amphibious invasion ever undertaken.'

Alan did not know what to say, and out slipped, 'Golly.'

'Golly indeed,' said Menzies with a laugh. 'Your part in all this is twofold,' he went on.

Alan knew not to ask any questions and remained silent.

'Firstly, you're to monitor enemy messages and report back any unusual movements of their forces. The second part is what we're calling Operation Fortitude. This is our own deception plan, designed to confuse German High Command about our intended landing zone.'

'May I ask roughly when this operation is likely to take place, sir?' asked Alan.

'Current planning is for May, but that may change. The exact timing will be kept secret to a very few. Now, the important factor for you is location. The aim of Fortitude is to convince Hitler that we're going to have a two-pronged attack, first landing in Norway, where their forces are weak, and secondly landing a sizeable Allied force at the Pas-de-Calais, forming a pincer movement.'

'Understood, sir, but ...'

Menzies held up a palm. 'I can't reveal the actual landing site, you just concentrate on Fortitude.'

With that, Alan was dismissed from the office, and he returned to Bletchley.

His mind was reeling with what he'd been told by Menzies. He was invigorated by such a bold plan, which he hoped would end the war. Knowing Fortitude would need his total attention, he had a small window of opportunity to concentrate on his new machine while the military put together their plans. He nicknamed his machine Nautilus, matching his Harrods password. It was time to put his own plans into action.

CHAPTER 9

Bletchley

February 1944

Alan couldn't build even part of his new machine at Bletchley, not without extreme scrutiny and suspicion from others. The problem with working with geniuses was that they were so damn clever.

Soon he was dividing his time between Bletchley and London, transporting equipment that was necessary to build and perfect Nautilus – and suffering countless failures, just as he had done with his earlier machine, Victory.

Finally, on the 31st of March 1944, he prepared to send his final test for the day. Suddenly a message appeared on the receiver. Alan plucked it up and checked the time stamp.

'Incredible,' he said out loud. It had been sent from two minutes in the future.

He looked at the message again, staring at the Morse code spelling out 'Test'. His heart was racing, and he could scarcely believe the consequences of what had just happened. It worked; Nautilus worked! He had broken the speed of light, disproven Einstein's theory. He wanted to shout, to dance or run down the street proclaiming his discovery, but none of this was possible. There would be no publication of his work, no accolades or Nobel prizes. Alan sat back down onto the small seat, evaluating the message one more time and confirming to himself and himself alone the magnitude of what he had just achieved.

The question now was how he could improve it, how he could make the time difference bigger.

As a precaution against any unwanted surveillance from the security services, he established a routine when visiting Nautilus. He would first visit the bank and withdraw £10, which he spent in various departments throughout the store, and finish with a visit to the tearooms. Here it would be easier to spot other single customers stopping for tea, potential agents sent to follow him. If all was clear, he would descend to the safety deposit room; if not, he would leave the store with his purchases.

One day, during a visit to Harrods, he recognised a man on the train from Bletchley. The man appeared again on the Underground and then followed him to the store. Alan diverted to the bank and watched from below as the tall man nervously searched around the store. Alan was convinced that it was him the man was looking for. He walked back up the stairs, keeping the tall figure in his sights. It was only when he saw the man reach the watch department and pull out a small paper package from his inside jacket pocket that he realised the man was simply having his pocket watch repaired and had no interest in him.

Despite the false alarm, Alan knew he would have to be careful, very careful indeed. His machine was getting more powerful by the day.

If he was discovered, he would lose Nautilus and probably be imprisoned. He could even be shot as a spy. The thought scared him as he realised that this was no longer a scientific project. The risks were huge; his life depended on secrecy.

CHAPTER 10

London, Savoy Hotel

June 6th, 2018

'So, what was Turing doing in America?' Annabelle repeated, still trying to follow all the threads of her father's story.

'Something to do with secure telephones. There's a suggestion he met up with Oppenheimer and Einstein, but he didn't work on the bomb – that was all Oppenheimer. He returned to England in 1943.'

'You were born in 1946, years after Joan and Turing broke up. Turing can't possibly have been your father.'

It was absurd that her father would believe this was possible. Her head swam as she tried to reconcile this wild story with the gentle, direct man she knew. Her instincts were scientific, always based on facts, and these were sadly lacking from this story. Was her father being targeted? Was she? Paranoia was creeping into the conversation.

'According to Joan, they remained incredibly fond of each other. She described it as a "special love". They continued to work together, spent time with each other, but then the preparations for D-Day took over everyone's lives.'

'That was 1944. What's it got to do with you and some ancient present from Joan Clarke, who I don't believe for one minute is my grandmother?

44

I can't help thinking you're putting me on, or – or something is wrong with you.'

David realised he was losing the conversation. His daughter's mind was analytical; she would need to see more evidence if he was going to convince her of the truth. He took a deep breath and drained his martini.

'I'm perfectly fine, Belle, but history is important, and D-Day changed everything,' said David. 'You'll see.'

CHAPTER 11

Operation Fortitude

February 1944

Alan and Menzies joined a meeting of the London Controlling Section – comprising high-ranking officers from the British Army, Royal Navy and Royal Air Force – alongside the teams in charge of Fortitude North, the fake invasion of Norway, and Fortitude South, the invasion of France from the Pas-de-Calais. Both Fortitude teams were responsible for convincing the enemy that their plans were real, with the aim of diverting as many forces as possible away from the actual invasion site, which was now revealed to be Normandy.

The plans were elaborate. A fake 4th Army, which was to be stationed in Edinburgh Castle, would cross to Norway and move south into Germany, while a fake 1st US Army Group would land at the Pas-de-Calais. It was crucial that the Germans believed in Fortitude. The more soldiers and Panzer tank divisions that moved north away from Normandy, the easier it would be for the real invasion forces.

In the north, the deception was concentrated on false radio messages, giving instructions to imaginary Allied divisions to move their bases to Scotland in preparation for the journey to Norway.

In the south, the ruse was even more elaborate, with the use of inflatable tanks, canvas aircraft and detailed reports of vast troop movements. Even General Patton, who was highly regarded by Hitler and the German High Command, officially resigned from his 3rd Army to take up command of the fake 1st Army Group.

As Fortitude went into full swing, Alan's role was to monitor traffic for any troop movements that might indicate that the Germans had taken the bait.

In his increasingly rare spare moments, Alan returned to Harrods to make improvements to Nautilus, adding power to the magnetic accelerator and improving the speed of the particle separation. He also finally solved the problem of how he would know when a message had been sent. He connected Nautilus to the Harrods telegraph wire so that when a message was received, he would be sent a telegram. The telegram was innocuous, just four letters, TEST, so as not to arouse any suspicions if intercepted by one of Menzies' agents.

At Bletchley, progress was also being made, with some encouraging results from the Fortitude campaign. Hitler had moved thirteen army divisions from France and Holland into Norway to strengthen his defences. Allied commandos raided the ports up and down the Norwegian coast, and RAF bombing raids were diverted to the fortifications around Calais, adding to the deception.

The second phase of Fortitude aimed to convince the Germans that any invasion would take place much later than May 1944 – the real invasion date decided on by Churchill and Roosevelt some six months earlier.

By early May, however, the lie had become truth, as General Eisenhower had to give up his planned invasion, delaying the D-Day operation until June 5th to amass a much larger force.

To keep the fictional timeframe moving, Fortitude engaged Australian actor ME Clifton James, who had a striking resemblance to Field Marshal Montgomery. James was dispatched on a tour of North Africa to inspect troops posing as the field marshal, with even Montgomery's closest officers duped by the ruse. This was a significant deception, as it would be unthinkable for Montgomery to be in Africa if an attack were imminent in Europe.

The Germans continued to reinforce Norway and the British stepped up their raiding parties, convincing the enemy that the invasion was likely to be in July or August, when the northern seas would be calmer.

Alan intercepted and decrypted Enigma messages confirming that additional German reinforcements were being sent to both Calais and Norwegian bases.

Fortitude was succeeding.

CHAPTER 12

Operation Overlord

June 1944

Eisenhower and the Allies had three separate but detailed plans for D-Day. They had plans for the Normandy beaches – their preferred campaign. They had plans for the Pas-de-Calais, which was the alternate landing zone should they encounter problems with Normandy. They even had plans for Norway, but this would be a delayed attack in July or August. Everyone had trained for each location; everyone was prepared. But the one thing they could never be fully prepared for – although always reliable in Britain – was bad weather.

The navy needed low wind and calm seas, the air force clear skies and a full moon, and the army a low tide to reveal the Atlantic Wall – beach obstacles that had been placed along the entire coastline from Norway to Spain.

D-Day was planned for June 5th.

On the 3rd of June, Eisenhower's meteorologist predicted bad weather for the upcoming week. But if they went past the 6th, they would need to postpone for a further two weeks to have favourable tides and moon, which would make secrecy almost impossible. The loading of thousands of men and their machinery had already begun.

On the morning of June 4th, the meteorologists said there would be a small window in the weather on the 6th of June, but it would be further up the coast and only for a few hours.

Eisenhower called a meeting attended by Churchill and Montgomery. Using the scrambler, they 'dialled' in Roosevelt to discuss the weather issues. Eisenhower wanted Calais or delay, Churchill pushed for Normandy now, and Roosevelt suggested they switch to Calais, arguing that they would still have the element of surprise, given the rapid transit time.

Ultimately, they agreed to initiate Operation Kingdom, the plan to invade Calais.

Eisenhower gave the order to recall any ships that were at sea and have them rerouted. The remaining troopships were ordered to leave Portsmouth and their anchorage behind the Isle of Wight and move up the coast, hugging the land in calmer seas, to Folkstone and Dover.

At 2100 hours on the 5th of June, the orders for Operation Kingdom were given to all Allied commanders up and down the country, who tore open their Kingdom envelopes.

At 2300, the British and American airborne troops took off and would be the first Allied soldiers to land in France, by parachute and glider.

Five hours later, at 0400 on the 6th of June 1944, the Allied fleet sailed across the English Channel for Calais, led by minesweepers and battleships that started their bombardment of the beach fortifications at 0500.

Alan was in early that day, a day that would change the shape of the war. Already on his second cup of coffee, he was tracking the traffic from France and plotting the progress of the fleet when he was joined by Hugh Alexander, who was also keen not to miss a moment of this historic day.

By 6am, Alan knew something was wrong. 'Hugh, have you seen this?'

'What is it, Alan?'

Alan placed his coffee cup on the chart table and handed over the sheet of paper that he had just finished reading.

'Communication from the invasion fleet. They're headed for Calais, not Normandy,' he said, his face showing concern and a little fear.

'Maybe it's a feint?' said Hugh.

Alan telephoned Menzies at MI6 but was told he was unavailable all day.

'I don't understand it, Hugh. If there was a change of plan, why were we not told?'

'Ours is not to reason why, dear boy. We're mere voyeurs of today's events. It's the time for men with guns.'

'Maybe so, but if they are heading for Calais, I fear guns will not be enough, and many of those men will not be coming home. We got lucky at Dunkirk. It's unlikely that we'll get that lucky again.'

Gordon, Joan and the rest of the team entered Hut 8, their chatter and excited laughter a sharp contrast to the silence of the room.

Joan sensed it immediately. 'What's wrong? What's happened?' she cried.

Everyone looked at Alan.

CHAPTER 13

Calais

June 6th, 1944

Calais was heavily fortified. It had seven large batteries with huge guns that could destroy oncoming landing craft, and MG 42 machine guns that could fire 1500 rounds per minute to wreak havoc and mayhem on approaching forces.

The German commander-in-chief was Field Marshal von Rundstedt. The local commander was Field Marshal Rommel, known as the Desert Fox for his exploits in Northern Africa. Rommel was a superb officer and highly regarded by both Hitler and the Allies.

Heading to his accommodation for the night on June 5th, Rommel queried his driver, 'Where is von Rundstedt?'

'Sir, in Rouen at the war games with half of our divisional commanders. I hope the invasion doesn't start tomorrow,' his driver joked.

'Relax, Hans. Look at the weather – no one is crossing the sea in this. The invasion won't be until July at the earliest,' said Rommel.

By 5am on the 6th of June, reports were coming into German command that Calais was being attacked by paratroopers landing all around the city.

The landing beaches started at Cap Gris-Nez, which had a heavily mined beach and a vast gun battery on top of the cliff. This battery was the prime target of Lord Lovat and his Special Service Brigade, whose job it was to disable and silence the battery's deadly power. Further landing beaches were north at Fort Lapin, Sangatte and Calais itself, all fortified with gun batteries and crack troops recently arrived from the Eastern Front.

The first landing craft delivered their human cargo, and wave after wave of infantry ran through the water and sand and a hailstorm of German machine-gun fire.

Despite heavy bombing, the gun batteries were all operational, as Lovat's men were embroiled in a massive firefight at Gris-Nez. Through pure grit and bravery, they finally took the guns, but at a huge cost, more than half of the brigade dead on the battlefield.

Rommel was in disbelief when he was woken in the early hours of June 6th. He repeated his demands to the caller on the phone from Calais HQ. 'You must keep them on the beaches at all costs!'

He ordered his two Calais-based armoured divisions to move in to support the coastal defences. In addition, his 21st Panzer Division, based in Normandy, was ordered to leave and give additional firepower to his forces in Calais. Rommel wasn't convinced that this would be enough and rang Hitler at his retreat, the Berghof in the Bavarian Alps, asking for the release of additional divisions held under the Führer's direct control. Unbelievably, the staff refused to wake the Führer and Rommel's requests were thwarted.

The beach defences at Calais were considerable, making it very difficult for the attackers to move in their heavy armour. The main attack was made up of soldiers with rifles, machine guns and hand grenades. The silencing of the guns at Cap Gris-Nez allowed the US 1st Army and 29th Infantry Division to move off the beach and become the second success of the campaign.

~

At Bletchley Park, Alan retrieved the early reports coming from the first wave of troops. He was nervous, expecting the worst as he quickly absorbed the detailed data from France. He re-read the report to be certain, a small smile forming as he looked up at the worried faces of his team.

'Hugh, take a look at these – the Yanks have taken the beach! Perhaps my pessimism was a little premature.'

'Great news,' said Hugh, finally letting out his held breath. 'Is there anything in there about Lovat's men? I have a cousin in his unit.'

'Certainly. You never said. What's his name?'

'Michael, Mike, he's been with the commandos for the last two years.'

Alan removed his cup from the table, eager to display the communications coming in.

'Place the map over here on the big table and get your chess set. As we interpret the reports, we'll put pieces on it as markers.'

Gordon and Joan helped Hugh place the pieces.

'The Allies will be white,' said Hugh. 'It's a common belief that, as white moves first, it has an advantage,' the chess champion explained.

'We'll take any help we can get,' said Alan.

~

The Americans teamed up with the remaining British commandos and headed off towards the town, only to be met by Rommel's 116th Panzer Division, consisting of 160 tanks and 15,000 battle-hardened German soldiers. The invaders did not stand a chance, and the Massacre of Cap Gris-Nez claimed the lives of 10,000 American and British soldiers, with a further 8000 injured or captured.

Rommel's Panzers secured the whole area around Gris-Nez, making any future attacks futile. Gun battles were raging on the streets of Calais with the brave but outnumbered paratroopers.

And then the final threat against the Allies came from the air.

Rommel had convinced his old friend from the North African campaign Major von Kutzner to fly two squadrons of Messerschmitt Bf 109s from their base outside Paris to strafe the beaches and approaches of Calais.

The effect was catastrophic, bloodied bodies littering the shallow waters. The men at the beachhead were caught in a pincer movement by the menacing, yellow-nosed German aircraft and the machine-gun fire from the cliffs above.

The sea turned red.

~

Alan pushed over the white king in surrender.

'I'm so sorry, Hugh. But don't give up hope for your cousin. Mike may have made it off or been captured.'

Hugh lit a cigarette and walked out of the hut, his head down, dejected, needing to be alone with his thoughts.

Joan went to Alan, holding his hand in hers. Looking into his eyes, she could see the pain.

'I'm so sorry, Alan,' she said, knowing her words fell on deaf ears.

~

Of the 150,000 men who went out in the first waves, only 28,000 made it back to the awaiting ships. A further 20,000 men were captured. The rest were killed or wounded, many of whom died on the beaches or in field hospitals due to lack of doctors, nurses and medical supplies. It was a devastating result for Allied High Command and a bitter and tragic loss of life. The biggest irony of all was that during these battles and bombardments, which had left the port town of Calais half-destroyed, there had been no rain, only light winds and even a sunset, the reddened sky a mirror of the beaches below. The weather was no different further down the coast, all the way to Normandy.

Rommel's men had the taste of victory in their mouths and a resolve that they had not felt since the early days of the war.

Finally, Rommel thought, *we can win.*

CHAPTER 14

London

June 8th, 1944

News of the size of the defeat in France shook the British nation. Despite brave and defiant words from Churchill, the people knew this was a major setback. He insisted that the RAF continue their bombing campaign against German cities and industrial locations, mindful that morale could change the very direction of an army and a war.

Alan went to see Menzies. 'What happened?' he demanded angrily.

Inside the Chief of MI6's office, a table was strewn with maps, reports and cold coffee cups. Menzies held a half-empty crystal decanter of single malt and poured glasses for both of them.

'I thought we were meant to be attacking at Normandy,' said Alan. 'What about Fortitude? We spent weeks convincing the Germans we were going to attack at Calais and then we did? Was this a double bluff?'

'It came down to a weather report,' replied Menzies.

'Weather?' asked Alan incredulously.

'Eisenhower was told that the seas at Normandy would be too rough and the landings too dangerous. The next available option for favourable conditions was going to be at least two weeks away. Obviously, this was far too long to keep everyone cooped up on the ships, and security would have been impossible. So, after a heated debate, they instigated Operation Kingdom, the attack on Calais, where the same meteorologist predicted calm seas and clearer skies.'

'Everyone signed off on it?'

'Everyone.'

'What were they thinking? Fortitude was successful. Rommel moved two Panzer divisions to Calais, thousands of troops. This is madness, sir.'

'I'm aware. It was a judgement call, the act of surprise, the overwhelming numbers, the conditions were good, we even took one of the beaches. But Rommel's Panzers were everywhere, hundreds of tanks, they came out of nowhere. It was a massacre, Alan.'

He took a gulp of whisky and sank into his chair, defeated. Alan had never seen him like this; it made him afraid.

'How many?'

'Too many. Only 20 per cent made it back.'

'A hundred and twenty thousand men gone. What's going to happen? What about all the men in reserve that as we speak should be loading onto ships to support the push for Berlin?'

'It's devastating. The top brass are meeting with Churchill right now, to confirm the losses and evaluate the chances of another attack this year, which seems unlikely. With most of our experienced paratroopers dead or captured, I don't like the odds.'

'And the conditions in Normandy?'

'That's the bloody rub of it. We would have made it.'

'The weather report. I don't believe it.' Alan turned to leave Menzies with his sorrow, but stopped. 'Sir, before I go, could I ask a favour?'

'Certainly.'

'It's Hugh – he has a cousin under Lovat, Mike Alexander. If you could find anything out, I'd appreciate it.'

'I'll do what I can. But Alan, not a word to anyone – no blame, just awful bad luck, understood?'

'Yes, sir,' muttered Alan, closing the door behind him.

~

If the mood of the nation could be judged by the looks on people's faces on the train to Bletchley, then the country was in a lot of trouble.

Alan arrived back at 5pm and went to look for Joan. Despite their break-up, they remained close friends with shared affection for each other. More importantly for both of them was their continued mutual respect for each other's work. The whole team, but especially Joan and Alan, had worked tirelessly to make Hut 8 the success that it was.

He found Joan concentrating over a map with a deep frown on her face.

'Have you heard, Alan? The losses have been announced. It's simply ghastly, so many men, so many families' lives ruined. Those poor boys!' she sobbed.

Alan embraced her, stroking the back of her head.

'I know, I know,' he said, trying to comfort her. He took her hand and led her outside for a walk on the grounds. The sun was still high in the sky, and on any other day this would have been a beautiful evening. But there was no beauty to be seen this day, just sorrow, which would soon turn to anger and then his masters would seek their revenge.

~

Two days later, Alan was invited to attend a top-level meeting at Eisenhower's HQ. All the chiefs were in attendance, army, navy, air force, US and British. Menzies spotted him and ushered him to sit by his side.

'They are trying to decide on our response to the debacle of D-Day. Just observe, Alan, and answer only questions directed to you.'

'Yes, sir,' replied Alan.

The discussion became heated. Air Chief Marshal Sir Arthur Harris oversaw Bomber Command, and he had a plan. He proposed that his men should carry out an intense week of carpet bombing from Calais to Normandy, starting at the beaches and moving thirty miles inland. The aim of the campaign would be to destroy the elusive Panzer divisions and weaken the beach defences.

'The Germans will see the raids for what they are, retaliation, and will be relieved that we have given some respite for their industrial cities,' said Harris. 'We would then launch a second attack at Normandy, using our vast reserves. The Germans will never expect a second invasion.'

'But what about the French civilians? There must be hundreds of thousands of people living in your strike zone. Your bombs will massacre them,' said Alan. Menzies kicked Alan under the table.

'Yes,' scowled Harris, annoyed at the question from a junior man. 'The cost of war is high, as we have just witnessed. I dare say the cost of victory will be higher.'

~

Alan returned to Bletchley unconvinced by the Harris plan, which seemed to him more murder than mayhem.

He was deep in thought as Joan entered his office.

'There you are, Joan. I need your opinion. What would you do if you could have prevented this disaster?' said Alan.

'What are you going on about? You can't change this. It has happened.'

'Hypothetically, say we had some intelligence that we could have placed at a high level, high enough to have changed events. But, in doing so, you knew that you were changing the course of history. Soldiers who died would be alive, getting married, having families. What would you do?'

Joan stopped and stared at him angrily.

'Did we have this intelligence, Alan?' she demanded.

'Of course not – how could we? I'm just asking, if you could change history, would you?'

'You talk such rot sometimes, but of course I would, anyone would. Now, can we please walk down to the pub? Our friends will be there drowning their sorrows.'

Alan followed her but continued his musing to himself. Was now the time to put Nautilus into action? The thought of changing history scared him and seemed so obviously wrong on every level. But by correcting an error – the plan, after all, had been to attack Normandy – he would simply be changing things to how they should have been.

They entered the pub, Alan still undecided over his next step.

~

The following day, Alan was yet again called to London to see Menzies. There, he was informed of the final plan to bomb the French coast for a week and then invade Normandy. Codenamed Operation Reciprocity, the invasion was planned for the 19th of June.

Alan was horrified by the idea. The generals and politicians needed to save face, but at what cost? Untold numbers of French civilians and countless more Allied soldiers. In despair, he left Menzies to his papers and walked off in the direction of Harrods. His decision had now been made – the prospect of further colossal loss of life brought absolute clarity to his mind.

Despite needing to act while he knew he still could, he followed his security protocols, visiting the bank for a cash withdrawal, followed by tea and savoury scones in the garden restaurant. Finishing his refreshments, he was convinced that the coast was clear and proceeded to the safety deposit room.

Once inside his strongroom, he thought carefully, scribbling down his message before destroying it, unhappy with his draft. He had to give as much information to his earlier self as possible to prevent the switch from Normandy to Calais on D-Day. But it had to be credible, it had to be convincing enough to make the largest egos in the world stay the course. He attempted the message again, explaining the weather change, Rommel's Panzers, the huge loss of life, not just from D-Day but from Operation Reciprocity. He had to justify to himself the dire need to avert this disaster.

An hour later, he was satisfied with the message. He looked at his machine and felt extremely nervous. Once he sent the message, there would be no going back. He was going to change the course of history. He placed the handwritten message back on the table, his head in his hands as he contemplated this monumental decision. He thought of Mike, Hugh's cousin, who was almost certainly dead – the consequences of this decision might save him and over 100,000 others just like him. But having that power frightened Alan. Should he do this? He went over the logic once more. It was more than D-Day. The French civilians who would certainly die from Harris's bombers were never meant to be killed; they were innocents, and he could, *should* save them. His resolve strengthened: he was doing a good thing, righting a wrong.

He reviewed the paper for the final time, pulled his chair closer to the table, placing his right hand on the Morse code sender, and started to tap out his message. His hand ached with the effort of the long communication.

It was done. Alan stared at the silenced Morse sender and let out a sigh.

It was history's turn to shoulder the responsibility. After turning out the light, Alan closed the door, at peace but silently hoping he would never have to return to this room in such circumstances.

CHAPTER 15

London, Savoy Hotel

June 6th, 2018

The waiter brought another round of drinks as David tried to explain the events that led to his conception and that of Nautilus.

'Okay, I get it, D-Day was the start of the end for the Germans, but why are you telling me all this?' Annabelle said, taking another sip from her drink.

'This is hard for me to explain, Belle, and will be even harder for you to believe. D-Day as we know it only happened because of Alan Turing. The Normandy plan was switched to Calais at the last moment due to bad weather and resulted in disaster. It would have changed the course of the war.'

'You've had too many martinis. D-Day was a historic success that changed the tide of the war in favour of the Allies,' stated Annabelle.

'Yes, Belle, but only after Alan sent himself a message, using his new machine, back in time, two weeks prior, and convinced Churchill to stick with Operation Overlord and the Normandy landings.'

'Are you mad? First you want me to believe that Turing was your father, and *now* that he built some sort of *Vernian time machine*. Why would you say such a thing?' said Annabelle.

'Funny that you should mention Verne – that's exactly what Turing did. In fact, he called the machine Nautilus. I know this all sounds crazy, Belle, I went through the same emotions, the same disbelief as you when I was told, but it's all true. You know that I don't lie to you. Just keep an open mind, that's all I ask.' He sounded exhausted with his own explanation.

Annabelle stared at her father. It was true: he was a lot of things, but he was no liar, and he had never lied to his daughter. Could he be telling the truth? It was too crazy, but why would he make it up? He would never do that to her.

Annabelle put her drink down on the glass table and looked into her father's eyes. She saw nothing false, no mask, no lie.

CHAPTER 16

Bletchley

May 27th, 1944

It was just over a week till D-Day. Alan was at work early, reading through transcripts and intelligence reports for signs of success from Fortitude. He was not disappointed. Rommel had ordered two Panzer divisions to the Pas-de-Calais; he had taken the bait.

At 9am, a military policeman arrived and knocked at the door.

'Telegram for you, sir,' said the soldier, handing over the flimsy brown envelope.

When the MP was out of sight, Alan open the telegram and saw the single word *TEST*. He tore up the message and grabbed his hat and coat and left for the train station. Throughout the journey to London, he was both nervous and excited at the same time. Thoughts ran through his mind: his last test of Nautilus had pushed the time gap to two weeks – had something catastrophic happened? More likely, he thought, it was just another maintenance test, perhaps from more than two weeks into the future.

Entering Harrods, he headed for the bank once again and followed his security measures. And gave himself the all clear.

He entered the room with some trepidation and retrieved his message.

Using his personal cypher, he decrypted the communication, dated the 11th of June 1944.

> *D-Day landing changed to Calais due to weather.*
> *Bad weather predicted for Normandy incorrect.*
> *Churchill convinced to change location by Eisenhower and Roosevelt.*
> *Wrong decision.*
> *Rommel has Panzer divisions available in Calais only 1 in Normandy.*
> *Massacre, 120,000 dead or captured.*
> *Must stick with Normandy or French Coast will be flattened as a reprisal.*

Alan couldn't believe what he was reading. How could they have changed the landing zones based on a weather report? This was a disaster, and he alone knew it. He had hoped that he would never be put in this situation, but the future outcome of the war was now his responsibility. He felt incredibly anxious and a little sick. Sensing a panic attack, he took six deep breaths to calm his body. He had to think, but not here.

He left the building and crossed Brompton Road to Hyde Park. The vast green expanse separated Knightsbridge from Mayfair and Bayswater and at this time of year was beautiful, with cherry trees in full blossom and flowerbeds still tended despite the war, providing a respite to Londoners from the misery of everyday life.

Alan took in his idyllic surroundings and thought about how much easier his life would be if he had not built Nautilus. The responsibility was tremendous, but the opportunity to right a wrong, to fix a mistake, ultimately to allow people to live who would otherwise have died: was this not the power possessed by gods?

Alan needed a plan.

He needed to see Churchill.

CHAPTER 17

Bletchley

May 28th, 1944

Alan doctored some reports suggesting that Hitler's reserve Panzer divisions were moving towards Calais and further north to protect the Belgian port of Antwerp. This would be a consistent response to the Fortitude plan.

He requested weather reports for Normandy, including long-range forecasts. The reports frustratingly took twenty-four hours to arrive from London but allowed Alan to start plotting all the variable elements – windspeed, sea state, tides, moon and cloud cover.

After two days of hard work and long nights, Alan created a formula showing that, even though the distance between Calais and Normandy was 200 miles, the landing conditions would be materially the same. In fact, his maps and graphs showed that the difference would be no more than 20 per cent, but that the fighting conditions, especially now with more Panzers arriving, would be considerably worse in Calais.

Now he was ready.

~

Churchill and his war cabinet operated from an underground complex staffed around the clock by officers of the Army, Navy and Air Force whose main task was to man the map room and produce an intelligence summary for the Prime Minister every morning.

Alan showed his pass to the entrance officer at the complex. Despite his high security clearance, he did not have direct access to the war rooms.

The officer of the day was an injured squadron leader from the RAF.

'What is your business, Mr Turing?' the officer snapped.

'I need to see Mr Churchill with critical intelligence.'

'Pass it through your regular channels or give it to me and I'll ensure that it gets looked at,' said the officer impatiently.

Alan tried to keep his anger under control. He could not go to Menzies with this. Menzies was a skilled spy, and he couldn't risk even the slightest chance of being questioned about his sources for the information.

Alan reached inside his briefcase and pulled out some papers covered in formulas and mathematical projections. He almost shoved the paper in the officer's face and said, 'Can you read this? Can you understand this? You sure as hell can't explain it, but I can. And believe me when I say the Prime Minister needs to see it.'

Alan took out a piece of paper and scribbled a note.

'Just give him this. I'll wait.'

The officer took the note.

'If he steps inside this building while I'm gone, shoot him!' the officer ordered a nearby MP, stamping his authority on the situation and saving his face in front of the enlisted man.

'Sir!' came the response.

The RAF officer went inside to find Churchill's secretary, Elizabeth Layton.

'Excuse me, miss, a Mr Turing is outside and he's most insistent that Mr Churchill receives this.' He handed over the unread note and waited for her return.

It was lunchtime, so Miss Layton knocked and entered Mr Churchill's private room, where he was dining, drinking his usual bottle of champagne and smoking his cigar.

'Excuse me, sir, but Mr Turing is waiting on the street, says it's most important that you see him, sir.' She handed him the note.

Churchill opened the note, which simply said:

OVERLORD CRITICAL

'Well, go get him!' he ordered through a puff of smoke. 'Get him off the street and bring him here.'

'Yes, sir,' she replied.

Miss Layton returned with Alan and once again knocked on the door.

As they entered, Churchill was pacing around the room, cigar in one hand and a glass of brandy in the other.

'Can I offer you a drink, Mr Turing?' Churchill enquired.

'No, no, thank you,' Alan replied, nervous not only about what he was about to say, but to be in the presence of such an imposing man, whose oratory skills and command of language could wound and maim as effectively as any rifle.

'Don't dillydally, then – what's so important that you're here interrupting my lunch?' Churchill said.

'I need to show you the recent reports from France. Fortitude is in full swing.' He opened his briefcase and started unrolling maps.

'Just speak, man, we can look at all this later,' Churchill commanded.

'Per the Fortitude plan, we've been passing information to our agents and allowing the Germans to intercept intelligence confirming that our pending attack will take place at Calais. In fact, this deception has been highly effective. I have in my possession evidence that Hitler has released three of his Panzer divisions to support Rommel at Calais and further north towards Antwerp, allowing them to deploy north or south.'

'Excellent news. Fortitude has been more successful than we could've expected, but I don't see why this is, as you put it, critical?'

'The weather,' said Alan.

'The weather? Now, Mr Turing, you have me at a loss.'

'Yes, sir, I've been studying the weather patterns from Calais to Normandy and obtained all the forecasts that the weather chaps are using for the D-Day crossings,' said Alan.

'I understand that the weather will be crucial to the actual day the invasion will begin and we've already suffered delays, but what in the devil's name brought you here?' Churchill asked.

'It's my belief, sir, that in the next few days, based on the forecasts from the meteorology department, they will inform HQ that the weather will be prohibitive to the Normandy landing zone, and that further they'll suggest that there will be a break in the weather further north, at Calais.' Turing paused. 'I will take that drink now, sir, if I may?'

Churchill poured a brandy. 'This is preposterous,' Churchill said. 'You mean to say that your charts and graphs and goodness knows what else you have in that briefcase of yours and no doubt turning around in your brain that you want me to believe that Eisenhower is going to ask me to change the invasion location after months of planning, with troops waiting on ships as we speak, Turing! He's going to suggest that we attack a fortified Calais because of some weatherman?'

'Correct, sir.'

'I'm not sure whether to have you arrested or looked at by a doctor,' Churchill said.

'All I'm asking is for you to keep these reports. If nothing happens, then burn them. But if I'm right, the documents will show that conditions in Normandy will be sufficient to keep to the plan. And the fighting conditions will be significantly better at Normandy. You must not be convinced otherwise, sir. We need to stick to the plan.'

'Mr Turing, this all seems to be an unnecessary fuss and quite frankly

I'm worried about your state of mind. However, I also have the utmost respect for your work, and I hope I can rely on you in time to come. Good day,' said Churchill, dismissing him.

~

Turing returned to Bletchley agonising over the meeting. Had he done enough? Did Churchill think him mad?

All he could do now was wait. In a few days, the armada of nearly 7000 ships would set sail for France. He could not be sure whether an attack on Normandy would be successful, but he knew in Calais lay certain death.

CHAPTER 18

London

June 4th, 1944

Churchill could not believe his ears. General Eisenhower had requested a meeting with himself and Montgomery to discuss the go order for D-Day. Roosevelt joined via the scrambler phone. Twenty minutes into the meeting, Eisenhower produced a report predicting bad weather at Normandy and the whole Channel for the 4th and 5th of June, but a small gap in the weather for the 6th. The only problem was the gap was further up the coast, towards Calais.

'How the devil did he know?' muttered Churchill.

'Excuse me, sir?' said Eisenhower.

'Nothing, nothing. Now, where did I put those damn reports? Miss Layton!' he shrieked. 'Get me those weather reports and tank movements from Bletchley, would you?'

She returned five minutes later clasping the reports, graphs and maps from Turing.

Eisenhower continued: 'If we wait for the right weather at Normandy, we will need to delay for a further two weeks at the minimum. This, I believe, would be impossible to handle, but there is a scenario where the invasion point could be changed.'

'To Calais, I suppose, element of surprise and all that,' said Churchill.

'Well, yes, sir, precisely, we should consider it.'

'Tosh!' he replied. 'Now, you've all seen the Ultra reports about the Panzer divisions moving towards Calais and Antwerp. These are Hitler's best troops, best commanders, and the Panzer tank is a formidable weapon in those hands, gentlemen. I'd also like to show you this analysis of all the weather fronts, and reports for the whole region. There's no need to go into all the detail, but the conclusion is that if your weather chaps are telling you that the conditions in Calais will be improving, then those same conditions are highly likely, in fact over 80 per cent likely, to be the same in Normandy. Now, what we can be certain of is the opposition forces on the ground will be entirely different,' concluded Churchill.

'Where did you get these reports, sir?' enquired Eisenhower.

'I've had the chaps at Bletchley complete a study on weather patterns just in case,' he lied.

'Just in case?' said Eisenhower, somewhat perplexed.

'Now then, gentlemen, let's return to the question at hand. When – not where. It appears to me that you are suggesting that we delay for a further day to give the Navy the best possible conditions for the crossing to Normandy. So, D-Day will be the 6th of June,' said Churchill.

'Yes, sir,' replied Eisenhower, still confused how his whole intention in the discussion seemed to have vanished in front of him.

'And how are preparations going, General?' asked Churchill.

'Very well, sir. The ships are already loaded with supplies, and we'll start the embarkation of the rest of the men tomorrow.'

'Excellent work, General, so let's review the attack plan one more time.'

CHAPTER 19

D-Day

June 6th, 1944

At 0500 hours on the 6th of June, the aircraft dropped their bombs and the naval destroyers unleashed their powerful guns against their military objectives onshore at Normandy. The German gun crews were thrown from their bunks, awakened by the bombardment causing terror and death.

The first communications came into Bletchley an hour later, confirming the Americans had landed at Normandy. The sense of relief Alan felt was visible to the team.

'Are you alright?' asked Hugh.

'Relieved that it has finally started. I think I'll pop outside for some fresh air,' Alan replied.

The Allies attacked across five landing zones.

Utah Beach and Omaha Beach were the furthest west. The American 4th Infantry, 82nd Airborne and 101st Airborne divisions targeted Utah, and the 1st and 29th Infantry targeted Omaha. The British and Canadians made up the forces attacking Gold, Juno and Sword beaches, in total an area of over seventy-five miles.

By 0630, the seas had calmed sufficiently for the Americans to land at Utah and Omaha.

The currents were strong and pushed their landing crafts one mile to the south. However, at this location the defences were relatively weak, and the combination of the 101st Airborne paratroopers attacking from inland and the thousands of troops being deposited from the grey metal US landing craft gave the attackers the advantage. The fighting was fierce, but the Germans were outgunned. By the end of the day, the Americans had landed 21,000 troops at a cost of only 197 infantry casualties.

Omaha was different. The US 1st and 'Fighting 29th' were tasked with securing the beachhead. The sea defences were intact and tank support soon arrived from Rommel's Panzers.

The battle raged on all day; men took cover wherever they could to avoid the onslaught of rapid German machine-gun fire. US casualties were high, and the men became tired and demoralised. The beach looked to be lost. Major General Omar Bradley decided to send in reinforcements to support the 29th. The beach commanders ordered the exhausted men forward, gaining ground one inch at a time. Darkness came, allowing the troops to move off the beach, and finally in the middle of the night they broke through and took the beachhead. The cost was great, with thousands of casualties.

The Canadians at Juno Beach encountered heavy resistance from the German 736th Grenadier Regiment and 21st Panzer Division. Their mission was to break through and capture the Carpiquet airfield and reach the Caen–Bayeux railway. Despite losing 340 men, sheer weight of numbers brought success, and by the end of the first day's fighting the Canadians had reached their D-Day objective, progressing further inland than any other of the attacking forces.

The British 50th Infantry Division at Gold and the 3rd at Sword under Lieutenant General Dempsey were both successful in achieving their objectives.

~

Alan had a handful of transcribed messages from the campaign, conveying the news to the team. 'Great news, everyone, it seems that all our work with Fortitude has paid off. All the beaches have been taken with fewer than expected losses.'

'What a relief,' said Hugh. 'And for the family too. I never told you, but I have a cousin attached to Lord Lovat's men.'

'Is that so?' said Alan. 'Well, by all accounts his brigade put on a good show, so I hope he got through.'

Alan was elated. According to his message from the future, 120,000 men would have died or been captured if they'd invaded at Calais. The death toll at Normandy was reported to be less than 5000. He had saved 115,000 soldiers – husbands, fathers and brothers, and at least one cousin.

Despite his joy, one thought clouded the moment. Now he fully understood the enormous power of Nautilus. His intentions with the machine were honourable – simply put, to save lives – but if Nautilus were captured and weaponised, it could hold the world to ransom.

He thought back to his meeting with Oppenheimer, who at this very moment was finalising the construction of his cataclysmic bomb. Alan did not envy him, to use his skills to kill. At least Nautilus in the right hands saved lives. He was pleased with his creation and in some way thought of it as an equation, the left balancing the right. Nautilus saving life where the atomic bomb would create death.

CHAPTER 20

Bletchley

June 21st, 1944

Alan was working with the team at Hut 8. The volume of communications had increased threefold since the invasion of Normandy, so when the motorcycle messenger arrived and handed over the envelope, he was most displeased with the demand from the Prime Minister.

Joan saw the look on his face. 'Bad news?'

'The Prime Minister has required that I see him on Thursday for lunch.'

'You're an odd fish, Alan,' said Joan. 'Lunch at Downing Street, with Winston Churchill, two weeks after D-Day – this is history! Perhaps he wants to congratulate you and the team, for all our hard work.'

Still annoyed about the imposition on his time, Alan did try to see it through Joan's eyes.

~

Alan arrived at Number 10 Downing Street precisely at midday and showed his pass to the duty policeman. After passing security, he was shown through the historic doorway.

'This way, sir,' said the butler. 'Lunch will be served in the drawing room. The Prime Minister will be in shortly and has asked that you make yourself comfortable. Can I get you a drink, sir?'

'No, thank you,' he replied. 'I'll wait.'

'Very well, sir.'

Alan walked around the room, admiring the paintings on the walls of past prime ministers. The room was not exactly elegant, but functional, befitting the state of the nation during wartime.

Churchill boomed into the room, whisky glass in one hand and cigar in the other. Alan's peaceful solitude was broken; his nervousness returned.

'Ah, Turing, there you are!'

The butler opened a bottle of champagne and poured two glasses.

'Sit, sit,' Churchill commanded. 'I want you to know, Mr Turing, that I and the war cabinet are extremely grateful for your work. I would ask that you pass on my most extreme thanks to your colleagues. It must be difficult to work without praise, wear no uniform and have no public recognition.'

'Thank you, sir, they will be thrilled to receive your kind message.'

The butler served lunch and Churchill urged Alan to tuck in.

'What baffles me,' Churchill said, and Turing felt his stomach knot, 'is how the devil you knew that I would be presented by the Supreme Allied Commander with exactly what you warned me of, a change of landing zone based on poor weather conditions. How did you know, Mr Turing?'

Alan had been expecting this question. He'd been certain this lunch was going to be an interrogation and had planned his answers on the train down to London.

'I didn't know, for certain, only that it would be possible. I'm a mathematician, and thus I work on probabilities. Having studied the past and present weather patterns, I calculated that there was a high probability that Group Captain Stagg, the chief meteorologist, would want to protect his team by suggesting a delay, or a change of location, or indeed both. Ever since the Spanish Armada, navies have encountered unexpected conditions in the Channel, and according to my assumptions, when Eisenhower was faced with such damning facts, it seemed entirely logical that he would at least want to discuss the option with you, sir.'

'I see,' mused Churchill. 'You would have me believe that you foresaw a meeting about arguably the most monumental decision of the war because you had a historical interest in the effects of weather conditions on navies and you created an equation determining human behaviour?'

'Exactly.'

'Extraordinary,' sighed Churchill. 'Of course, we'll never know the outcome had we attacked Calais, but I should say that based on the opposition that the Yanks faced at Omaha from one Panzer division, I'm certain that the casualties would have been significantly higher against three of them.'

Churchill continued to quiz Alan over the latest intelligence reports from Bletchley. Although the subject of his subterfuge did not come up again, Alan was not entirely sure that Churchill was convinced by his explanation.

With lunch finally over, both men said their pleasant goodbyes and Alan returned to Hut 8. But Churchill was not finished with the topic.

Passing his secretary, Churchill asked her to summon Menzies for a meeting at 10pm that night.

Menzies arrived on time but looked decidedly tired.

'I apologise for the hour, Mr Menzies, but I have need of your services,' said Churchill. He recounted to the spy his encounters with Alan, both before D-Day and earlier that afternoon.

'Quite extraordinary,' agreed Menzies. 'However, he does have the most unique brain I think I have ever come across and, like most academics, is prone to eccentric behaviour. Why do you doubt his explanation, Prime Minister?'

'I'm not sure, Menzies. There is a nagging doubt that I'm feeling. It's just such a coincidence. I mean, who, in the middle of all the work they were processing with Fortitude, decides to study weather patterns? Just keep an eye on him, would you?'

'Certainly, sir.'

Menzies' driver took him back to his office. He re-read the surveillance report on Alan. Apart from his expensive taste in shopping, nothing appeared to be out of the ordinary, but he made a note to conduct a search of his lodgings and increase his personal surveillance. If there was something untoward about Alan, he would get to the bottom of it.

CHAPTER 21

France

September 1944

In July, there had been rumours around Bletchley that Hitler had survived an assassination attempt by one of his most trusted officers. Following this, Hitler ordered his troops to fight to the death, and by September the Allied advance had severely slowed.

Yet again Alan and his team were engaged in supporting a new plan to end the war.

Montgomery devised a plan to parachute 35,000 airborne troops into Holland, from Eindhoven to Arnhem, with the aim of securing all the bridges to allow the British Guards Armoured Division to drive through, crossing the Rhine into Germany. Codenamed Operation Market Garden, it was a complete failure, wasting scarce resources and costing thousands of lives.

Alan contemplated using Nautilus a second time. He had the power, should he choose to wield it, to save 15,000 men – how could he not? He sought out Joan, desperate to talk to her and to share his burden.

'Did you see the losses from Holland?' he asked.

'Such a terrible waste of life,' she said softly. 'I wonder whether these generals actually know what they're doing. But what can we do? We give them all the intelligence to help them make the best decisions, and if they're wrong there is nothing you or I can do to change it.'

Alan was virtually bursting to say, *You are wrong, I can, I have!* But her words were true: battles were inevitable; some would be successful, such as D-Day, where casualties were relatively light, and others would be worse.

Despite the losses from Market Garden, progress was still being made.

And the thought of approaching Churchill or Menzies with yet another wonderful theory scared him to the core. Now was not the time to risk another visit to his creation.

~

As winter approached, it became clear that the war was going to continue into yet another year.

In December 1944, reports came into Bletchley that Hitler had convinced his High Command to launch a counterattack through the Ardennes Forest. Due to bad weather, Allied aircraft couldn't fly, giving the Germans significant successes. Heroic battles took place with huge losses in Bastogne and St Vith. Eventually, the weather improved and Allied air superiority destroyed the German advance; the defence of Germany began. Alan and his team received intelligence communications from all over the theatre of war.

When Allied bombers flattened the German cities of Dresden and Cologne, there was carnage on an epic scale. There was shock among the team, and Alan found himself in the uncomfortable position of defending the strategy, pointing to the horrors being discovered by the advancing troops as they came upon the concentration and death camps.

By April 1945, the Soviets had captured Berlin. Mussolini and his mistress were killed on the streets of Rome, and with no hope left, hiding in his bunker, Hitler took his own life.

THE TURING PROTOCOL

On the 7th of May, the Germans formally surrendered, and Victory in Europe or VE Day was announced the following day by Churchill, who proclaimed, 'This is your victory! It is the victory of the cause of freedom in every land.'

CHAPTER 22

London, Savoy Hotel

June 6th, 2018

David was trying to keep Annabelle calm.

'I felt the same way as you do when Joan Clarke told me what I'm telling you in this very same hotel.'

'You don't know how I feel,' Annabelle said, 'my father telling me such a crazy story.'

'Let's go back to your ancestry – let me explain how I came into being. If I can get you to understand and believe that, we can move on to somewhat more tricky subjects.'

'As long as you're picking up the tab, I'm all ears,' Annabelle said, trying to bring levity to a matter about which she didn't know how to feel.

Annabelle was fiercely independent and disliked being at a loss, especially with her father.

'I assume that you checked Joan's story with your "parents" in Scotland,' she said.

'Of course. There were a lot of tears from your grandma, apologies and excuses, mainly that she had given Joan her word never to reveal the truth. In the end, of course, it was me who felt bad, reassuring your grandmother that I would always consider her as my mother. But yes, she confirmed

Joan's course of events exactly as she'd told me, so as you can see there is no doubt, no doubt at all, that Joan and Alan are my biological parents, ergo your grandparents.'

'I don't understand any of this,' said Annabelle. 'And the other nonsense of time machines and messages travelling back in time – it's preposterous. I'm not saying I believe it, because I do not, but even if I believed such a thing were possible, how does anyone know about it now? Clearly it would have died when Alan died, if it ever existed. So why tell me now?'

'Alan Turing was a meticulous planner and admired all over the world for his talents, but he was also an intelligence officer, engaged by MI6. He feared for years that he was under surveillance from many, including the very department that employed him. So he made contingency plans, protecting his creation. But I assure you, it was real. It is real. Nautilus is very much alive,' said David.

CHAPTER 23

London, VE Day

May 8th, 1945

It was finally over.

The celebrations in London had begun. More than one million people descended onto the streets, dancing, kissing, laughing, an emotional outpouring after nearly six years of war.

The mood in Hut 8 was euphoric. Everyone danced, hugging each other, throwing top-secret communications into the air like confetti.

'Come on, you lot, let's drive down to London and join the party!' Hugh said.

'We still have work to do here,' Alan said, who was finding it difficult to transition to a time of peace after so long at war.

'Poppycock! It will still be here tomorrow,' Joan said. Grabbing his hand, she picked up his hat and stuffed it on his head sideways. 'You're coming with us whether you like it or not!'

Hugh drove the ecstatic band of cryptographers to Regent's Park. Alan sat in the back seat with Joan, gazing at the skies no longer filled with enemy aircraft. It was hard to understand that the war was over. Change would be coming, he thought, for better or for worse, but it was coming. So many revellers crowded the streets, arm in arm, trying to reach

Piccadilly. It grew impossible to drive, so Hugh abandoned the car and told the group they would have to go the rest of the way on foot.

They joined the crowds, waving their flags and singing songs from Vera Lynn. Alan hated such large crowds, finding them claustrophobic, and his head told him to return to Bletchley and the security of Hut 8. But the atmosphere was electric, and with Joan holding his hand he had the confidence to stay, to enjoy the moment.

The throng inched through the streets of SoHo and the theatre district until finally Joan, Alan and Hugh found themselves at the Statue of Eros at Piccadilly Circus. They were surrounded by men and women, many in uniform, dancing for joy. The cheeky American GIs took full advantage of the gaiety, stealing a kiss from any girl who would allow it.

Hugh secured a bottle of champagne and suggested that they make their way to Buckingham Palace.

'Churchill and the King are going to make an appearance! We can't miss this moment – it's over! Let's go!' Hugh cried.

Churchill addressed the nation by wireless, declaring the unconditional surrender of the German forces. He suggested a brief period of rejoicing should be allowed; however, he warned the populace there was still toil ahead. The treacherous Japanese and their cruelty demanded justice and retribution.

'You heard the Prime Minister,' said Hugh, 'a brief period of rejoicing, it's virtually an order. Let's go to the Savoy for dinner and rejoice!'

The Savoy was full of high-ranking officers and the British aristocracy, all impeccably dressed. The mood was somewhat more serene compared to the masses a mere one hundred yards from their dining tables. But even in these opulent surroundings, the excitement in the room was real and contagious.

Dinner was delicious and Hugh's generosity was unbounded. By the time Joan suggested a dance, everyone was merry: even Alan took little persuading to join the ladies and gentlemen gliding around the ballroom.

Hugh grabbed a young woman and led her to the dance floor, leaving Alan and Joan alone at the table. The Savoy was vibrating with excitement as the patrons danced too long, drank too much and revelled too hard.

There was still work to be done, but for one night they were free.

Joan looked across the table at Alan, the only person in the room who seemed to not be counting his blessings.

'You have done something remarkable,' said Joan.

Alan didn't respond. Instead, he picked up a knife from the table, inspecting it.

'You have saved countless lives. You should be proud. Look around you. The world is celebrating.'

Alan kept his eyes down, continuing to rub his thumb along the serrated edge.

'I've booked us a room,' Joan continued.

Alan's thumb suddenly caught the blade, and a little blood began trickling down onto the pristine white tablecloth. Joan grabbed a napkin and wrapped it tightly around his finger, forcing him to look at her.

'We can't be what society tells us to be. I accept that. But tonight, just for one night ...' Joan locked eyes with Alan, not letting him look away. 'Let me be with the one person I truly love. The only person who really understands me,' said Joan.

They held each other's gaze for what felt like an eternity. Alan nodded.

Seeing Hugh enchanted and distracted by his beautiful young dance partner, they made their escape and walked off to their room. Tonight, not even the Savoy staff would begrudge the unmarried couple their enjoyment.

Inside the room, Alan became nervous, not quite knowing what was expected of him.

Sensing his state of mind, Joan walked over to him and gently held his hands. 'Relax, we have all the time in the world.'

'And no pyjamas!' he replied.

Joan giggled, the effects of the champagne making her giddy and mischievous. 'Why don't we have a lovely hot bath?' She walked over to the bathroom and turned on the taps, sprinkling bath salts into the steamy water. She turned towards Alan and slowly unbuttoned her blouse.

Alan stood in the middle of the room, transfixed, watching Joan as she undressed in front of him, silhouetted by the lights, the steam enveloping her naked body.

She stepped into the hot bath and beckoned him to join her. Alan had slept with a woman before and found the whole experience unexciting, but his feelings for Joan were strong. There was love between them. He knew he had to try.

He folded his clothes neatly, placing them on an armchair. Embarrassed by his nakedness and at over six foot tall, he stepped clumsily into the bath, treading on her toes. Joan laughed as yet another 'sorry' ensued from Alan's mouth.

The heat of the water mingled with the sweet-smelling aroma from the lavender bath salts, calming Alan's mind.

Joan was in a playful spirit, washing her breasts with the soapy bubbles, her nipples responding to her touch. She took the foamy liquid and stroked Alan's legs. Edging closer and closer, she reached between his thighs and made Alan hard as they kissed, passionately. She slid up his legs and placed Alan inside her, letting out a small moan of pleasure, which surprisingly for Alan made him respond. He pulled himself closer, deeper inside her. They continued to make love, oblivious to the water splashing over the side of the bath, until they climaxed and fell into each other's arms. Their passion spent, the coupled relaxed, holding each other – two people in love, if only briefly.

Joan broke the silence. 'I'm getting cold, Alan, let's go to bed,' she said gently.

They dried themselves and slipped into their luxurious, fluffy dressing gowns. In contrast, the Egyptian cotton sheets were cold but soft. Joan put her head on Alan's chest and drifted into a peaceful sleep.

They woke late, their headaches a reminder of the celebrations of the previous night, their nakedness an embarrassment to Alan as he recalled their bathroom activity. Both dressed hurriedly.

'I think I'll go to visit my parents,' Joan said.

'Do you mind terribly if I don't?' Alan said, turning the memories of the previous night around in his head, confused by the conflict of what he felt for Joan and the physical consequences of continuing a romantic relationship. Last night had been enjoyable, much to his surprise. He knew that he could love Joan, but he also knew he would want to be with other men – how could that be fair? He would be living a lie, and he cared for her too much for that.

Joan kissed him tenderly on his cheek. 'Go – it's okay. I'm not going to demand that you make an honest woman of me,' she said. 'Anyway, as I recall, it was I who ravished you, not the other way round. So, fear not, go back to Bletchley. It's alright. I'm sure that's what you want to do.'

Alan knew that he should stay. It was cowardly to escape to the sanctity of Bletchley, but he wasn't ready to face this new reality. He crossed the room and hugged Joan, squeezing her tightly and returning her kiss.

'What was that for?' asked Joan.

'For last night, for right now, for being you. Thank you, Joan.'

Alan left the room, caught a taxi to the station and returned to Bletchley – and a new world, in so many ways.

CHAPTER 24

Bletchley

May 30th, 1945

The team had returned to Bletchley, but Alan started to think of his life ahead in peacetime. He knew exactly what he wanted to do. He could go back to Cambridge and take up where he left off before the war. But no, if war had taught him anything, it was to think bigger. He believed there was going to be a technological revolution that could impact society even more profoundly than the industrial revolution of the 1800s.

He wanted to build an *electronic brain* – or, more precisely, a computer.

He didn't have to wait long for an opportunity to pursue this. He was recruited as a Temporary Senior Scientific Officer at the National Physical Laboratory at Bushy Park, near Richmond in the south-west of London. Run by the UK government, the NPL was set up to standardise equipment for testing materials and to advance the fields of physics and technology. The director at the time was Sir Charles Darwin, the grandson of the famous theorist on evolution.

Alan went in search of Hugh and Joan, finding them tidying the offices and tables in Hut 8. 'There you are,' said Alan. 'I've come to say goodbye. As you've probably heard, I've been offered a position at the NPL. They're letting me build a new machine – it's thrilling. The computer age is here and we're going to be at the forefront, pioneers.'

Joan and Hugh listened politely. Joan held him and gave him a hug. The physical contact took her back to the Savoy, a happy thought, a special night that she knew was never going to be repeated as their relationship returned to one of professionalism and deep respect for each other as colleagues and friends.

They all promised to write to each other, but as Alan walked out of the door, Joan turned to face Hugh, both knowing that Alan had already moved on to the next project, the next phase of his life.

Alan took lodgings at 78 High Street, Hampton, close to the NPL offices, and started work on his new machine, called the Automatic Computing Engine or ACE. But in July, before he could completely devote his time to peaceful domestic matters, he was summoned by Menzies once again.

As Churchill had warned, even though the war in Europe was over, the Japanese continued to fight in the East. Their loyalty to the Emperor and their code of honour demanded that they fight to the death. There were tens of thousands of soldiers dotted across the island archipelagos of the Pacific, and they were dug in and heavily fortified.

The Americans had suffered substantial losses flushing them out. The Battle of Iwo Jima cost 26,000 casualties and Okinawa 50,000. An invasion of Japan would cost more. For the new president, Truman, this was unacceptable and he was looking for an alternative.

Emperor Hirohito realised that the war was over, but many of his generals wanted to fight on to the last man, under a rallying war cry to every Japanese citizen called the Glorious Death.

Following the successful testing of Oppenheimer's atomic bomb on July 16th in New Mexico, Truman had shared the data with his British allies.

Alan interpreted the test results for Menzies. 'If these numbers are correct, then the Americans possess the most destructive device ever imagined by man. Have they said whether they are actually prepared to use it, sir?'

'Yes, Alan. Truman has authorised its military use.'

The answer was horrifying, but ever since Alan met Oppenheimer he knew one day it would come to this, and now that day would soon arrive.

'They informed Churchill yesterday that they were no longer prepared to fight island to island, and if the Japanese refuse to surrender, the United States will deliver a message to their military high command that they will not be able to ignore.'

'I fear that when this message is delivered, we may hear it in Whitehall,' said Alan.

~

On the 6th of August 1945, the uranium bomb codenamed 'Little Boy' was loaded on to a B-29 bomber called the *Enola Gay*. After a six-hour flight, Colonel Paul Tibbets dropped his weapon from 31,000 feet above the Japanese city of Hiroshima. The bomb exploded 1500 feet above the city at 8.15 in the morning, destroying every building in a one-mile radius.

Alan read the headline: ATOMIC BOMB DROPPED ON JAPAN ... A 'RAIN OF RUIN'.

He immediately thought of Robert Oppenheimer and wondered whether he would be judged as a hero or a villain. When the numbers came in, 70,000 dead, he thought opinion might swing to the latter.

Three days later, the 'Fat Man' bomb was dropped on Nagasaki, killing 40,000 people and injuring a further 60,000, most of whom would die of their wounds. Six days after the destruction of Nagasaki, Emperor Hirohito ordered the surrender of Japan.

The war was over, but the world had changed forever.

The military use of atomic bombs had a profound effect on Alan. He knew that, through technology, weapons would get more powerful, faster and smaller. He was determined that Nautilus and its power should never be weaponised.

Nautilus's legacy should be to prevent the horrors of war, to save lives. He considered whether Nautilus could be used to prevent such an atrocity, but came up short. The Americans would never have changed their minds and the Japanese would never have surrendered solely from the threat of destruction. His only hope was that once the world experienced the power of atomic weapons, they would never be used again.

When the atomic bomb had been tested, Oppenheimer quoted from the ancient Hindu text of the *Bhagavad Gita*: 'Now I am become Death, the destroyer of worlds.'

Alan was determined to be Life, not Death.

CHAPTER 25

London

August 1945

As the atomic age dawned, nations began a race to catch the Americans and build a nuclear bomb. Stalin was paranoid about the power that the Americans now possessed, keeping his own scientists under strict surveillance, while his intelligence services captured talented German physicists to work in his programs, often against their will.

Joan and many from the Bletchley team stayed in intelligence and moved to North London and a new home, GCHQ or the Government Communications Headquarters. Alan took a consultancy role within the government that, critically, retained his top secret security clearance.

Menzies called upon him almost immediately.

He was to join four British scientists and six Americans and travel to Germany. Their cover was to improve German communications, but the real mission was to seek and recruit scientists who could aid the UK and US defence programs.

Joan settled into her work at GCHQ and was pleased to see many more women working in the large team of cryptographers. She made a particular friendship with a young lady called Sally Flowers, who, like Joan, had studied mathematics at Cambridge.

During a morning stroll one day, Joan suddenly grabbed Sally's arm for support and vomited onto the grass.

'Oh, my goodness, are you okay, Joan?' asked Sally. Worried, she started rubbing her friend's back.

'Fine,' replied Joan. The bout of nausea passed and she managed to stand up straight. 'I don't know what's wrong with me. It started last week. I feel fine, then suddenly quite ill, then I feel fine again.'

'I see,' said Sally. 'If you don't mind me asking, and this will sound quite odd, but have you noticed whether your breasts have grown or if your nipples are sore?'

Joan was visibly shocked by the question from the younger girl. 'I'm sure I don't know, but perhaps a little.'

'Do you have a husband, boyfriend?'

'Well, no,' she replied honestly. 'Are you suggesting that I might be pregnant?'

Sally nodded.

'Oh my,' was all Joan could say. The sudden possibility of being pregnant sent her mind spinning. What would happen to her career? How would she care for a baby? So many questions – she began to panic and feel dizzy.

Seeing that her friend was distraught, Sally held her hand and guided Joan to a nearby bench, shaded by a large oak tree, where they could both sit and talk in private.

'Everything will be alright – the war was a crazy time,' Sally said.

'It wasn't like that,' protested Joan. 'I suppose it was a bit, but he was a dear friend. We were even engaged to be married at one point.'

'I'm sure when you explain, he will do the right thing.'

'If only that could be true.' A small tear fell onto Joan's blouse as she looked up at her friend.

'He's not dead, is he?' said Sally, concerned that she had upset her friend even further.

'No, he's quite alive, but it's impossible, Sally, it will never work. We cannot be a couple.' She began to sob.

The following day, Joan saw her doctor, who confirmed what she feared.

Joan considered her options. An abortion was illegal and dangerous, and Joan didn't want to destroy the baby that was growing inside her.

But to have the baby would mean giving up the job that she loved and moving back with her parents, not to mention bringing dishonour to herself and to her family.

Perhaps I should speak to Alan, she thought. He would do the right thing, as Sally had put it, but then what would she do? Become a housewife, married to someone who was devoted to his research, who could not love her? She would die of boredom and most likely resent her child. There was no easy choice; she needed help.

During her time at Cambridge, she had befriended her mathematics professor, David McIntosh, and his wife, Claire, who also taught at the esteemed college but was never recognised as a professor. The mathematical couple saw in Joan her exceptional brilliance, but also a sadness and loneliness, so would invite her for luncheons, often ending in a long walk along the river debating her theories and challenges to established thought. They'd kept in touch since they left Cambridge, with the McIntoshes moving to Edinburgh.

Joan boarded the overnight sleeper train at St Pancras Station. Sleep was hard to come by due to the constant noise of the changing tracks and the raucous businessmen who had bribed the barman to keep the bar open to 2am. Finally, at 7am, the locomotive pulled into Edinburgh Station. It was bitterly cold. She had declined her friends' offer to pick her up from the station and, despite the cold, decided to walk to clear her head in anticipation of the conversations ahead.

Joan pulled her coat tight around her body, wrapping a woollen scarf around her neck to protect herself against the cold northerly wind that blew through the city as she walked in search of the university.

Soon she found herself among the beautiful gardens surrounding the ancient college. She gazed upwards to the imposing domed tower that now housed the law faculty, adjacent to which she would find the mathematics department. She darted inside as it started to rain and went in search of her old friends. David and Claire had received her telegram and were waiting for her inside the master's lodge. As she entered, David added another log to the fire, a burst of sparks illuminating the cosy room.

Claire spotted Joan and rushed to embrace her.

The two women hugged, Claire squeezing Joan's shoulders almost too tightly.

'My dear girl, what a sight for sore eyes.' Claire held Joan at arm's length, inspecting her old friend. 'Let me look at you.'

'That's enough, Claire, let the poor lassie catch her breath,' David said in his broad Scottish accent.

'Don't mind him, Joan, he's just a brute of a man. Since leaving Cambridge, he's regressed back into a savage highlander.' Claire reached up to her husband and kissed him firmly on his lips.

Joan felt so relieved to be with her friends. She knew they would not judge her; here she was safe. She reached for Claire's hand and the two women marched off towards their lodgings, talking and laughing, while David picked up Joan's suitcase and followed.

The couple lived in a three-bedroom townhouse belonging to the university. Claire showed Joan to her room and helped her unpack. David kicked open the door, a bottle of Laphroaig whisky in one hand and three glasses in the other.

'Shall we start with a welcome toast?' asked David.

'I don't think I should,' Joan said.

Claire looked concerned. 'Is there anything the matter, lass?'

Joan burst into tears and was immediately comforted by her friend. After a few minutes, she was able to compose herself, helped by a small nip of David's whisky. Sitting on the bed, she recounted her more recent life, culminating in her current predicament.

'I don't know what to do. I'm so confused. Should I have the baby? Keep it, not keep it, I just don't know! I thought maybe I could stay with you for a while. And you could help me decide.'

Claire and David looked at each other in silence. David took one of Joan's small hands in his and Claire took the other.

'You can stay here with us, Joan, everything's going to be just fine. We'll see how you feel when the bonnie wee thing arrives,' said Claire.

'There's no need to make any more plans than that,' said David.

Claire looked into her husband's eyes lovingly.

With everything settled, Joan finally managed a smile.

'I'll leave you two to chat while I prepare brunch,' said David.

'Thank you, thank you, both. You're so kind,' said Joan, smiling warmly as he left the room.

'Right. Now that we're alone, let's talk about the father,' said Claire.

CHAPTER 26

London

October 1945

Alan opened the door to his house, weary from his trip to Germany. Picking up his mail, he was excited to see a letter from Joan, immediately recognising her handwriting. He tore open the envelope. She wrote that she was exhausted and had taken a leave of absence from GCHQ, and that she was going to Scotland to stay with friends and recoup.

Concerned but preoccupied with more pressing matters, Alan had to discard the letter and write up his report for Menzies.

Over the next few months, Alan worked tirelessly, creating his dossier on the concept of his machine for the Director of the NPL.

His plan promised that the machine would be able to solve mathematical problems using stored formulas. Problems that would take thousands of humans many months to compute by hand would be solved in minutes.

Funding for the pilot machine was approved, and Alan's embryonic idea came to life.

~

Five hundred miles away, another baby was born, a healthy boy whom Joan immediately named David after her dear Scottish friend.

Joan and baby David continued to live with her friends. Everyone helped, and in their own ways they all fell in love with the boy. Despite her feelings for the baby, Claire secretly wished that Joan would enjoy motherhood so much that she would pick up her life and find a way to move back to London and start afresh with Alan, as a family.

Then, when David was four months old and the two women were taking their daily walk through the park, Joan addressed her friend anxiously. 'Claire, we need to talk,' she said. 'About the future. I love baby David, with all my heart. But moving to London and coercing Alan into marriage and a family – it's impossible. It will never work.'

Claire was stunned. 'You don't need to decide now. You are welcome to stay with us as long as you like.'

'You're so lovely, and thank you, but I have put a lot of thought into this. I need to choose what's best for the baby. You're going to think I'm being terribly cruel, but I honestly believe that he's better off if he stays here with you. Could you do that, Claire? Would you and David raise him?'

'I'm not sure what to say, Joan, it's a huge decision. Are you sure this is what you want? I can't imagine the pain you must be feeling even to suggest such a thing. I think we should go home, have a cup of tea and discuss it with my husband.'

David Senior listened to Joan's request.

'We all love baby David, but you are his mother, Joan. And I still think you should tell Alan. Will you not think about it, explore all the options before you consider such a drastic plan?'

Over the following weeks, the three adults discussed the options over and over, until ultimately the two women reached agreement and David's objections were overcome. The formalities were completed, the Edinburgh authorities never doubting the local professor's story that the baby was the child of a cousin who had died in labour. Baby David was adopted and formally named David Alan McIntosh.

Leaving the baby at home with his new father, Claire took Joan to the railway station.

'I will never forget this,' Joan said.

'We will write every week and keep you informed of baby David's progress. You have nothing to worry about.'

'Thank you. But not for a while, please. I need to adjust to being on my own. Write in a few weeks.'

Joan boarded the train, holding on to Claire's hands as they said goodbye. The train let out a shriek from its whistle, steam appearing from under the carriage.

'Thank you, Claire. I love you both,' said Joan, tears mixing with the sooty smoke from the engine. The train gave a final hiss and moved slowly from the platform, transporting Joan back to her life in London. As the train picked up speed, Joan's heart was telling her to scream, pull the emergency break and run back to her baby. But her head guided her to her seat, where she would spend the rest of the journey in sorrow and grief as she came to terms with her decision.

Heartbroken but resolved, Joan started to rebuild her life without her baby or his father. However, she was to see Alan again, and much sooner than she could have imagined.

CHAPTER 27

London

June 1946

In the summer of 1946, the British government awarded them both a medal: an OBE for Alan and an MBE for Joan. When Joan was notified of the awards, she invited Alan to have dinner with her after the ceremony. She had decided it was time to tell Alan about their child. She knew it was going to be a tough conversation, but nevertheless one that had to occur.

The ceremony was held at Buckingham Palace, where they received their awards for wartime services from King George VI. After the ceremony, as planned, they went for dinner at the Savoy. Alan was clearly upset.

Joan could only think that with what she was about to tell him, his mood was unlikely to improve.

'What's the matter, Alan? You look like someone who has just been punished, not awarded a medal by the King,' she said.

'I am peeved. We're both still subject to the *Official Secrets Act* and continue to report to the head of MI6,' he said grumpily.

'What is your point, Alan?'

'It's okay for you working at GCHQ – everyone is covered by the act. I, on the other hand, work with engineers and mathematicians. It's bad enough that I can't tell them how I know certain things will succeed, because of our work at Bletchley, but now I've got this damn medal. They're asking, "Why? Why you? What did you do in the war, Alan?" Honestly, you'd think Menzies would have seen this coming.'

'As I see it, the answer is really rather simple. You are known to be a bit of a loner, grumpy and often, well, damn right rude. So just be yourself and the engineers will leave you alone!'

Joan poured them both a glass of champagne, and Alan gave her a cheeky smile.

'I'd better be careful after what happened last time we got drunk at the Savoy.' His mood was softening, as it always did when he was in Joan's company.

'Talking of that, there's something I need to tell you.' Joan set her champagne flute down. 'That night, which was simply lovely, by the way, well, afterwards – there is no easy way to say this. I became pregnant.'

Alan was silent, staring at the bubbles in his glass. He twisted the glass around and around, using his thumb and forefinger. Joan knew the look: it was always the same when he dealt with a problem he couldn't quite understand.

'What happened?' he finally said. 'Where's the baby? Did it ... live?'

Joan explained her trip to Scotland and the arrangements made.

'I named him David.'

'How dare you, Joan!' he raged. 'You had no right to make these decisions alone. We could have married, you could've lived with me, and raised him, our son, together! We still can!'

Joan placed her hand on his, but he withdrew it quickly, knocking over his glass. Joan mopped up the liquid with her napkin. 'Leave it!' he barked.

Joan folded the napkin, placing it in front of her, and regained her composure. Sitting up straight, she spoke directly to Alan, holding his gaze.

'I knew what your reaction would be, but it would be a miserable life, for all of us. You are just not built like other people, to be a father, a husband. It's for the best, trust me.'

Alan stood up from the table, placing the empty glass next to the champagne bottle. 'Stay away from me.'

He stormed out of the dining room and onto the street.

~

Alan returned to the NPL and threw himself into his work on his electronic brain. The work soothed him, gave him time to think. He thought about his work, the long hours, working at weekends, and wondered if he had been too harsh with Joan. Would there have been room for a baby? Would he have been prepared to sacrifice his work for the role of a father?

He decided to respect Joan's wishes, but still – he had a son, an heir, living in Scotland. He wanted to know about the child and hoped they might know each other.

Progress on Alan's ACE computer was slow, and competition was increasing. A gifted mathematician and early supporter of his called Max Newman was working on a similar machine at Manchester University, and the pressure on Alan to complete the designs for his new creation intensified. The Director of the NPL wanted to be first, constantly pushing Alan for progress.

For months Alan slogged away at his designs, changing and improving the outcome. When he was finally finished, though, the Director ruthlessly decided that Alan's presence was no longer required, suggesting he should resume his fellowship and return to Cambridge. Alan was hurt by the suggestion and mystified that he was not going to be retained to help with the final construction of his machine.

Reluctantly, in late 1947, he moved back to King's College and made new friends among the faculty, determined not to feel bitter and twisted by the Director's actions. The freedom of college life gave him lots of spare time to work on his theories and to visit Nautilus, enhancing its power and adding security features.

One day, he was visited at Cambridge by Max Newman, who offered him a position within his team at Manchester University and access to building a new machine, not just designing one. Alan was unsure. He was having a good time at Cambridge, but the challenge and freedom to build a new computer was tantalising. Accepting Max's offer, he left Cambridge and took great pleasure in informing the Director of the NPL of his new position with the competition.

Alan settled into his work at Manchester with enthusiasm, even though progress at times was incredibly slow. His partnership with Max grew rapidly, Alan having always had genuine respect for Max's intellect. Alan's ideas made an instant impact on the team and its progress, growing his status from week to week, which pleased him enormously. He wasn't exactly a social butterfly, but peer respect and accolades were important to Alan, even if he didn't want to admit it to himself.

His move north, however, was not without its dangers.

CHAPTER 28

Manchester

1950

Tired of landladies and suitcases, Alan purchased a house in Wilmslow, Cheshire, twelve miles outside of Manchester. The house was big, enabling Alan to bring his work home with him. Just off from his lounge was a large office, which he converted into a laboratory housing a variety of machines connected by electrical wiring. He also stored bottles of chemicals – many of which were extremely dangerous, such as mercury and cyanide – for his experiments.

His interests expanded into the area of neuroscience, and the differences between a human brain and an electronic one.

As comfortable as he made his home, though, Manchester was a hard city, and being a gay man in 1950 was dangerous. Alan was constantly worried if his latest friend was in fact a plant: if he were caught, the press would be brutal, his reputation would be tarnished and he would likely be dismissed from his work at the university. But he had needs and wants like any man, and it angered him that straight men could do as they pleased whereas homosexuals were ridiculed and sent underground to dark and dangerous streets and the smut-filled tunnels near the train station. These areas were unsafe for anyone, but especially so for the inexperienced and naive university professor, who never knew what he might find.

Returning from work, he would often walk through these streets as casually as he could, but he lacked the confidence to approach the men there, scared that he would say the wrong thing. Instead, he would return to the privacy of his home, alone and frustrated.

By November 1950, both the Manchester Mark 1 computer and Alan's earlier machine, the ACE, were complete, although neither of them resembled his earlier designs. The British atomic agency and GCHQ bought multiple copies of the machines, but Alan was neither pleased nor interested as he started to distance himself from the computing departments of the university.

In October 1951, Churchill won the general election, returning to Number 10 Downing Street as prime minister after six years of Labour government. Menzies was still the Chief of MI6 but had his reputation damaged when two senior diplomats, Burgess and Maclean, defected to Moscow. Both were Cambridge University graduates working in the Foreign Office and had been passing secrets to their Russian handlers for years – including the years Burgess had worked directly for MI6.

Outraged by this development, Churchill summoned Menzies to Number 10.

'Now, look here, Menzies, these defections from within your ranks are, quite frankly, an embarrassment. The Americans are using the situation to withhold their intelligence and referring to the Secret Intelligence Service as a leaky ship! It will not do. It will not do at all.' Churchill paused to light a cigar and continued. 'I require you to investigate your officers fully, especially those who attended Cambridge – clean house! We cannot have any more egg on our face, do you understand?'

'Yes, sir. What about Turing?' he said.

'Especially Mr Turing. There's something very odd about that man – extremely bright, of course, but he'd be a prime target for the Soviets, so we must be certain of his allegiances. What are your thoughts on the matter?'

'We have kept tabs on him ever since his days at Bletchley. Everything points to him being non-political but a target just the same. And he has, of course, as we discovered during our surveillance, a weakness for young men, which may allow him to be compromised.'

'Keep an eye on him, Menzies,' ordered Churchill.

~

Alan spent most of his time working from home in his makeshift laboratory, searching for chemical reactions within plants and other natural materials. The work was interesting but solitary, and soon he became lonely.

As winter approached, the afternoons got darker. Alan walked through the bitterly cold streets, his coat collar turned up against the biting wind, and once again found himself on Oxford Street. This time, he was going to be courageous; he was determined to speak to someone.

He caught the eye of a boy who looked around nineteen. Despite the youth's winter coat, Alan could tell that he had an athletic build. He had short, dark hair slicked back, which contrasted with his bright blue eyes. Alan was excited by the young man; overcoming his shyness, he approached the youth with a smile.

'Hello,' said Alan softly. 'It's a little cold to be outside. Are you hungry?'

'Starving,' said the young man, in a broad Mancunian accent.

'I know a lovely little Italian restaurant just a few minutes from here – would you like to join me?' Alan asked.

'If you want.'

Alan walked in the direction of the restaurant, followed by the young man.

'What's your name?' asked the youth.

'Alan – and you are?'

'Arnold. Arnie if you'd like.'

During dinner, conversation was difficult at first, but the company pleasant. Arnold's fresh face was attractive.

'Do you live locally, Arnie?'

'I live with my parents in Moss Side. It's a bit rougher than around here. What about you?'

'I live in Wilmslow.'

'You must be posh, then. What do you do?' asked Arnold.

'I work at the university. If you'd like, you could come to my house at the weekend. Would you like that?' asked Alan.

'Write down the address and I'll come by Saturday night after the football.'

Alan thought the young Arnold was beautiful and seemed genuinely interested in him and his invitation. He passed him his address written on the back of a serviette and summoned the waiter to pay the bill.

'Thank you for a lovely evening, Arnie, and I look forward to seeing you on Saturday, around six o'clock. Is that okay?'

'See you Saturday,' replied Arnold.

When Arnold failed to show up, Alan felt disappointed, and not a little annoyed. This was exactly the reaction that Menzies had planned: the young Arnold Murray had played his part perfectly.

Alan spent Christmas with his family but could not shake the image of Arnold from his mind. The dangers of seeking male company were very real, yet there was something about Arnold – he'd seemed intrigued by Alan's knowledge. Alan relished the opportunity to teach anyone new things, but especially a young man like this. He returned to Manchester for the new year and immediately went in search of the youth, soon finding him chatting to his young friends, who disappeared as Alan approached.

Alan was very uncomfortable, even scared to be in this neighbourhood, half-expecting to be mugged or arrested, but the power of his desire pushed him forward.

Arnold kept his head bowed, avoiding Alan's eye contact, clearly nervous.

'I was sorry that you didn't make it to my house.'

Arnold shuffled his feet on the spot, still not looking at Alan.

'I got nervous,' the young man said. 'Thought you might be a copper. You can't be too careful.'

'I suppose you can't, and I assure you, I'm not a policeman, far from it. Why don't we try again? Would you like to come back to my house for a drink?'

Looking up finally, Arnold locked eyes with Alan and nodded.

Alan flagged down a cab and the two men went to his house. Once inside, Alan gave Arnold a brief tour.

'This is my laboratory, where I'm experimenting with the effects of various chemicals on plants and looking at the behaviour and brain patterns of small animals when stimulated by light or certain substances.'

'What's that?' Arnold reached out to a glass apparatus containing a rainbow of colourful liquids connected by steel tubes and rubber hoses.

'Don't touch that,' Alan yelled, scaring the young man. 'Sorry, it's just very fragile and some of the chemicals are extremely dangerous. Perhaps we should go to the lounge, where we can relax. I will light a fire to take the chill off.'

The log fire gave out an immense amount of heat, soon warming the room and its occupants.

'Tell me about yourself, your family,' Alan said.

The conversation continued for some time, the room becoming extremely warm.

Against the heat, Arnold removed his shirt, his muscular torso glistening in the light of the fire. Alan admired his athletic body and ran his hands over his chest. Arnold edged closer, slowly unbuttoning Alan's shirt, and leant over to kiss him slowly.

The two men were oblivious to the noise of the shutter on the camera outside, from the man who had followed them home.

Arnold spent the next two weeks visiting Alan at his house and, as in any new relationship, the excitement and passion was bountiful. Alan taught his new friend about biology, plants and the natural world. They visited museums and galleries, and Alan even took Arnold to the university to show off the computer department where he worked. Arnold responded just as Alan had hoped: he was eager to learn and extremely attentive to Alan's teachings and desires.

After every meeting, Arnold returned to his parents' house, going straight up to his room. He had been instructed by the man from London to write detailed notes of everything he had learnt, accompanied by dates and places they had visited together, even their activities and conversations in bed. He felt a little guilty about betraying Alan; he did genuinely like him. But the money from Mr London was too tempting and tempered his guilt as he placed the large letter in the postbox on the corner of his street.

~

A few weeks later, Alan returned home to find the house ransacked. Broken jars, papers scattered about the floor. Oddly, though, very little was missing: some cash, a watch and – oddest of all – some letters from Arnold. The cash and watch were easily replaced, but the letters concerned him – although not graphic, they would clearly show that two men were having an affair, and could be extremely dangerous if they fell into the wrong hands. His hope was that the thief would see no value in them and throw them into the rubbish bin or, better still, the fire.

Except for the cash, it all was now locked in the safe at MI6. But then everything went terribly wrong.

Far from simply tidying up his house, Alan in all his naivety reported the break-in to the police and, worse, told them that he suspected it may have been his *friend*, Arnold Murray. Two detectives searched the house, taking fingerprints and a detailed statement from Alan. The nature of the questioning changed, moving from the robbery itself to his relationship with Arnold. Alan foolishly admitted to the detectives that he was having an affair with Arnold, giving them the dates and details of their connection in a five-page statement.

Menzies' plan to use the threat of exposure against Alan was blown to dust; he now had a much bigger problem.

Five days after the death of King George VI in February 1952, the two detectives returned to Alan's house and knocked on the door.

Alan was arrested and placed in handcuffs.

'Are these necessary, officers?' he asked, horrified and alarmed.

'It's the rules,' he was told abruptly.

Alan felt humiliated as he was led from his house to the waiting police car. Curtains twitched as his neighbours gave in to the temptation to be nosey and see what all the fuss was about. As Alan was placed in the back of the car, his neighbours started to form the questions and theories that would fill their week of gossiping at the bingo hall.

Alan was charged with gross indecency, a crime that carried a two-year jail sentence. He was shocked and scared; he was going to pay a price for his stupidity, and it was going to be high.

As the court date edged closer, he thought to contact Joan – but what would she be able to do except to be supportive and hold his hand? No, it was time to call in a real favour. He went to London to see Menzies.

'Take a seat,' Menzies said, ushering him into his office. 'I got your message and a copy of your file from the Manchester Police.'

'I see.' Alan's face was gaunt, with dark patches under his eyes from lack of sleep, and there was a slight tremble in his hands as he received a glass of whisky from his boss. 'I can't go to jail. Surely you can help.'

Menzies opened Alan's file, which, unbeknown to his companion, he had already studied many times over. The plan had always been to create a tool to control Alan, not to humiliate him or have him incarcerated. Churchill could make the charges disappear with a stroke of a pen but had told Menzies that the public interest in the case was too strong. The papers were having a field day, making it hard for the Prime Minister to intervene. The government and MI6's hands were tied.

Four weeks later, Alan had his day in court. His lawyer came out of the judge's chambers and sat with his client.

'If you enter a guilty plea, the judge will give you an offer to keep you out of jail.'

'What's the offer – a suspended sentence, a fine?'

'Not quite,' he replied. 'The charge carries a minimum two-year sentence, but no one wants to see you in jail. They will offer you a chemical procedure, an injection of hormones that will reduce your libido and stop you from reoffending. It's a good deal, Alan, I strongly advise that you should take it.'

'But which chemicals? What if there are side effects?'

'They didn't say. I don't think they know, but how bad can it be? You wouldn't survive in jail,' urged the lawyer.

Neither the judge, Menzies nor Churchill for that matter understood the effects of the hormones that Alan would have to endure, but they considered the option to be extremely lenient, considering his predicament was caused by his own actions and signed confession.

Alan could not face going to jail, giving up his work and his liberty. What choice did he have? He did consider using Nautilus – a simple message warning him about the break-in and his careless confession. But he had not built the machine for personal gain, and his life was not in danger. How bad could an injection be? It would be a dishonour to those people who died in the war without his intervention. He would suffer the consequences.

Reluctantly, he accepted the deal.

CHAPTER 29

London

June 1952

Menzies was full of trepidation as he entered Churchill's office.

'Sir, again, I apologise for the Turing fiasco. What I can tell you is that in my professional opinion Mr Turing is nothing but a loyal and valuable individual who, despite his unhealthy appetites, should be honoured for his talent and his past endeavours, which were and remain vitally important to the country.'

Now that the spy's career was coming to an end, Menzies wanted to demonstrate his admiration for Alan in the hope that the mathematician's reputation could be repaired.

He handed Churchill his report and his resignation, the latter reluctantly accepted by the elderly statesman, who thanked him for his many years of service. Menzies left Downing Street with his conscience slightly clearer, but deep inside he knew that Churchill and MI6 would never fully trust Alan and would certainly never leave him alone.

~

Alan heard the clatter of his letterbox. There was the usual hate-filled mail from prejudiced bullies, local flyers and one fancy envelope, beautifully decorated, containing an invitation to Joan's wedding.

The happy day was to be held at Chichester Cathedral on the 26th of July.

He wrote back to her:

Dearest Joan,

How happy I am that you have found someone to love and who will be able to love you back in the way that you deserve. I understand that your future husband is a former army officer and works like you at GCHQ. How perfect. I'm sure you have lots in common and I extend my heartiest best wishes to you both.

As much as I would love to attend your wedding, I do not think it wise that I accept your invitation. Apart from feeling ghastly most of the time from these infernal drugs, I do not want to cause any unease at your glorious event. I know you accept me as I am, for which I do love you, but I fear others and possibly the press might be interested in my attendance and cause trouble.

However, I do so wish to visit before you 'tie the knot', and to that end I propose we see each other in London on the 20th of July. For old times' sake, shall we meet at the Savoy at four and take tea?

Affectionately yours,

Alan

Joan arrived at exactly 4pm.

'Darling Joan, how lovely to see you,' said Alan.

Joan took in the appearance of her dear old friend, shocked at how he looked. He had put on weight, but his skin was pale and his eyes listless, surrounded by dark circles. She bit her lip and reached out to take his hand.

'Alan, you poor thing. Excuse me for saying so, but you look quite awful.'

'I feel awful. I still have another six months of treatment to go. But I haven't come here for pity. I want to hear all about your plans.'

Joan played along with his determined, hard-worn positivity and was genuinely excited as she laid out in detail the plans for her wedding day.

'Does your fiancé know about David?' Alan asked quietly once they had covered the easier ground.

Joan folded her arms across her chest. 'He does not, and nor will he. David is happy in Scotland. That is simply the way it will always be. It would be too confusing for David and unfair on John to complicate their lives.'

'I understand why you want to keep David's life as uncomplicated as possible, and I respect that, but for myself, I do wonder about the boy. Could I ask that you also keep me informed of his progress, maybe a photograph or two? I would like to leave him with a future and my legacy.'

Seeing Alan's affection for the boy warmed her heart. She stroked his face with the palm of her hand.

'I'm sure that can be arranged, but what do you mean by a legacy? Do you want him to inherit one of your machines?'

'I do, but it comes with complications ... The only real way to explain it to you would be for you to see it for yourself.'

'And where is this legacy of yours?'

'Harrods,' he replied.

Joan burst out laughing, spilling her Earl Grey tea.

'I'm serious, you must tell no one. Just meet me tomorrow, please, at nine o'clock, and all will be revealed. You are the only person I can trust this to, Joan, and when you understand the nature of what I'm going to show you, you'll see it is imperative that it remains secret.'

At nine the next morning, Alan led Joan down the staircase to the safety deposit boxes and gave his password to the ever-present guard. Joan was in awe. 'I never knew this place existed,' she said.

'You don't know the half of it. There are underground tunnels and offices sprawling all over Knightsbridge.'

Alan entered the code and opened the door, switching on the light. Once inside the small room and with the door firmly closed behind them, he said, 'Let me introduce you to Nautilus.'

Joan stared at the machine, puzzled. Taking a step closer, she tried to comprehend its purpose. She glanced around the room, which was filled with maps and documents, some of which she recognised from her days at Bletchley.

'Is it for Morse code?' she said. 'A communications device? Why is it down here and not at the university? Is this one of your special projects for Mr Menzies? The government does know about this, do they?'

Alan hesitated. Joan knew the answer to her question.

'I'm not sure I should be here. I still work at GCHQ, for God's sake,' Joan said with increasing nervousness.

'It is a communications device,' Alan said. 'It can send short messages, but what is unique about it is that the messages travel at such a speed that they can be sent backwards in time. No one knows anything about it, except me and now you.'

'Stop being ridiculous,' Joan said and laughed at the outrageous idea.

'I assure you, it's possible.'

'Oh really? How far back are we talking?' Joan said sceptically.

'Initially, it was minutes and hours,' Alan explained patiently.

'And now?'

'Six weeks.'

'Six weeks! What the hell, Alan? You haven't used this thing, have you?'

'I had no plan to use it, but then I got this message, from myself.' Alan reached into a drawer and retrieved the original message in Morse, together with his translation, and handed them to Joan.

Joan read the document, confusion clear across her face. 'I don't understand, Alan – we attacked Normandy. There was no massacre at Calais.'

'Look at the dates. The message was sent by me several days after D-Day, when Eisenhower changed the invasion to take place at Calais. I received the message on the 27th of May, and I convinced Churchill that he might get a proposal to switch locations based on bad weather reports, and that it was imperative that he hold firm with Normandy.'

'What did he say?'

'I'm sure he thought I was barking mad, but the important thing is that no switch happened. Normandy was a success and there was no massacre. I changed history, Joan.'

'You are barking mad. Even if I accept that it's true, and that is a big if, you can't go around changing history. You're not God!'

'I had no choice. If I had done nothing and Churchill was persuaded to invade Calais, according to that message that you are holding, over 80 per cent of our troops would have died. We could have lost the war. I had to act. If you think of it, it's no different to when we were at Bletchley. We knew where all the ships were, we knew when and where the U-boats would attack, and we decided who survived and who didn't. Were we not gods, Joan?'

Joan could hardly believe her ears.

'I understand your motivations, but I'm struggling to accept that what you're telling me is true. But if it is, if this machine can do the things you say it can, then you need to destroy it. Can you imagine what would happen if this were to fall into the wrong hands? And I would include the British government on that list.'

'I know, believe me. I had no intention of using it. But destroy it? No. What if I had heeded that advice in 1944? We would now likely be governed by Adolf Hitler and another four million Jews would be dead. Is that what you want?'

'No, of course not. But this is so incredible – so terrifying. You need to prove it to me, prove to me it works.'

Joan sat on the only chair in the room, rubbing her temples with her fingers, alleviating the small headache that was growing in her head.

Alan took Joan through all the physics and the electronics, explaining how Nautilus would send a telegram, to alert him there was a message waiting on the receiving station.

'It's amazing, Alan, terrifying but amazing. What I find most impressive is that 100 per cent of the electrons not only break the speed of light, but when they reassemble in the past there is no redundancy. Is that because of the magnetic accelerator? Are the electrons attracted to the magnetic field surrounding the core? And therefore stay together?'

'Correct. Joan, your brain is still a marvel to work with.'

'I see why you called it Nautilus.'

Joan was becoming convinced, and the lure of complex machinery, physics and power were hard to resist.

Alan said, 'I suggest we agree that the machine should never be used except as an absolute last resort, and only when the problem facing the world is on a global scale, where humankind is severely threatened. This should be our defining and abiding Protocol.'

He desperately wanted Joan as his co-conspirator, sharing the burden and immense responsibility that came with the knowledge of Nautilus's existence.

'Why have you told me now?' asked Joan.

'Three reasons. Firstly, I'm worried that I may get found out. I'm sure that I'm being followed and have been for some considerable time, whereas I believe that you will suffer less scrutiny.'

'And the second reason?' asked Joan.

'I wanted to tell you before you got married. You see, this way, it is a pre-existing secret, like David.'

'You are very cunning, and a little cruel. Go on.'

'The last reason is my health. It's not the best, and although I do believe I will recover when I stop the treatment, it did make me think. I would hate the idea of leaving Nautilus unattended, or worse still, allowing it to be captured, if something were to happen to me.'

'And how does David come into this?' asked Joan.

'Well, that, I believe, should be part of the Protocol, our legacy. We should only pass on Nautilus's secret to family. Should one of us die, providing that David is old enough, I would say thirty or forty years of age, only then should the secret be passed on to him.'

'You're going too fast, Alan. I'm not sure that I want anything to do with this. As for David, he doesn't even know that we exist.'

'There's plenty of time, Joan,' Alan said. 'Shall we continue?'

Alan talked for the next three hours, going through every detail of Nautilus's operation. The more complicated it got, the more fun the two academics had, reminding Joan how much she missed working with her friend, the genius mathematician.

When they finally finished, Alan gave Joan a copy of all the codes, passwords and combinations, assuming that she was engaged with the project.

'I think we should have a failsafe,' Joan said. 'A code word, in case something terrible happens to us, or if Nautilus is about to be discovered. A destruction code.'

Alan was reluctant to agree to such a code but desperately wanted Joan to be involved with Nautilus, and, more importantly, with him. The idea of working with Joan again excited him more than he'd imagined.

They agreed on the code word and committed it to memory.

As they left the brightly lit store, Alan embraced her and gave her a beautifully wrapped gift. 'For your wedding day,' he said. They kissed.

'Please be careful, Alan, and promise me that you will take care of yourself.' She blew him a kiss as she walked away, the gesture making him smile.

He took a cab to the station and waited for his train, happy that Joan had accepted his proposal. Closing the door to his carriage, he caught the reflection of a man staring at him. Could it be that he was being followed, or was he simply recognised as the disgraced professor? His unease lasted the long journey back to Manchester.

CHAPTER 30

Manchester

1953

Relations between the Americans and the Soviets were at an all-time low. Communism had swept across many parts of the world, and the West was determined to stem the flow. From Cuba on America's doorstep, to Europe, with the creation of East Germany and the USSR's Iron Curtain, and Asia, where China's communist leader, Mao Zedong, had defeated the American-backed Kuomintang. Only five years after World War II, the Americans were already fighting another war, in Korea across the 38th Parallel, and this was continuing in a desultory way three years later.

Today, though, the troubles of the world were far from Alan's thoughts. This was going to be a rewarding day. His probation had ended, and with it the torturous hormone treatment. He had also received a letter notifying him that Manchester University was extending his contract for a further five years. He looked in the mirror: his refection was pale and sallow. He felt awful, but his research had told him that the effects of the chemicals were reversible with time. Today would be the beginning of his recovery. As a first step, he decided to go for a short run, knowing exercise and fresh air would make him feel better.

As a next step in the recovery program, Alan decided to go on holiday, to enjoy himself and get some sun. A few days later, he visited his friends in London and enjoyed the spectacle of the Queen's coronation. Shortly after that, he boarded a ship to France and travelled to the beaches of St Tropez, and then onwards to the Greek islands, where he could be himself without fear of arrest. The sun-soaked Mediterranean and its free-living locals were such a contrast to England and his life in Manchester. The tanned, athletic bodies on the beach were a feast for Alan's eyes, and the beach crowd moved to the surrounding bars to watch the crimson sun set over the glistening Mediterranean sea. He made friends easily and was astonished at how relaxed and confident he was in Europe, in sharp contrast to his life in England and the archaic rules and attitudes that had nearly ruined his life. Alan did not want to leave this paradise, but return he must.

Docking in England, refreshed and ready to restart his life, he was met by a messenger. His old masters required his presence. Churchill was still prime minister, despite suffering a stroke earlier in the summer. Alan was to meet the new head of MI6, Major General John Sinclair, who'd sent a car to pick him up and deliver him to Downing Street.

Alan entered the austere building and was shown into the dining room, where the two men were engrossed in conversation. Despite everything he'd been through, he was saddened to see Churchill looking so frail.

'Ah, there you are, Turing, you look uncommonly well. I trust your holidays were enjoyable. Can I offer you a glass of champagne?' Churchill said in a friendly manner.

'Thank you, sir. How can I be of service?'

'The Russians are up to their old tricks again, pushing their weight around in places they shouldn't. In fact, Sinclair here has gathered intelligence that the Soviets have developed a hydrogen bomb, which may be tested at any moment.'

'We tested our own atomic bomb last October, did we not, sir?' asked Alan somewhat sarcastically.

'Not the point!' Churchill chided. 'Eisenhower has asked us to cooperate and form a joint team of individuals from both the CIA and MI6 to collect as much information as we can about the Soviets' capabilities and the location of their missiles. I've told Sinclair that with your vast experience at Bletchley and your uncanny knack for operational success, I'd like you to head up the British contingent. What do you say?'

'I foresee a few problems. Firstly, I have lost my security clearance, and due to my conviction I'm banned from travelling to the United States. Then there's my position at Manchester University to think of.'

'Nonsense! Sinclair will have your clearance reinstated and we'll speak to the university and explain that you are needed for vital work with the government. They'll agree to hold over your tenure, don't concern yourself. Of course, you will be compensated – we're willing to offer you a fee of £5000.'

The money was, of course, always useful to a university professor, but for Alan, having his security clearance reinstated and his US restrictions lifted was music to his ears. He could finally move on from his conviction and recover elements of his earlier life and reputation.

'That's very generous, sir, and I'm happy to help. I take it you would like me to start right away?'

'Quite so, Mr Turing, and welcome back to the service. Let's have another glass, shall we?'

~

Over the next months, the joint team was assembled at GCHQ, now based in Cheltenham, and Alan used his newly regained influence to recruit his old colleagues from Bletchley, including Hugh Alexander. Joan reluctantly declined due to the poor health of her husband. Also joining the team in operations was Harold 'Kim' Philby, suggested by the new head of MI6.

GCHQ provided detailed analysis, intercepts and photo imagery from across the Soviet Union. By the spring of 1954, the team had provided a comprehensive analysis of the strength of the Russians' thermonuclear capability, unhappy reading for Eisenhower and Churchill, as the threat of the Soviet bomb became very real.

Alan's team was proving its worth. Despite the Americans' earlier fears about a joint operation, they were pleased with the results, so much so that Alan was invited to Washington to brief the CIA Director and meet with President Eisenhower at a state dinner.

On the 6th of June 1954 – the tenth anniversary of D-Day – Alan returned from Cheltenham to his house in Cheshire, eager to pack for the trip to Washington.

The house was exceptionally clean and tidy, his efficient housekeeper having taken full advantage of Alan's absence. Frustratingly for her, there was one room she couldn't work her magic on, his laboratory. Alan had given her strict instructions never to enter the room, explaining that it was far too dangerous for her as he kept deadly chemicals. This was only a half-truth, though: the real reason he did not want her there was that he knew she would tidy things away that would waste his time and upset his system.

He tinkered with his experiments into the night, recording measurements, taking detailed notes. He retired to bed just after midnight. Despite the next day being a bank holiday, Alan rose early. With the trip to Washington only a week away, he had so much to organise. He visited his friend Max at the university and they had lunch at a nearby Greek restaurant, where Max brought Alan up to speed on all the developments of the university's latest computer. Alan was eager to talk about the future, the expansion of the computing department and the positive possibilities that might develop from their work.

Alan thanked his friend for a delightful day, and they promised to see each other after he returned from his US trip.

He walked home, his head full of thoughts, preparing in his mind the presentation he was to give to President Eisenhower.

It started to rain, the grey cloud cover darkening the sky and Alan's mood. He reached the corner of his street just as the heavens opened. Running the last hundred yards to his front door, he opened it, quickly discarding his hat and coat in the hall. Entering the lounge, he found a man sitting in his armchair.

'Philby! What the devil are you doing here?' demanded Alan.

'We need to talk,' Philby said, calmly but firmly.

'About what precisely? And what the hell do you think you're doing breaking into my house and scaring me half to death?'

'When we last met, you said you were not politically minded, despite your support for the Labour government at the last election. But with everything that has happened to you, the way you have been treated by your own government, after everything that you did for them during the war, why are you not outraged, Alan? We do not understand, why are you still supporting the capitalistic ideals of the Americans and their British puppets?'

'You say "we"? Who exactly are "we"?'

'I and some others, Cambridge men like yourself, have been working for the Russians, for communism. We all truly believe that this is the only viable economic system that can sustain a fair and just world for humanity, and Russia the only country that has the strength, which you have seen for yourself, to defeat fascism.'

'In Britain, this could be called treason, so don't tell me any more, Mr Philby, and please leave,' Alan demanded.

Philby rubbed his fingers slowly along the felt edge of his hat, which was placed on his lap. Raising his head, he replied, 'I have an offer for you. My masters in Moscow, in return for certain intelligence, will provide financial reward and the provision of certain "friends" that will be to your tastes. Further, should you ever be in any danger, you will be protected and offered an apartment in Moscow, status, rank and all the money you need to carry out your intellectual requirements and your social needs. But more importantly, you will be helping the world, stopping American capitalism from serving the few rather than the many. It is noble, Alan.'

Alan shook as a sense of panic went through his body. He was frightened.

'And if I say no? You have exposed who you work for here tonight. I'm sure you're not just going to leave disappointed. Do you have orders to kill me?'

'We want to recruit you, not shoot you.' Philby tapped a bulge in his left breast pocket, the threat clear, despite his words of reassurance.

He reached inside his jacket. Cold sweat ran down Alan's face.

'A lovely boy,' said Philby, handing over the picture of David, now aged eight.

'How on earth do you know about him?' Alan replied, stunned.

'Moscow has been interested in you for a very long time. One of my colleagues even worked at Bletchley, not in your team, but he knew of your reputation. When Joan disappeared to Scotland, we had her followed. We soon discovered why she was there.'

'David does not even know that Joan and I are his parents, so you need to leave him out of this.'

'We have no intention of involving the lad, but we do need you to cooperate.'

Alan paced around the room, trying to work out a plan. When he was near the door to his laboratory, he darted inside and came back out clutching two containers of white liquid.

'This is potassium cyanide, Mr Philby. If you shoot me and these bottles break, we will both die from the gasses that are released. Now, I want you to tell Moscow that I have no intention of becoming a traitor but that I recognise the threat to my son. So your identity and everything that you have said tonight is safe, and will remain that way, as long as no harm comes to David. Now, please leave before I drop one of these.'

Philby drew his gun and walked towards Alan, ordering him to put the canisters down.

In a panic, Alan threw one of the containers at the Russian agent. Philby was well trained and avoided the deadly missile, the bottle landing harmlessly on the chair behind him as the spy tackled Alan to the floor. The second container smashed against Alan's leg as he fell to the ground. He felt a searing pain below his right knee. Looking down, he saw a shard of glass protruding from his flesh. The wound was frothing with pink bubbles as the deadly noxious liquid mingled with his blood.

Philby froze, trying to avoid the broken glass and staring at the fatal wound. 'What can I do?' he said.

In a final act of kindness, Alan looked at the spy and said, 'Cover your face, man.'

Philby did exactly that, covering his mouth and nose with his jacket. Carefully getting off the floor, he rushed over to the windows, opening them wide open, gulping the fresh air into his lungs and in the process saving his own life. He looked over at Alan, his body lying on the floor, motionless, his eyes still open, staring but lifeless.

The poison had taken less than two minutes to finish its agonising journey through Alan's body.

Philby was angry with himself. This had not been his intention; he'd merely wanted to frighten Alan into working for the Soviets. Moscow would not be happy, and there would be an almighty stink back at MI6 in losing such an asset. He needed to think.

With a scarf wrapped around his face and wearing his leather gloves, he went about tidying the scene of the crime. First, he removed the piece of glass from Alan's leg and cleaned the wound. He searched the bathroom and found a plaster, which he placed over the small cut, and then pulled up Alan's socks to cover the wound. Dragging Alan's body to the bedroom, he placed him peacefully on his bed. He saw an apple on the bedside table and took a few bites, then dipped it in the remaining cyanide from the half-broken canister. Rubbing the poisoned apple inside Alan's mouth, Philby watched as froth formed over his lips, accumulating around the face of the corpse.

With the body dealt with, Philby spent the next twenty minutes clearing up the broken glass and washing the floor where the poison had spilt from the canister. Satisfied that the house was now devoid of any signs of struggle, Philby checked in on Alan one more time to confirm there were no signs of life. Looking around, he was certain that the scene would point to a suicide. He placed the remains of the apple next to Alan's right hand. He would tell Moscow that Alan had killed himself before he had time to contact him, putting himself in the clear.

The next evening, Alan Turing's body was discovered by his housekeeper, who, shocked and distraught, reported it to the police on the morning of June 8th, 1954.

PART 2

CHAPTER 31

London

June 1954

Joan stared with disbelief as she read the headline on the front page of the *Daily Mail*: PROFESSOR ALAN TURING COMMITS SUICIDE.

She was devastated, enraged. She arranged to meet up with Hugh Alexander.

'The police and the papers are saying Alan committed suicide. I just don't believe it, Hugh.'

Hugh put his arm around her tenderly as they sat on a bench in Hyde Park overlooking the lake. The day was glorious, with families feeding bread to the ducks and couples rowing on the glistening water. The two friends were impervious to the serenity around them, shrouded in grief and full of unanswered questions.

'I only spoke to him last week,' Hugh said. 'He was excited to be returning to America and said he was looking and feeling much better since the hormone treatment had finished. Without wanting to sound dreadfully callous, I could've understood this a year ago, when he was so depressed, but now it just doesn't make sense. I think I will go to Manchester and talk to the police.'

'Would you? I would come too, but my husband is not well. I have to return to Scotland on tonight's sleeper train, and anyway the police won't take any notice of me.'

'I'll go up in the morning and get to the bottom of this,' said Hugh.

When he arrived in Manchester the following day, he asked to see Alan's house and was accompanied by a local detective, who instructed him not to touch anything. He was also shown pictures of Alan's corpse lying so peacefully on top of his bed.

'There was no sign of a forced entry, no evidence of a struggle and the neighbours heard nothing out of the ordinary,' confirmed the detective.

Hugh walked around the dimly lit room and approached Alan's writing desk, which was messy as always, made worse no doubt by the investigating officers.

'We found several tickets and papers, including his upcoming journey to America and an invitation to the Royal Society next month.'

'Do you not think it odd, Detective? That a man who has already suffered the shame of a court declaring him a homosexual, already persevered through hormone therapy for over a year and now was finally rid of all this and about to embark on a long journey, to a country that he is fond of, decides to end his life?'

'I'm sorry for the loss of your friend, sir, but I've been doing this job for over twenty years, and nothing surprises me anymore. I can only go by the evidence, which I have to say points exactly to a man in turmoil who had the means to end his life swiftly and chose to do so.'

The two men left the house and parted company. Hugh returned to London by train and wrote a letter to Joan confirming that, despite all that they knew of Alan, it seemed as though their dear friend had sadly decided to end his life.

For the next eight years, Joan and her husband, John, lived a quiet life in their house in Crail, near St Andrews in Scotland. Both had a keen interest in history and in particular the history of Scottish coins. With time on her hands and being so close to Edinburgh, Joan concocted a plan with David's adoptive parents to see him when he was playing in the park or playing football for his school team. She resisted the temptation to talk to him, happy with her voyeuristic love for him and avoiding the pain that he would suffer if he knew the truth.

She paid regular visits to Harrods; Alan's will confirmed that the contents of his storage unit, among other items, had been bequeathed to her.

The world remained far from peaceful. The Korean War finished in July with the two Koreas facing off across the 38th Parallel. Britain invaded Egypt in 1956 and Russia invaded Hungary the same year. However, despite these events, Joan, as she had remarked to Alan when he was alive, had no intention of using Nautilus.

But she had made him a promise, and she would keep it. Nautilus would be maintained; her first test messages would be sent to confirm its continued operation, and improvements would be made as technology changed. The final and hardest part of the promise would be to eventually hand over Nautilus to their son, David.

CHAPTER 32

1961

Joan's husband had a series of treatments for his chest that, with much rest and recuperation, saw him return to reasonable health, allowing them the opportunity to return to England and GCHQ.

The arms race was at its height. America had increased its nuclear arsenal from just nine weapons in 1946 to 28,000 by the early 60s. Russia was not far behind. The Soviet-backed Fidel Castro had taken control of Cuba. Too close for American comfort.

With the threat of missiles that could reach Washington in a few minutes, President Kennedy authorised the invasion of Cuba at the Bay of Pigs using CIA-trained exiles. The operation was a disaster and added to the Cold War conflict. By October 1962, the construction of nuclear missile silos had started on the island, with Russian weapons loaded onto a convoy of ships, bringing the two superpowers to the brink of war.

Joan received various pieces of intel showing troop movements and weapon manifests that convinced her the island was a powderkeg that could set off a global conflict between the two superpowers. This was a potential global threat to humanity, and for Joan meant a threat to her son. The Protocol that she and Alan had established was satisfied. But what could she do? The time range of Nautilus even in 1962 was restricted to only eight weeks, a security measure that Alan had introduced a decade earlier, explaining to Joan that he considered the time sufficient to change an outcome, whereas a longer period, a year for example, would be extremely dangerous – too many events could change, causing a paroxysm in time.

Kennedy and the Russian president, Khrushchev, both had all the facts and were in stalemate, neither side wanting to back down. The US Navy had formed a blockade of the island and the Russian ships were steaming towards them. Time was running out, and Joan could not conceive of how to help.

The answer came to her, of all places, in the staff kitchen at GCHQ, where one day, while making coffee, she had a conversation with Harold Philby, who was talking quite freely about his opinion that Kennedy had finally met his match in Khrushchev and that the Reds could be walking down Pennsylvania Avenue by Christmas. Philby had been widely suspected of being a double agent. However, he had survived and been cleared of any suspicion by MI6 and had the support of several prominent politicians. Philby oversaw the Greek and Turkish desk at GCHQ. He showed Joan one of his recent intercepts, explaining that the US missile divisions based in Turkey had recently been placed on high alert. However, it also stated that the president of Turkey, Cemal Gürsel, was objecting to the use of missiles. Turkey had only gained independence in 1923 and was neutral during most of World War II. Although the country was part of NATO, the Turkish president was nervous to provoke his Russian neighbours.

Joan went to see Nautilus. She didn't know whether her plan would work, but she felt she had to try.

She instructed her earlier self to send an encrypted message to Philby purporting to come from the US Embassy in Ankara. It would state that the Americans were operationally ready to utilise the full force of the

Turkish arsenal at the president's command and, critically, had the full backing of the Turkish government.

Philby received the message at 10am on October 24th, 1962. Two days later, Khrushchev sent an unexpected message to the Americans, offering to withdraw his ships and halt the construction of the missile sites in Cuba in return for Kennedy's undertaking that there would be no invasion of Cuba, now or in the future, a promise Kennedy gave with a sense of relief.

The change of heart from the Russian president convinced Joan that Philby had sent her message directly to Moscow, confirming that he was a Russian agent. Joan's dilemma was that she couldn't produce evidence of this to MI6 without revealing the presence of Nautilus.

Later that year, though, Anatoliy Golitsyn, a major from the KGB who had defected to the West, identified to Dick White, the new head of the Secret Intelligence Service, that Philby had been working for the Soviets for years. Unfortunately for White and MI6, Philby had got wind of the defection. Travelling to Beirut, he took a ship to Russia and completed his own defection. He remained in Moscow until his death in 1988.

This was to be the last time that Joan used Nautilus. Even when the assassination of President Kennedy took place in 1963, she decided against action. Saving an individual, even a US president, did not meet the strict criteria that she and Alan had established as the Turing Protocol. Wars would follow in Vietnam and throughout the African continent, but none presented a global threat. History would run its course unchanged by Joan or Nautilus, as it should be.

She missed Alan every single day.

PART 3

CHAPTER 33

David's Story

In 1959, when David turned thirteen, his parents decided to send him to boarding school at Gordonstoun, in the Highlands on the coast of Scotland near Elgin. The school had a reputation for hard discipline and tough challenges, matched only by the harsh climate of the country. Prince Philip had attended the school, and three years into David's time there Gordonstoun would receive another royal, Prince Charles, the future king of the United Kingdom.

What it lacked in comfort was made up for in the form of physical activities. David had inherited his birth father's athletic prowess and excelled in cross-country running, climbing and kayaking. The students swam and sailed on the lochs and honed their survival skills with weekend orienteering adventures in the mountains. His academic skills were equally impressive, making him a popular pupil with masters and students alike, culminating in him becoming Head Boy in his final year.

In 1964, David was accepted into King's College at Cambridge, and like his biological parents he studied applied mathematics, graduating three years later with a first. His graduation was joyfully attended by his parents, Claire and David, and observed quietly and secretly by Joan, her pride and love nearly bursting her heart.

David had inherited Joan and Alan's skill in the field of mathematics, and he applied this to the science of computers and advanced calculus, culminating in having several papers published by his university that caught the attention of the National Aeronautics and Space Administration. He worked briefly with the American agency on the periphery of the Apollo program, but he quickly found the work monotonous, with his supervisors constantly checking his work and forcing him to redo it several times over. He was about to leave the program when the excitement levels went up a notch as they announced a launch date for Apollo 11. As a team member, he was able to access the command centre and watch this incredible journey unfold – in between fetching coffee for the men at the consoles. Everyone was on edge as Neil Armstrong guided the lunar module towards the surface of the moon, landed successfully and took his Giant Leap for Mankind.

David joined the celebrations, humbled at being present at such a historic event. But the celebrations soon died down as the team concentrated on getting their boys back to earth, while David considered his future, certain that it was not in the stars.

He returned to England and Cambridge, where he received a scholarship to complete a PhD in electronic communications and was spotted by the recruiters at GCHQ and, more importantly, MI6. One year into his studies at Cambridge, he was invited to an interview in London by the intelligence services. He sat various exams, covering mathematics and science, and was set puzzles and codes to break using different cyphers. The written papers were followed by a series of interviews carried out by an array of different individuals, ranging from severe military types to psychologists and code breakers. A week after the tests, David was invited back to the new MI6 headquarters at Westminster Bridge Road in Lambeth, where he was presented with two offers.

The first came from GCHQ, which would utilise his academic brain and his inherited skills of problem-solving and code-breaking. The second came from MI6, which was to be wholly more interesting.

Little had changed in the Special Intelligence Service since the end of the war. The recruiter was a typical Foreign Office type – probably went to Eton or Harrow, thought David – pinstripe suit, shiny black shoes and a tie with a crest he couldn't quite make out. When he'd entered the building, he'd been struck by how very modern it was, lots of light, as it was made mainly of glass, with polished tiled floors, a stark contrast to the windowless, sparse office he now found himself in. He wondered whether he was about to be interviewed or interrogated.

'Right, McIntosh,' said the recruiter as he flicked nonchalantly through a thin file. 'You have scored extremely well in the written tests, but what has impressed the Service most are your physical test results, which are quite exceptional. There is one thing that is bothering us, though, your background check. I'm sure you're aware that the people who raised you aren't your biological parents, and we can't find any trace of who they are. Can you shed any light on this?'

'As far as I'm concerned, they are my real parents,' David replied directly. 'They explained to me that my real mother was their cousin who died in childbirth. They didn't know who my father was.'

'This is consistent with the interview we carried out. When we questioned them about the subject, they confirmed that the identity of your father is still unknown to them. His name is blank on your birth certificate.'

'And is that so important?'

'Just a loose end. This sort of thing was not uncommon during the war among certain people.'

David resented the recruiter's tone. 'Have you ever seen your parents' birth certificates?' he asked.

'Let's move on, shall we?' the recruiter said. 'The service would like to invite you to join our organisation as an intelligence officer. Should you accept, your training will start next week.'

Putting aside the brief flicker of defensiveness about his parents, David accepted immediately.

The training was to last six months and was called IONEC – Intelligence Officers New Entry Course. Splitting his time between GCHQ and MI6, David and the small team of new recruits were taught and tested across a wide range of disciplines, from code-breaking, at which David excelled, to tradecraft, where they learnt how to follow possible targets and avoid being followed by foreign agents. Surveillance techniques, communication drops and interrogation were all part of the course.

The second phase of the program was brutal: a six-week training camp at Fort Monckton, Gosport, on the south coast of England.

David was one of six, including two women. At nearly six foot tall and eighty-five kilograms, he cut an imposing figure. His favourite classes were hand-to-hand combat and weapons training, where he could use his speed and agility. The trainers were most impressed by his electronics skills in both bombs and weaponry, grading him A+.

The last phase of training was in the field. Each recruit was teamed up with an active case officer and sent to work on live cases, mostly in London but also other cities throughout the UK. This phase lasted three months and was considered an apprenticeship. David had a very approachable personality: people liked him, would talk to him and were comfortable in his presence. This skill would be developed and honed and become one of his greatest assets.

With the training complete, David was to be sent to his first post. He was curious which country it would be. He had passable French and Spanish but no Arabic. He was completely taken by surprise when he was told to report to the embassy in Dublin.

CHAPTER 34

Northern Ireland

1972

Conflict in Ireland had gone back centuries. The Easter uprising in 1916, which was suppressed by the British, led to the partitioning of the country in 1921. The south formed a new state, comprising mainly Catholics, while Northern Ireland remained part of the United Kingdom and had a majority Protestant population. There were, however, many Catholics living in the north, which led to tensions, demonstrations and violence. David's task was to seek out informants from both camps and report all information to his superiors in London.

At the end of January 1972, there was a large demonstration in Derry, a Catholic community. David's agents warned him there would be trouble, and he argued with London to have the march cancelled. His calls were ignored; indeed, the only action taken by the government was to put more troops on the street. The British paratroopers were met by 10,000 demonstrators. Overwhelmed, the soldiers tried to make arrests but were resisted. Instead of retreating, they opened fire on the civilians, claiming fourteen lives.

Three days after what became known as Bloody Sunday, the British Embassy in Dublin was burnt to the ground. David was furious with the military; there was no need for the bloodshed and there were sure to be reprisals against the army. The loss of life could have been avoided if they'd acted upon his intelligence. The Irish Republican Army became very active, with shootings, car bombings and physical punishments becoming commonplace.

Through his network of informants, David managed to prevent several high-ranking assassinations, and two car bombs were safely defused thanks to his intervention – which did not go unnoticed back at HQ. The stress of constantly watching over your shoulder, checking your car every time you parked and wondering whether the person next to you had a gun or a knife took its toll, though. Paranoia began to set in and made David withdraw from his colleagues. After two years of active duty, it was time to consider a change.

In the spring of 1973, he requested a transfer and was rewarded for his hard work in Ireland. He was posted to what was considered in the Service to be a cushy number: Madrid, the capital of Spain.

There, he ran an intelligence team of four, reporting directly to the Madrid Station Chief. The job came with a furnished two-bedroom apartment in the fashionable area of Plaza de España, situated off the busy shopping street Gran Via, in the heart of the city.

Spain was still under the control of the fascist dictator Francisco Franco, though the old dictator was frail, suffering from ill health. After decades of control, Franco wanted to leave the country with a democracy and re-establish the monarchy, restoring as king Juan Carlos I.

But on a gorgeous Saturday morning in April, David had no thoughts of politics. Leaving his apartment early, he walked to the Plaza de Oriente, absorbing the beauty of the architecture and the stunning gardens with views across the Casa de Campo. The spring sunshine was warm, and he revelled in the opportunity to sit at an outside table at the Café de Oriente. He ordered a coffee with toast and jamon, and drenched the fresh warm bread with olive oil, the green liquid sparkling in the morning sun. David sat back in his chair and took in his surrounds, relaxed, and like any normal tourist started people-watching.

But David was not a tourist: he was trained to notice the unusual, and soon he caught a furtive glance from a lady sitting three tables to his left. He returned the stare of the dark-haired woman. She was beautiful, olive-skinned, slender and well dressed in a slim skirt and tight white blouse that accentuated her figure. The woman moved out of her seat and approached David's table, his eyes on her the whole time.

'May I sit?' Her English was fluent but accented with a sultry Spanish tone.

'Please.'

'I'm impressed,' she said, 'ordering like a local. No tea, toast and marmalade like most of your countrymen?' She smiled.

'May I get you something, señorita?'

'Lydia. Lydia Barrera-Martin, Spanish Intelligence. I'll be your liaison during your time in Spain, señor.' His question went unanswered. 'We were to be introduced on Monday at the embassy, but with such a beautiful day I thought I might find you here.'

'As my liaison, perhaps you could show me around your beautiful city and recommend somewhere for lunch,' David said.

'Unfortunately, I have to visit my family today, but meet me here tomorrow at 2pm and we can have lunch and talk.'

Lydia removed her sunglasses, revealing her large brown eyes, and shook David's hand. 'Mañana,' she said.

David watched her leave. There was no engagement ring or wedding band – encouraging – but she was bound to have a boyfriend; she was too beautiful. As she turned the corner and disappeared, David sat down at his table and started to plan out his conversation for the next day.

CHAPTER 35

Madrid

April 1973

Lydia was already at the cafe when David arrived as requested at two o'clock. She was dressed casually in tight jeans and a T-shirt, with her sunglasses perched on her head. David thought she looked like a movie star.

Hailing a taxi, they went to the Salamanca District, in the old quarter of the city. For lunch, Lydia chose a charming street cafe shaded by the beautiful old apartment blocks that characterised this part of Madrid.

They enjoyed delicious prawns cooked in garlic, tortillas and thinly sliced octopus sprinkled with olive oil and paprika. The architecture was ancient, and the streets were bustling with Madrileños, shopping and talking in a hive of activity.

'Your city is beautiful and so alive, I can't wait to explore it more,' David said.

'I'm glad you like it, and I'm happy to practise my English with you. I must apologise that I cannot spend more time with you, but I have a big meeting at the British Embassy tomorrow with their new liaison officer. You may have heard of him,' said Lydia, smiling.

'Of course, and I'm sure he will be delightful,' David said, continuing the joke.

'Until tomorrow,' said Lydia, kissing David on each cheek.

~

David's work at the embassy was mundane and uneventful, but after the chaos of Ireland he wasn't complaining, especially if it meant spending more time with the stunning Spanish intelligence officer. They had lunch or dinner at least twice a week, talking about their families and upbringing and the culture of their prospective countries. They were opposites. Lydia had an extremely close, large family, whereas David didn't even know who his actual parents were but instead explained his love and admiration for his adoptive parents in Scotland.

Lydia loved to dance, which was not a skill David possessed. But dance he would, often into the early hours of the morning, watching the sunrise with Lydia as the late-night revellers spilt onto the quiet streets. By now he knew he was falling for his Spanish colleague. He was concerned that Lydia was less interested in him; she never invited him back to her apartment or suggested she go to his.

With the season, that was about to change.

'You know next week I have holidays,' said Lydia. 'Nothing much happens in Spain during the summer, and the office runs on bones staff.'

'You mean skeleton staff,' David corrected, laughing gently.

'I'm going to my hometown for two weeks and wondered if you would like to visit. I can show you a different part of my country. It's a small town called Pedraza, in the province of Segovia. It's only two hours by train, and there's a lovely hotel that I could book for you. What do you think – would you like to come?'

'That would be wonderful,' replied David. 'Are you sure your family won't mind?'

Lydia squeezed his hand and kissed his cheek. 'I'm sure, but I can't invite you to the house. Spain and my parents' generation are still much behind your country with relationships, and, well, it's just better if we see each other in the town. Come next Wednesday – it's a wonderful time of year, we have a festival of light. Every house and building will have candles in their windows and on the street. It's a magical fiesta. I'll make a reservation for you at the Hotel de la Villa.'

~

After arriving in Pedraza, David checked in to the hotel and met Lydia at the Bar Andres in the central plaza of the medieval town. The sun was setting, casting a golden orange glow that gradually sank below the town walls. The townspeople lit their candles and the whole area was basked in flickering flames of yellow and gold.

'Could you have asked for anything more romantic?' said Lydia. 'Let's walk a little.'

Lydia held David's hand as she showed him around the ancient town, a sense of excitement in her voice as she recounted her childhood memories, pointing out every building that held a place in her heart.

They went for dinner and enjoyed succulent lamb with sliced potatoes followed by sweet chocolate desserts, the culinary specialty of the area. The night was jet black, the sky full of stars, the summer air made even warmer by the thousands of candles that were burning brightly all around the town. They walked again in silence, soaking up the peaceful atmosphere, the flickering flames adding to the calm that swaddled the small hamlet.

As they completed their tour, they found themselves back at the hotel, too soon.

'I hope you enjoyed your evening,' said Lydia. 'It's hard in our profession to talk openly, which is why I brought you here, to show you everything that is close to me, that I love. This is my expression of trust in you, David.'

'I love it, Lydia – the town, the people! It's been a magical night, it's truly wonderful and I feel, well, humble that you chose to share all this with me. I hope one day I can show you England and Scotland, where I grew up, but it will be impossible to compete with this.'

For a long moment, they didn't say anything further, just sharing a meaningful gaze.

'Will you stay?' David asked quietly.

'Not tonight. We can wait,' Lydia said, smiling but with a hint of regret.

'I'll say goodnight then,' said David.

Lydia kissed him gently.

'Are you sure I can't walk you home?' he said.

'I'm quite safe in my hometown, and anyway I have fifteen cousins who will kill anyone who harms me. Remember that, guiri,' she said teasingly.

In the night, David was awoken, his senses disturbed – someone was in the room. He quietly slid his hand to the gun in his bedside drawer. He opened his eyes wide and saw the shape of the intruder moving behind the chair by the window. David cocked the gun and gave a warning: 'I'm armed.'

The intruder moved at lightning speed; David squeezed the trigger.

Click.

Nothing.

'Are you looking for these?' a familiar female voice said. The bullets from his gun dropped onto his chest.

'I couldn't wait,' said Lydia, pulling him into her arms.

~

David and Lydia soon returned to Madrid but would spend as many weekends as they could in Lydia's home town, he staying in the hotel, her visits getting longer and longer as time passed.

'I've been thinking, David, that it's time for you to be properly introduced to the family, especially my father,' she said one day.

'Not something that I will look forward to, but at least I've been trained in interrogation techniques. Although I'm not sure my Spanish will be up to it,' he replied.

'Don't worry, I will be there to translate – you will be fine.'

David's first visit with Lydia's father was terrifying. The Spanish Inquisition was clearly alive and well, although with Lydia translating he was not entirely convinced his answers weren't censored in some way.

~

On the 20th of November 1975, the Spanish ruler Franco died, and the authorities expected trouble. Lydia was transferred to Barcelona, where she had to infiltrate the pro-Catalan independence movement, which wanted to exploit the transition to democracy and plotted to carve out the large industrial province from the rest of Spain. David was ordered to remain in Madrid.

Lydia was gone for weeks on end with very little communication. The country was in a panic, with rival factions vying for power, the memory of the Civil War still very much alive, and mistrust was everywhere. David spoke to business leaders, politicians and ordinary citizens, developing a feel for the temperature of the country. Basque separatists called ETA carried out several bombings, injuring passers-by, and killed several right-wing politicians and a high-ranking police officer. David's informants would need to start delivering active intelligence; his boss wanted results and wanted them fast.

Lydia returned intermittently, exhausted, and angry at what was happening to her country. The stress of her assignment required all her attention and there was little room for David, which led to disappointment and arguments. For the first time, David started to doubt whether their relationship would survive.

But with time, the political situation began to calm; democracy was winning, and the extremist factions were tempered, though not eradicated. As security in the major cities grew, the people relaxed, and much to David's relief Lydia returned to Madrid two weeks before her twenty-fifth birthday.

David was invited back to Lydia's hometown, Pedraza, to celebrate. As they were now an established couple, David was allowed to stay at the house, although his bedroom on the ground floor was separated from Lydia's by the creakiest staircase he had ever heard. He told Lydia that he was convinced it was designed by the Catholic Church, probably by the Pope himself.

Finally able to relax, the couple walked her father's land, followed by two wild cats who played and fought, tumbling over each other.

The sun was setting over the town, golden shards of light extinguishing as the bright orb sank further behind building after building until it disappeared completely.

David stopped. He pulled Lydia close to him, the warmth of their bodies making them shiver in the cooling night air. She squeezed him even tighter, listening to his heartbeat, the steady rhythm getting faster and faster.

'I want to tell you something, something important,' David said.

'They're not sending you back to England, are they?'

'Nothing like that.' David held Lydia's hands and stared into her deep-brown eyes. 'I'm in love with you. Ever since I've met you, my life has changed. I feel loved by you, and I never want it to go away. I want you to become my wife. Will you marry me?'

'No,' she replied. David was stunned and wholly unprepared for this reply.

'Darling,' she said, a wicked smile on her face. 'In Spain, you must first ask for my father's blessing. Then, and only then, I will say yes.'

'You horrible woman!' David laughed with a sense of relief.

'If you're going to ask for my father's blessing, I cannot translate for you. You must do it all yourself. Let's go for a walk and I will teach you.'

For the next hour, they walked through the town, stopping to admire views, and practising the correct Spanish to have the conversation with Lydia's father.

David was nervous, silently reciting his speech in his head.

'I can't do this in front of the whole family,' he panicked.

'We will speak to him privately. I just wish my mother were here.'

Lydia's mother had died of cancer when she was only six years old. Her father and his family had raised her; he was everything to her, but he was conservative, clinging to the old ways, and here she was asking him to bless a marriage to a foreigner. She was worried.

'Let's find Papa before dinner,' Lydia said, 'so you can enjoy your food later.'

David stumbled through his words, rushing the speech, too eager to get to the end. Luckily, though, his Spanish was good enough to be understood.

Lydia's father took her hands and started to speak, slowly and directly, never taking his eyes from his youngest daughter.

Lydia translated for her father: 'This is not easy for me to agree to.'

David was surprised and concerned as a tear fell from Lydia's eye. She continued to speak her father's words.

'I see you as a good man, and I can see that you love my daughter, but you're not Spanish. You will return to England, or your government may send you to another country. What, then, will become of my daughter? If she is your wife, it is clear she will go with you. When you have children, they will be raised in England. So, when you ask me to bless your betrothal, you're asking me to give up my daughter.'

'But Papa, I love him – this is the man I want to spend my life with,' Lydia pleaded.

David asked Lydia to translate for him as he made his case.

'It's true that we both live dangerous lives, doing the jobs that we do, and I'm certain they will not leave me in Spain forever. But I love your daughter and I love your country, so I can promise you that we'll make our "home" here. Even if we are posted abroad, our heart and our family will be in Spain.'

'Please, Papa, say yes and make me happy,' Lydia begged.

Her father leant forward, holding one hand of each of them, looking directly at David. 'Make her happy, and if you cannot, send her back to me.'

Lydia hugged and kissed her father.

'Thank you, Papa,' said Lydia. She smiled at David, grabbing his hand. 'Now we must tell the family, and tomorrow the whole town will know. Last chance to run away!'

~

The wedding was attended by David's parents, who spent the day nodding and smiling, as they spoke no Spanish, and with their thick Scottish accents even the English contingent from the embassy found them hard to understand. Lydia's family were particularly impressed when they learnt that the British ambassador and his wife had accepted their invitation. The final attendee wasn't on the list and sat quietly at the back of the church, out of sight of the happy couple. Joan looked on with a sense of love and pain as she witnessed her son complete his vows.

'Oh, Alan, if you could see what I see,' she whispered to herself. She left silently through the back doors.

CHAPTER 36

Madrid

1978

The next two years were the happiest of the young couple's lives. They travelled extensively throughout Spain, visiting the Alhambra in Granada, skiing in the Pyrenees and sailing around the Balearic Islands. It was hard to believe that they were both professional spies, a profession hardly associated with a happy family life.

To complete this joyous existence, Lydia soon gave birth to their daughter, who they named Annabelle, born on the 6th of June 1978, the anniversary of D-Day. Perhaps it was an omen, as their life was about to change.

The IRA had stepped up its bombing campaign, not only in Belfast but also on the British mainland. This reign of terror intensified as the Provisional faction became more ambitious. During the summer of 1979, the Queen's cousin Lord Mountbatten was murdered when a bomb exploded aboard his boat off the coast of Ireland. This was followed a few hours later by an ambush on British soldiers at their barracks at Warrenpoint, Northern Ireland, where eighteen men were killed.

David was immediately recalled to London. They decided that Lydia would stay in Spain with the baby while he got settled.

He was sent back to Ireland to reconnect with old informants, seeking intelligence on the spate of recent bombings. But things had changed: the Provisional IRA were powerful, frightening. No one was willing to talk. David returned to London empty-handed and reported as much to his superiors.

~

In the spring of 1982, David was joined by his young family in a small two-bedroom apartment near Paddington Station. David was moved from the Irish desk as MI6 focused its attention on Argentina following the invasion of the disputed Falkland Islands.

A bloody war ensued through the tiny cluster of islands in the South Atlantic. Both sides sought political gain from the conflict, but the Argentine gamble failed as the British prime minister, Margaret Thatcher, committed superior forces to the region. Despite the loss of 200 British lives, Britain and her prime minister were able to announce victory only seventy-four days after the initial invasion.

Lydia saw little of her husband during the campaign. When he was at home, he either slept or appeared briefly for a change of clothes. To alleviate her boredom and loneliness, Lydia invited her sister Elena to visit, and they busied themselves with long walks through the London parks to Tower Bridge before returning by taxi. The sisters talked all day, soaking up the atmosphere, treating themselves with visits to the Harrods food halls, returning home to make lunch from their exquisite but costly purchases.

One morning, Lydia and her sister left the apartment for their customary walk in Hyde Park. Lydia had Annabelle in her pushchair and was talking to her sister about Spain and the friends and family she missed desperately. Suddenly, there was a thunderous explosion no more than 500 yards from their location – the shock wave knocked them down, the pushchair landing on its side.

Lydia, deafened by the blast, sought out her crying daughter, cradling her to her chest. Elena, a nurse, stood up, shaking, and walked towards the blast.

'Stop,' cried Lydia, 'there could be another bomb!'

'I must,' Elena replied.

David had heard the explosion from his office. He ran towards the park, the smoke rising in the sky guiding him to the location of the blast. He ran the two-mile distance in less than fifteen minutes, and soon found his wife and child being helped by medical staff, thankfully uninjured, his pulse reducing from combat mode as he found them safe. His sister-in-law was still helping the emergency services tend to the wounded before she was relieved by the arrival of further ambulance crews.

This was not to be the last bomb in Central London. The following year, on the 17th of December, at arguably the busiest location at the busiest time of year, a car bomb exploded outside Harrods itself. Despite a warning given by the IRA more than half an hour prior to the detonation, the area was not evacuated. Six people were killed and ninety injured.

The bombing shook the magnificent building, and also had a serious effect on a particular individual many miles away in Scotland. Joan visited her strongroom in the new year, relieved to find that Nautilus was unharmed and fully functional. The recent bombings made Joan uncomfortable, though. She realised that, should something happen to her, she would fail in her promise to Alan, and Nautilus could be destroyed or captured. She rented a safety deposit box in David's name and, before returning to Scotland, wrote out a complete dossier explaining how Nautilus functioned, the Protocol, codes and past uses, placing the documents in the box.

When she arrived back in Scotland, she gave the key to her solicitor with instructions to send it to David upon her death.

Of course, it would have been far simpler to contact David, who was nearly forty years old, and explain everything, but she wanted to wait, and not burden him with the weight of responsibility that came with the guardianship of Nautilus.

~

Nine months later, there was an attack on Margaret Thatcher and her party at the Grand Hotel in Brighton that killed five people and injured thirty. The Prime Minister was angry and upset that such a breach of security could occur and demanded results from the intelligence services.

David's workload doubled, and they decided it was best for Lydia and Annabelle to return to Spain. David would join them for Christmas.

Life back at the sleepy hamlet was rejuvenating for Lydia. With her family as doting babysitters to the six-year-old Annabelle, Lydia was able to spend time in Madrid visiting old friends and colleagues at the Spanish intelligence service.

The Spanish authorities wanted her back and offered her a position at the embassy in London, to start the following year. Lydia accepted immediately and was excited to call David with the good news.

Spotting an empty payphone across the street, she ran towards it before anyone could occupy the kiosk. Seeing the lights ahead change to red, she darted out between the double-parked cars. The driver of the lorry that ran the red light didn't see her and accelerated, killing Lydia instantly.

CHAPTER 37

London

November 1984

When he returned to England after the funeral, David volunteered for any mission that took him out of the country. The focus required to work in the field blocked his grief, only for it to return when he was alone at home. Lydia's perfume was still in the bathroom and on her clothes, still hanging in the small wardrobe. He remembered joking with her that they would need to move to a bigger apartment to house all her clothes and shoes.

He saw her everywhere: a glimpse of someone in the park, a smile on a stranger. Soon he realised he would go mad if he stayed in England. Thankfully, the world was a dangerous place, and the Service took full advantage of his skills and his desire for violence.

~

Four years later, Joan suffered her own grief following the death of her husband. The loneliness was unbearable. She needed her family, she needed David in her life and she was desperate to meet her granddaughter.

David was in Scotland for a break between missions, catching up with his parents and Annabelle, now ten years old.

Since the death of Lydia, Claire and David Senior were thankful and eager to raise Annabelle. Lydia's father agreed. After all, they lived in a small hamlet in Spain with a tiny school. Annabelle spoke a little Spanish but not enough to study.

Lydia's father knew that lack of contact would eventually estrange his granddaughter from him, but without her mother, his daughter, he released David from his obligation. David's recollection of the conversation at Lydia's funeral brought tears to his eyes.

Despite a wonderful week with his parents, he returned to London, a teary daughter begging him to stay longer. David realised that his absence from his daughter's life was getting harder, and that if things didn't change, she would grow used to him not being there for her and he could lose her – but return he must.

When he arrived at his apartment, there was a letter waiting, inviting him for afternoon tea at the Savoy. The venue was tempting, but he was in no mood to socialise and was about to discard the invite when he saw who it was from. When he'd studied at Cambridge, the mathematics professors would talk avidly about past alumni. They were particularly proud of the work achieved by Turing and Clarke, so the opportunity to meet such an esteemed individual, an Enigma code breaker, could not be ignored.

Two days later, he found himself walking excitedly through the lobby of the Savoy, realising he had no clue what Joan Clarke looked like. He took a seat at a small table and waited. At precisely 4pm, a small elderly lady walked towards him. Her pace was steady and determined; she was clearly a woman in fine health.

'I'm Joan Murray,' she said, introducing herself, 'but you may know me better as Joan Clarke.'

'An honour to meet you, Mrs Murray. I have to say you have me at a

163

complete loss as to why you'd want to meet me. All the same, I'm pleased that you do. Would you like some tea?' he enquired.

'Earl Grey and some of those delightful scones that they serve here would be lovely,' she replied.

David ordered, then sat patiently for a while, waiting for Joan to speak, but she was just looking at him, taking occasional sips of her tea.

'How can I help you?' he prompted.

She paused. Picking up her bone-china cup and saucer, she gave her tea a stir. 'As you know, the McIntoshes are not your biological parents.'

'Yes, my mother was their cousin.'

'That is not exactly true, contrary to your birth certificate,' said Joan. 'The McIntoshes are my dearest friends, and your mother is not their cousin and is very much alive. You see, the truth is that I am your mother, and I can also tell you who your father is.'

'I seriously doubt that anyone knows. I'm not sure what you are hoping to achieve here, but if you were my mother, I think my parents would have told me by now,' he said, upset with the conversation.

'Please hear me out, David,' she said. 'Your father was Alan Turing, God rest his soul.'

David sat back, looking at the woman, wondering who she was and what she was up to. Alan Turing being his father was ludicrous.

'Impossible,' he said finally, resolutely. 'I think I should go. I don't want any part of this conversation.'

He got up to go, but Joan laid her hand gently but firmly on his arm. 'Please stay,' she begged.

Joan signalled a waiter and ordered two whiskies. Reaching inside her bag, she retrieved a large brown envelope. She showed David photos of her much younger self with Claire and David McIntosh Senior. She was holding a baby, David Junior. She showed him her passport and a copy of his misleading birth certificate, together with several letters and photographs from the McIntoshes keeping Joan up to date with his progress.

The waiter brought over two crystal glasses of single malt, placing them on the table with a small glass jug of water on the side.

Gradually, the evidence mounted for David – but there was one part he still couldn't accept.

'Alan Turing was gay – how can that be possible?'

'It was just one night. We were drunk and celebrating and I, well, I cared for him deeply—'

'But why have you waited so long to tell me? And if any of this is true, why did you give me up in the first place?'

'I agonised over my decision. Alan was furious, but it would've been impossible for us to be a family. He and I weren't cut out to be parents. Please don't blame Alan, or Claire and David for that matter. I swore them to secrecy. It was my decision, mine alone. I chose, I hope, a better life for you, with people I trusted and who I knew would give you the love that you'd need.'

'You chose well – I'll not argue with you against Claire and David, they're my parents in my eyes and my heart. I love them dearly, as much as any son can,' he said. 'But why tell me now? Why cause this pain? Why tell me at all? What good can come of this? I'm sorry, Joan, but this is very confusing for me.'

Joan could see the anguish in her son's face, but she forced herself to continue.

'Two reasons, really, both entirely selfish. I've followed your life closely, with the generous help of your parents, my dear friends. I attended your graduation and even saw you briefly at your wedding to your beautiful wife. I was so sorry to learn of her death.'

David nodded, closing his eyes for a moment.

'After the war, I married an ex-soldier. We lived happily for over thirty years, and I kept my secret from both of you. He died, and as I said, for purely selfish reasons, I find myself not wanting to be alone when I have a son and a granddaughter.'

The mention of his daughter jolted him to the present.

'What am I going to tell Annabelle?' he said in panic.

'If you can ever forgive me, I would very much like to be involved in your life, and Annabelle's. There would be no need to tell her who I really am, and I certainly do not want to interfere with Claire and David's position as her grandparents, but perhaps you could introduce me as an ancient aunt?'

'You seem very adept at living a lie, Joan, but I'm not. I don't want to have that relationship with *my* child.'

The accusation was clearly understood by Joan.

'You said there were two reasons?' he said coldly, refusing to decide on this matter on the spot.

'The second is more complicated, and I suppose could be considered a gift or a curse from your biological father. It also necessitates a trip to Knightsbridge to fully explain the matter.'

David was confused and upset, finding it hard to hide his feelings. Why had his parents not told him? And if this was true, why should he hide the lie from his own daughter? He would phone home to Scotland tonight, an unpleasant call but a necessary one, to confirm what he had heard from this woman claiming to be his mother.

'I know nothing about you except your reputation,' he said. 'What you are telling me is upsetting, disruptive and hurtful. I need to talk to my parents.'

'I'm sorry for so many things, but please know that I love you. I want you to know where you came from, and if you can find a little space in your heart to forgive me, it would make an old woman very happy.'

Finally, David could take no more. He agreed to meet her the following week outside Harrods, if only to end the conversation so that he could make his escape.

CHAPTER 38

London

November 1986

David called Claire that night. She was expecting the call. Joan had rung earlier to warn her and recounted the conversation she had with David. She apologised profusely for putting her friend in this position but explained her predicament and how lonely she felt. Claire was upset but forgave her old friend.

David was less forgiving.

Between her sobs and saying sorry a hundred times, Claire confirmed the identity of his biological parents. David was immensely angry; he felt a sense of betrayal from his parents, more so even than from Joan for abandoning him. He didn't know Joan, so there was no emotion there, but with his mother there was loss. It felt like his life was a lie.

He hated being angry with his parents, though, and agreed to return to Scotland after his appointment with Joan. He spent the next few days researching his unknown family, Joan and Alan. He even visited Bletchley Park to see where they'd met, and learnt more about Enigma and the effect they both had on the war. He couldn't help but feel a little pride regarding their achievements and, surprisingly, his own heritage.

He met Joan as agreed outside Knightsbridge tube station, directly opposite Harrods. 'Why are we here?'

'Follow me and say nothing,' said Joan, all business.

David didn't know what to make of this behaviour. What could this woman possibly want with him at Harrods? Still, he followed.

Once inside the strongroom, Joan explained to a dumbfounded David the different machinery in the room. Every detail of Nautilus's operation. She explained how it worked and the circumstances that necessitated its use by Alan for D-Day.

'This is ridiculous! You're saying that Alan Turing – who you purport to be my father – built a time machine and changed history regarding the D-Day landings in World War II. And you want me to believe that this collection of antiques still has that power?'

'This is the second reason I had to see you. It was Alan's wish that the guardianship of Nautilus be passed on to you, his son. He would be so proud of your achievements, David.'

'What do you know of my achievements, Joan?' he said sceptically.

'Quite enough, thank you, David. I still have a few friends in the Service,' she said.

'To be clear. You're not saying that we, as humans, can travel back in time, but the machine you're calling Nautilus can send a message back in time to yourself.'

'Correct.'

'If what you say is true – and I'm not convinced, not even close – but if this machine can do what you say it can, I could warn her, Joan, I could save Lydia. Show me how to do it – send me a message about the truck in Madrid.'

Joan bit her lower lip, tears welling up in her eyes. 'The messages can only go back eight weeks. Alan built it this way fearing that anything further back could be catastrophic, too much intervention.'

'You could've warned me! If you were watching me like you say, why didn't you intervene? You could've saved her, Joan.'

'By the time I found out, I'd been in France for three months, well outside the time range.'

David was distraught, desperate to find a way to bring back his wife.

Joan chose not to mention that even if she had known in enough time, she wouldn't have acted, because of the agreed Protocol, that Nautilus could not be used for saving a single life.

Now was not the time to discuss the Protocol.

'Surely when you did find out, you could have sent the message back twice?' he asked.

'You are clever, but your father was extremely worried about that precise capability and the possibility of creating a paradox. Nautilus has a built-in timing device that only allows one message to be sent or received during a six-month period. I know this sounds incredibly cruel, but Alan designed all these restrictions to prevent multiple usage.'

David slumped into the chair, placing his face in his hands. His shoulders and chest began to convulse. The glimmer of hope snatched from his grasp felt like losing his wife all over again and the pain was intolerable. Joan could only look on, observing her son's grief, unable to console him.

She placed her hand gently on his arm. 'Let's go for a walk, David. You have been through enough for today. You must be feeling very confused, betrayed and God knows what else,' said Joan.

The biting wind whipped through the trees, giving flight to the fallen leaves. The harsh conditions seemed to flick a switch in David's brain and his survival instinct kicked in as he tried to make sense of all this new information. When he next spoke, there was no trace of emotion in his voice.

'This is a crazy story. Arguably the most important machine or weapon to exist, in the basement of Harrods. No wonder you never told anyone – they'd think you were senile.'

'When Alan told me for the first time, I had the same reaction as you. In fact, I wanted nothing to do with it. I even suggested it should be destroyed. But one of the main reasons I agreed to continue with Nautilus was because of you, and more lately Annabelle,' she said. 'You must never use Nautilus's power except as a last resort. The power is very much real, and with that power you can protect mankind, most likely from itself. Go home and let's meet tomorrow. I'll answer all the questions I can.'

David and Joan said their goodbyes and walked off in different directions through the park. The freezing wind helped David think clearly. The information he had received over the last days was incredible. But Joan Clarke was clearly not crazy, she was lucid, she was intelligent and had accomplished wonderous things. How could he not believe her? Everything he had been shown to support her words looked true. He had interrogated many people and in his professional opinion he could only conclude that she was telling the truth, however crazy it seemed.

Inside his apartment, he poured himself a whisky and went through the evidence one more time.

~

They met as agreed the next morning, at the Albert Memorial.

'We can walk through the park and talk some more,' Joan said.

'Tell me about Alan Turing.'

'Where to start?' said Joan. 'He was a brilliant man. Breaking the Enigma code saved untold lives and certainly shortened the war. But his unknown intervention with D-Day was most probably even more important, saving hundreds of thousands of lives and preventing Hitler from reversing his fortunes. It is for events such as these that he built Nautilus. And, should you accept, it will be your responsibility to carry forward his legacy.'

David had many questions, which Joan answered honestly and with love until it was time to part.

He continued to walk through the park, pulling up the collar of his coat tight around his neck to fight against the chill as he watched the small figure disappear into the grey winter's day.

He had spent the last few days learning so many things that would change his life, both personal and professional. The question now was whether he would accept everything that he'd been told. And if so, what would he do with this power?

CHAPTER 39

London

1990

Annabelle was living a complicated life for a girl so young, splitting her time between her grandparents in Scotland and her father in London, when he returned from his work overseas.

Her time with her dad was so precious that she would often miss school to join him at the London apartment or for a brief holiday in Spain with her Spanish family.

But the holidays were becoming less frequent. Her father seemed to be overseas nearly all the time.

When Annabelle turned eleven, she was with her father at home, so she decided to have a conversation with him about school. 'Daddy, next term, I'm going to high school.'

'Are you worried about it?'

'No, not really, but I've been thinking it might be better if I board.'

'You have?' said David quizzically.

'I just think with all your overseas work, it will be better for both of us. The school is near Grandma and Grandad, so I can see them at weekends, and when you're back you can come to Scotland or I can come down to London. What do you think?' she asked.

'I think you're only eleven years old, Belle. I've spent a lot of time overseas lately. I can try to cut the trips down if you like?'

Annabelle saw the guilt in his eyes, the pain that he was suffering, and wished she could take it away.

'I know you don't like to talk about your work, but I'm not stupid, Dad. I know you work in intelligence and you have to travel. I'm very proud of you. I just think it will be easier for me if I can have a routine at school and with you. I have lots of friends, so I won't be sad,' she said.

David's heart was fit to burst with the thoughtfulness displayed by his daughter, wise beyond her years.

'You're an exceptional young lady, Belle, and your mama would be very proud of you, just as I am. Are you sure this is what you want? That you'll be happy?'

'I'm sure.'

David hugged his daughter, kissing her on top of her head.

'Have you spoken to your grandparents about this?'

'Yes, Dad, they just want me to be happy, and let's face it, it will be easier for them if I'm at school during the term.'

David recognised the generosity being offered by his impressive daughter and nodded.

'Okay, Belle, let's get you to the station and back to the oldies. They'll be waiting for you as usual on the station platform.'

~

With his daughter settled into school, David informed MI6 that he wanted to go back into the field. He didn't have to wait long.

In August 1990, Saddam Hussein's Iraqi forces invaded Kuwait.

Despite diplomatic attempts to force his withdrawal, the dictator refused. Within months of the invasion and with the invitation from King Fahd of Saudi Arabia, 500,000 troops from multiple nations were deployed to the area. David was attached to the SAS to provide communications support between MI6, the military and their CIA liaison.

The allied forces launched a massive air strike against the Iraqis. However, they were well defended with Scud missiles and the elite Republican Guard, who were experienced soldiers, respected by the special forces.

David put forward an idea to plant a virus in the Iraqi early-warning system, but he would need access to an Iraqi military computer. Three days later, he set out under the cover of darkness to capture the device, accompanied by twelve men from the regiment. As they passed into enemy territory, David could feel the adrenaline coursing through his veins as he and the raiding party sought out their prey.

They travelled slowly and silently through the desert terrain, stopping suddenly for any noise, scouring the horizon with their night-vision goggles, looking for any human contact. They'd been walking for three hours when a glare appeared around a hundred yards in front of David's position. The platoon froze as they all saw the faint glow of a lit cigarette.

Drawing their knives, four of the soldiers moved out, two going to the right of the lookout post and two to the left. David lay on his stomach watching the four soldiers slide into the foxhole. Within seconds, he was tapped on the shoulder and signalled to join them.

He climbed in, passing four corpses with their throats cut, and searched for the military-grade laptop. One of the sergeants found the machine, and David quickly uploaded the software. Satisfied that his virus had been accepted by the Iraqi system, he gave the signal to leave and joined the rest of the platoon waiting for him above.

One week later, the Desert Storm air offensive commenced, and the skies were lit up with thousands of missiles that rained down on the unprepared defenders. David's plan had worked: the defenders were overwhelmed, and hundreds of Iraqi soldiers surrendered to the allies.

When the ground offensive began in February 1991, the sheer scale was incredible. With superior artillery and air support, the allies were unstoppable. Within a week, Kuwait was returned as a sovereign nation and David returned to London.

~

Fighting in the field excited David: his skills served a purpose, often saving the lives of his comrades, who were happy to have him as a member of their team. The overwhelming combination of fear and euphoria also meant it was the only time he didn't think of Lydia.

It became addictive. So when, only a year later, a civil war broke out in what was the old communist Yugoslavia, David volunteered to go out with the UN peacekeeping force deployed there, reporting back to MI6 in London.

Yugoslavia was a collection of republics – Bosnia, Croatia, Serbia, Slovenia, among others – but the ethnicities were complex, with a large Muslim community in Bosnia, Serbs living in Croatia and Croats living in Bosnia. When Slovenia declared independence on June 25th, 1991, Bosnia followed suit three months later, and Serbia declared war. The Serbian army was brutal, as was its leader, Slobodan Milošević. What followed was a bloody genocide, with massacres under the Serb commander Ratko Mladić killing thousands of Muslim refugees in Srebrenica.

What was more appalling for David was that these atrocities were carried out under his own eyes and the eyes of 400 UN peacekeepers. They were powerless to intervene. The rules of engagement allowed them to fire their weapons only if fired upon.

David sent report after report detailing the horrors that he witnessed. He supplied photographic evidence of mass murders and other atrocities to his superiors in London, begging them to send more troops and a change in their orders. The request fell on deaf ears, the conflict continuing for another three years.

During his second tour, David joined a British patrol in a Croatian village. David had received intel that a company of Serbian soldiers led by two tanks were on their way to the village. The British soldiers and David were urging the villagers to flee; most had. With the village nearly empty, David entered what he thought was a deserted house, only to find twelve children guarded by two nuns. With the Serbian approach only minutes away, David quickly loaded the frightened children into the British Humvees to aid their escape. But the British officer, a captain, ordered his men to evict the children from the vehicles. The men knew the Serbs would murder the children and do untold acts to the nuns before killing them.

'Please, sir,' begged a corporal, turning to David. 'Can you convince the captain to take them? You know what's going to happen to them if we leave them here.'

'I'll try, corporal, I'll try.'

David approached the captain, who was busy offloading a young boy who could have been no more than eight years old. David put his hand on the captain's outstretched arm, causing him to twist round violently – his eyes, full of murder, locked on to David's face.

'For pity's sake, captain, we can't leave these kids here. They will be slaughtered, you know they will,' pleaded David.

At first, David thought he saw the fight leave the captain, but he was mistaken. It wasn't anger in his eyes; it was ambivalence. The captain said nothing and returned to his task of ejecting the children from the Humvee.

David drew his gun, placing the barrel behind the captain's head. 'I really must insist.'

The captain withdrew his hand from a five-year-old girl and stood still, silent, while his men hastily reloaded the refugees, until finally the column drove off, the soldiers smiling at David, saying silent thank-yous.

When they returned to base, David fully expected to be arrested, but the military police didn't come. The captain simply walked to the mess without saying a word. The soldiers, still smiling, took their precious cargo to a neighbouring village where they would be safe – at least for a week or so, thought David.

It felt so futile in Bosnia. The rules tied the hands of the British soldiers, and the Serbians knew they wouldn't be attacked, giving them free rein to commit further atrocities. He thought about Joan Clarke and the machine, Nautilus. Could they help – could the machine change the situation in the Balkans – could he stop the murders? But he realised the answer was no. MI6 and the UN already had all the information from his own reports. What possible further information could he send back to himself that would change the situation on the ground? None.

He began to see that the power of Nautilus could also be a curse.

CHAPTER 40

Scotland

1995

David's experience in the Balkans had a profound effect on him. The unwillingness of powerful nations to intervene when barbarous acts were being committed upon innocent civilians made him question his own purpose and the organisation he worked for. It also made him think about the nature of war, and Nautilus. If what Joan Clarke had told him was true, he could have the power to change a major global war or even prevent one altogether. Now that, he thought, would be a real purpose. There was honour in saving life.

With this shining glimmer of hope easing his soul, he planned a visit to Scotland. First to see Annabelle, now a beautiful, intelligent but sometimes precocious seventeen-year-old, and then to see Joan.

Annabelle was taking her final exams and would, her grades permitting, be moving south to study biochemistry at Oxford University, much to the chagrin of her father, who, being a Cambridge man, could not help but consider the esteemed university as the old enemy.

He spent a wonderful two weeks with his daughter. In between her studies, he talked to his parents, drinking whisky and telling stories about his adventures, albeit censored so as not to upset them with the real horrors that he had seen.

With Annabelle knee-deep into her books, he visited Joan to talk more about Nautilus and the Protocol. When he arrived, he was shocked by her frailty. She was dying. Over the next few days, they talked as much as Joan's body would permit. She battled to stay awake, determined to tell him as much as she could, to enjoy his company. She was frustrated with her weakness.

Holding his hand, she said, 'Don't fret, dear, don't grieve for me. These last years with you, watching Annabelle grow, have been the happiest years of my life. Thank you for accepting me.'

He looked at the sallow old face looking up at him, her love still shining through her watery eyes. She inched herself up on her bed pillows, the effort causing a coughing fit that left her exhausted.

'Rest,' David said.

'Nonsense, I need to speak to you,' she said, still stern despite her fragility. 'You must enjoy your life, David, enjoy your daughter, don't worry about getting old, just be thankful you had the opportunity. Be the best man you can be, the best father, do you hear me?'

'Yes, Mother,' he replied.

'Yes, Mother,' she repeated in wonder.

Joan smiled at her son and closed her eyes, for the last time. David searched her face, her calm expression. She was at peace, and he was glad to have known her.

David attended the funeral with Annabelle. He felt guilty not telling her that they were burying her grandmother and not some friend of the family. He finally accepted why Joan had kept herself hidden. But now was not the time to reveal the family secret. Annabelle was too young to carry such a burden, and he wondered whether he would ever have the strength to pass on the legacy to his daughter. Protecting Annabelle was his most important mission.

~

After the funeral, a package arrived from a firm of solicitors in Edinburgh. Opening it, David saw a letter from Joan explaining that everything necessary to maintain and operate Nautilus was in a safety deposit box at Harrods that could be opened with the key that he slid into his hand from a small envelope.

David considered throwing the key and letter away, letting Nautilus rot within the strongroom. But Nautilus was a connection to his family and – no matter the reason that Alan Turing had built the machine – he, David, was now its guardian. He made the choice to guard its secret for future generations.

Remembering his promise to Joan, he spoilt Annabelle at every opportunity during the years of her undergraduate studies, with holidays in Greece, France and, mostly, Spain, the land of her mother. The long summer nights and carefree attitude of the Spanish lifted the melancholy from his heart. The joy of watching his daughter torment the local youths with her beauty added laughter to the family gatherings.

'Come on, Belle, leave those poor boys alone, we need to pack,' he said one evening. 'We're going to Málaga tomorrow, and we need to catch an early train.'

'What's in Málaga?'

'A surprise. Now, let's get some sleep.'

The train journey was long and stifling in the heat, but finally they arrived in the Andalusian city. He hired a car and drove them to Mijas, a small town in the mountains overlooking Marbella, on the Costa del Sol.

David parked the car in the central plaza, surrounded by white-painted houses with orange-tiled roofs. Together they walked the last 200 yards shaded by palm trees that swayed nonchalantly in the light summer breeze.

He stopped in front of a large iron gate. Taking a set of keys from his pocket, he unlocked it, stepping into the gardens. Annabelle stood still and gazed at the sights. The cottage was over two floors, the sun beating off the white walls typical of southern Spain. A pagoda covered in vine leaves with bunches of grapes threatening to drop to the ground provided a shady oasis where springwater flowed into a well. The garden was bursting with colour from wildflowers and fruit trees, scented with olives ripening in the evening sun, still high in the sky despite the late hour.

'Whose is this place, Dad?' Annabelle asked in awe.

'Ours. I've bought it for us. You can study here when you don't need to be at home, escape the English winters. I might retire here.'

'It's divine. Mama would have loved it too, making a home in Spain.'

Annabelle walked around the garden, picking fruit and popping strawberries into her mouth.

They spent the week exploring the town and the beach in Marbella. They discovered local bars and restaurants and savoured delights from freshly caught fish to succulent steaks cooked on the fire of the Asador, a small family establishment only a quarter of a mile from their house. The food was amazing and the views over the mountains and sea breathtaking. The holiday was what both needed, but it came to an end too soon and it was time to leave.

When they returned to London, Annabelle kissed her father goodbye and took the coach to Oxford to continue her studies. When she arrived at the university, there was a letter waiting for her. The faculty had offered her a doctoral scholarship, with funding for a three-year PhD exploring viral diseases. She was so excited that she phoned her father immediately with the good news.

David was proud of his daughter; her future seemed to be on the right track. Maybe it was time to think of his.

Work was incredibly boring at his Vauxhall Cross office. Like every company or organisation in the world, MI6 was preparing for the new millennium, running tests on their software and security against the Y2K bug.

On the 1st of January 2000, the world woke up to hangovers and memories of stolen kisses, some regretted, some not. But there were no planes falling from the sky, ATMs were working and government records remained intact, much to the disappointment of some.

David would become eligible for early retirement in two years. He'd had enough of chasing bad guys but was getting tired of the desk. A role came up in recruitment and training, an area in which he thought he could add some real value, so he jumped at the chance. The roster was six weeks on, six weeks off, which suited him down to the ground, allowing him plenty of time to visit the villa in Mijas and spend time with Annabelle.

However, his plans for a more serene life were about to be turned upside down.

CHAPTER 41

New York

September 11th, 2001

At 8am on September 11th, 2001, the people of New York were making their way to work like any other day. Collecting their coffee from Starbucks, taking the subway and basking in the glorious clear blue skies of this autumnal Tuesday morning in the Big Apple.

Forty-six minutes later, the world changed.

Osama bin Laden and his terrorist organisation, Al Qaeda, had been planning the attacks for years. It had taken extraordinary training, funding and, most of all, security. They caught the world's best security forces completely off guard. The network of spies, counterterrorism agencies and confidential informants were impotent before this terror. Billions of dollars had been invested in preventing events like September 11 – the return on that investment was now looking extremely poor.

Nineteen Islamic terrorists from Saudi Arabia and three other Arab nations had arrived in the USA, many of them more than one year prior to the attacks. They took private flying lessons at commercial aviation schools and blended into society as unremarkable foreign residents.

On the morning of this fateful day, they boarded four planes destined for California, which ensured that they had full fuel tanks for the cross-country flight. They smuggled on board box cutters and knives. The pilots' cabin doors could be opened from the outside.

At 8.46am, American Airlines Flight 11, a Boeing 767 loaded with 80,000 litres of fuel, was flown by the terrorists into the ninety-sixth floor of the North Tower of the World Trade Center, instantly killing all on board and hundreds more. Thousands were trapped on the floors above in the 110-storey skyscraper.

At first, authorities believed it was a freak accident. Seventeen minutes later, that idea was squashed when United Airlines Flight 175 entered the New York skyline, turned rapidly and plunged into the eighty-first floor of the South Tower. People began to realise that they were being attacked – an attack against America, and on American soil.

Two further flights, American Airlines Flight 77 and United Airlines Flight 93, were to attack the Pentagon and the White House. At 9.37am, the American Airlines flight crashed into the west side of the Pentagon, its jet fuel igniting into an inferno, incinerating the passengers and killing a further 125 military personnel from the Department of Defense.

As United 93 approached its target, many passengers had made calls on airphones and learnt of the attacks on the Twin Towers. Even though the terrorists had already taken over the plane and killed the pilots, the passengers knew they had to act or die in the planned suicide mission.

The terrorists were attacked, the courageous passengers and cabin crew arming themselves with anything that they could find, from cutlery to boiling water.

As the aircraft approached its destination, three F-16 jet fighters from the 1st Fighter Wing at Langley Air Force Base had been scrambled. Due to poor communication and total confusion at the Federal Aviation Administration, two of the fighters were ordered out to sea by the North American Aerospace Defense Command. The third jet picked up the airliner on its scope as the flying bomb approached the White House. The unexpected flight meant that the F-16 had not been armed. The pilot was undeterred: he was clear about his mission – the airliner had to be intercepted. The lieutenant guided his plane to intercept the passenger aircraft. United 93 was in rapid descent, passing 5000 feet and travelling at over 700 miles per hour. The F-16 was converging at a combined speed of Mach 1.5.

The Boeing 757 was only 500 yards from the White House when the two planes collided. The courageous fighter pilot never considered ejecting from his aircraft; his mission was to protect the President, his commander-in-chief. The impact was spectacular. Despite the fearless actions of the aviator, the remains of United 93 struck the residential block of the White House, killing twelve people, including four members of the Secret Service.

Thanks to the Secret Service, the First Family, including President Bush, were now safe inside the bunker, the Presidential Emergency Operations Center.

The live feeds coming out of New York and Washington were being broadcast around the globe. For long minutes, the world seemed to stop. People watched in horror as the cameras picked up the images of office workers jumping out of the towers to certain death to avoid the pain of being burnt alive. Emergency crews had entered both buildings to find anyone alive so they could lead them out, to safety. The terror of the onlookers on the ground and of the billions watching their televisions suddenly changed to horror as they witnessed first one tower and then the second collapse under the extreme heat generated from the burning jet fuel.

For a moment, there was shock and then anger. The streets were silent as Lower Manhattan was shrouded in a fine grey dust. Residents and workers walked from the scene stunned by what they had witnessed.

~

David called Annabelle. It was a natural reaction to tragedy: he wanted to reassure her that she was safe and that he, her father, would make things right.

'Oh my God, those poor people,' Annabelle said.

'It's awful, no one seems to know what's going on,' David said. 'The whole country has gone onto high alert. Stay where you are – don't catch any trains or buses. I have to stay at the office but will call you when I can.'

In London and the rest of Europe, there was a sense of selfish relief, as the non-US population realised this was happening in a far-off land, mercifully not at home.

But that was about to change. This attack was global, and bin Laden had orchestrated a simultaneous campaign across the world.

In London at 3pm local time, a barge on the Thames filled with high explosives rammed into the wall of the Houses of Parliament, killing over one hundred Members of Parliament who were finishing their late lunches on the terrace overlooking the normally innocent riverscape.

David saw the explosion from his office, and within seconds smoke rose from what he instinctively knew to be the target.

He stood and stared out of the window, joined by his colleagues on the fourth floor of MI6 headquarters, dumbstruck, useless. When he found himself able to act again, he grabbed his jacket. 'Come on, you lot, pick up a weapon and let's go and see what we can do.'

He knew they were going to be of little help, but he couldn't stand still. At the very least, they could all go to St Thomas' Hospital and donate blood. He had a feeling it would be needed.

Boats were also used in Moscow and Sydney, where their targets were more symbolic than life-threatening. Two teams, each with six terrorists, used rigid inflatable boats to get close to their firing positions. Employing FGM-148 Javelin anti-tank missiles, the first team fired their high-explosive warheads into the Kremlin and St Basil's Cathedral in

Moscow, while the Australian-based team fired at the famous Sydney Opera House, destroying the iconic sail-design roof completely.

In Paris, a terrorist-controlled Boeing 757 flew into the Eiffel Tower, killing over 1000 people. In Hong Kong, a British Airways jumbo jet took off with 350 passengers; an hour later, with the flight crew murdered, the aircraft retuned to Hong Kong airspace and flew into the Bank of China Tower.

Within hours of the North Tower being struck, carnage and mayhem had been delivered to five other cities around the world. Panic ensued; every major city thought it was going to be next.

Hours passed without further attacks, but security forces were still too nervous to believe it was over. The death toll soon reached 10,000. The world was stunned and outraged that something of this scale could be perpetrated by a terrorist organisation operating from a third-world country, Afghanistan. How could this happen, thought David.

President Bush and his fellow national leaders were asking the same questions.

Bin Laden and his Al Qaeda followers had struck fear into the bellies of the infidels. Planes were grounded and the world stock markets began to tumble, exactly as he had planned. Governments were looking for answers among the chaos. News crews reported around the clock, adding unwanted pressure on government agencies and their employees.

The success of the attacks was so profound that they resulted in bin Laden appearing in a rare interview on Al Jazeera, claiming that the Jihad, or Holy War, against the West and its allies had begun and that Islamists from every nation should join the fight against the infidel.

This situation could not go on; it had shaken the very foundations of life on earth. President Bush called his counterparts in the UK, Russia, France, Australia and China, as well as many others within NATO.

He called for a War on Terror, a decisive act that would seek out and destroy not only Al Qaeda but any country that assisted it with arms, shelter or funds. These nations would suffer the wrath of reciprocity, and an ultimatum was delivered to the Taliban, Pakistan and Iraq, even the Saudis: deliver Osama bin Laden and all Al Qaeda terrorists to US or NATO forces.

The deadline came and went without a single prisoner being yielded. At Camp David, President Bush and his allies prepared their response.

CHAPTER 42

The Middle East and Central Asia

October 1st, 2001

Operation Reciprocity was to be unique. It was the first time that Russia, China and the US – along with its NATO allies – had agreed on a combined military campaign, one that would use weaponry and troops from all nations.

The campaign started with air strikes from Russian and American aircraft carriers in the Arabian Sea. Seasoned naval commanders looked on in disbelief as American and Russian ships sailed side by side, coordinating missile attacks from their vast arsenal of weaponry. Their targets were the Taliban training grounds situated around the capital of Afghanistan, Kabul. The attacks found their targets and the Taliban withdrew to the Spīn Ghar mountains and their intricate Tora Bora caves, which formed a natural haven. These caves had harboured the Taliban and Mujahideen for many years and were thought to be impenetrable. Many other fighters fled across the border to Pakistan, seeking refuge in the tribal villages, but this time they were pursued.

Russian and Chinese fighter jets and stealth bombers attacked the villages, releasing the full force of their payloads, wiping out every living soul.

In Iraq, NATO forces bombed military bases throughout the country, including the capital, Baghdad. The air strikes lit up the sky by night. During the day, the smoke was so intense that the sun was obscured, as if nightfall approached. Wave after wave of aircraft delivered their fatal cargo. Most of the military targets were destroyed, but the collateral damage, thousands of innocent civilians' lives, was a high price to pay. The Iraqi military resorted to their old tactic of using human shields, basing their command posts within hospitals or in civilian offices. This time, there was no quarter – cruise missiles were guided into their quarry, wiping out soldier and patient alike.

Five hundred thousand Russian and Chinese soldiers entered Kabul and the surrounding mountain ranges, seeking out insurgents, Taliban, anyone sympathetic to the cause of terrorism. In Baghdad, 300 US tanks and 200,000 NATO troops surrounded the city.

Pakistan made an idle threat to oppose the military forces, but when faced with overwhelming firepower it chose to fight in the United Nations rather than the field and street.

The hunt for bin Laden intensified.

~

David was sent to Baghdad to help with intel gathering and the questioning of prisoners.

When large cash bribes failed to bring in intel, they were replaced by brutal interrogations, some resulting in death. Bin Laden was cunning, moving from place to place. Despite the huge resources available to NATO, he couldn't be found.

Disappointed to not have seen results, David returned to London.

Due to his extensive skills, he was seconded to MI5, domestic security being the government's top intelligence priority. His task was to find out who had attacked the various target nations and to arrest and detain all known associates and sympathisers within the UK. Hundreds of people were detained in a makeshift prison camp at Wembley Stadium; barbed wire now surrounded the hallowed ground, and armed guards patrolled the terraces. David interviewed religious leaders, troublemakers and extremists, searching for anyone with a connection to the attacks.

Finding the identities of the actual perpetrators was easy. Their names were posted online, where the terrorists were hailed as the protagonists of the Jihad. What was distressing and fast becoming political gold was how many were known to the international security services. The pilot terrorists had mostly trained in US flight schools, one of which had filed a report to the FAA, noting that one of the pilots had poor English and even worse flying skills. But like many such reports, it had joined many more waiting to be read, no action taken until it was too late.

The mood around the world had changed. There was a new fear, mistrust of anyone who looked like the photos that were plastered across the newspapers. Female Muslims wearing burqas might as well have had the word 'terrorist' stitched into their clothing. Even at Annabelle's AstraZeneca laboratory in Oxford, all ethnic workers were screened and reassigned to projects that did not involve possibly harmful viruses such as Ebola. One of Annabelle's team, an Iranian doctor of viral medicine, was taken away and sent to Wembley despite her protests and those of her colleagues. Annabelle was so enraged by this action that she decided to visit her father.

David returned home to his apartment mentally exhausted after a particularly gruelling interrogation. All he wanted to do was take a long shower, enjoy a large single malt and sit on his couch watching a mindless movie. Seeing his daughter's coat on the hook behind the door, though, he knew that wasn't going to happen. Well, maybe the whisky.

'Hello, Belle,' he called, hanging up his coat next to her much more expensive Burberry jacket.

'I'm in here,' shouted Annabelle.

'I thought I told you to stay in Oxford,' he said.

'You did, but judging by the mess in here and all these plastic dinners, it looks like I've arrived just in time,' she said.

David was too exhausted to argue with his daughter, so he kissed her and opened a bottle of Rioja from their wine cellar in Spain. He poured two glasses of the aromatic wine and savoured his first sip. The oaky liquid slipped down his throat, taking away a small piece of the day's stress; he felt better with every mouthful.

Annabelle served a steaming plate of perfectly prepared pasta with crab, prawns and smoked salmon tossed in a creamy sauce and garnished with fresh parsley and chilli.

'Wonderful,' he muttered through a mouthful of the delicious food. 'Is this a social visit or is something on your mind?' He was slightly suspicious of the star treatment.

'A daughter can't cook dinner for her father without suspicion?' She pouted.

'I know you. What's the problem?'

'These attacks of course have been ghastly, and I'm sure you are up to your eyes in work, tracking all the perpetrators down. But have you seen what's going on in our own country? The neo-Nazis are having a field day, the police are abusing their powers and, well, quite frankly, if you're not white you are being told that you should stay inside and keep your head down, otherwise you could end up in that pitiful excuse of a camp at Wembley! What's next? Will they come after me, being olive-skinned and half-Spanish? I've already been mistaken before for someone born in the Middle East – it's bloody frightening.'

He took another sip of wine, unwilling to debate the backlash against immigrants within the UK. Instead, he tidied the dinner plates to the sink.

He sighed. 'What's your friend's name?'

Annabelle became coy, her not-so-subtle manipulation of her father having failed at the first hurdle. 'What do you mean?'

'Who have you lost?'

'Her name is Dr Armani Raja. She's not even Afghani, she's Iranian, been here for over five years.'

'I'll find out what I can and let you know.'

'There has to be a military response to the attacks, and homeland security obviously will be at a heightened state, but there's a fine line between what's happening across Europe and America right now and, well, fascism. I think that if we were in Germany in 1936, it would feel very much the same. I know you can't tell me what you are doing at MI6, but please don't let anger and revenge replace your humanity, Dad.'

Dinner finished, Annabelle turned on the television and poured a whisky for them both. The news revealed what David already knew. The names of the terrorists and the number of times they had visited the US, the UK and Afghanistan without raising any red flags.

'That's a bit embarrassing for your team,' said Annabelle. 'None of this was being looked into? Was there nothing you guys could have done to prevent this?'

Her question stuck in David's mind. He knew he had the power to make a change. If he used Nautilus, he could save lives – but should he?

He toyed with the conundrum all night. His first reaction and go-to position was, like Joan's, that the use of Nautilus should be avoided at all costs.

He had already considered it, on the day of the attacks, which was weeks ago, but despite their horror, the actual death toll was insignificant compared to a world war. More people had died in Operation Market Garden during World War II, and significantly more in Japan with the atomic bomb, both instances receiving no intervention from his father. On that basis, in his opinion, 9/11 failed the Protocol test. However, it was the events following the attacks that were beginning to concern him.

Had he misjudged?

The problem he saw was the changing mood of the people. The voice of the angry mob was quick to rise, to protest, to create violence. Memories of his experience in the Balkans, where ethnic tensions led to genocide and racial hatred not seen since Hitler's Germany, made him shudder. Could his daughter be right? Was Europe on the brink of another Nazi uprising? There was certainly very little opposition to the current measures: no marches, no cries for human rights. He evaluated his options.

Even if he wanted to change the course of events, he pondered whether he could. The simplest solution would be to supply the names of all the perpetrators, dates, flight numbers and so on to the intelligence services. But no crime had been committed at that point; the security forces would need evidence, warrants. He would be personally investigated for knowing such information; he could even be suspected of being a terrorist himself.

The other problem was time. It was already six weeks after the attacks. He would only be giving himself two weeks to disseminate the intelligence and prevent some, but probably not all, of the attacks. He needed to decide, and he needed to do it as soon as possible.

He eventually fell asleep undecided, but the kernel of an idea was growing in his mind.

~

The key to David's plan was the Americans. If he could prevent the attacks on the White House and the World Trade Center, the Americans would not be in play. The Chinese, Russian and Australian attacks were largely against property, symbols of society and power. Buildings could be rebuilt and symbolic attacks largely forgotten. Deadly attacks on France and the UK alone would not create the same scale of response, not without the US. He needed to give his earlier self all the relevant facts.

It was time to take a visit to the Knightsbridge store.

Early the next morning, he put on his running gear and left the apartment, telling his sleepy daughter that he would pick up some breakfast when he got back. The partial grunt that he got back in reply meant he would have several hours before she woke.

The run through Hyde Park was invigorating. The autumnal mist still lay in the trees like a cloak, the cold air filling his lungs and clearing his mind. He ran to the southern end of the park, arriving at Brompton Road. Turning right, he walked briskly to the brightly lit store. Making his apologies to the guard for his attire, he proceeded with his own security measures to enter the secure space that housed Nautilus.

He checked and re-checked all the data that he would need to avert the attacks and fired up the amazing machine that was Nautilus. The device no longer used telegrams for the TEST message: he had replaced that part of the machinery with the latest mobile phone, a Nokia 8310. He prepared the sub-messages relating to the six targets. When he was happy that the information was correct and gave a clear explanation of what would occur, he tapped out his message in Morse code.

This was the first time he had used Nautilus for anything except confirming the mobile-phone alert functioned. Would it work? He had wasted six valuable weeks before changing his mind, setting an almost impossible task to be accomplished in just two weeks. But the prize would be worth it – not just saving thousands of lives but preventing a rise in nationalism, and the re-emergence of ethnic cleansing, of fascism. He had to take the risk that his earlier self would succeed.

CHAPTER 43

Mijas

August 28th, 2001

David and Annabelle were enjoying a splendid lunch, the ingredients hand-picked from their garden in Mijas. The summer was coming to an end, but the land was producing wonderful fresh produce. Lettuce, tomatoes and peppers were mixed with last year's olives to make a refreshing salad, finished with an olive oil dressing, lemon juice and balsamic vinegar. David had been down to the port early in the morning to procure two lobsters from the local fishermen, which formed the main course of their feast. The temperature was in the early thirties Celsius, so dessert consisted of fresh fruit: grapes picked from the pagoda, ripe plums and figs from their sole fig tree.

'We should just live here, all the time,' Annabelle said, olive oil dribbling down her chin. 'No wonder the Spanish live to a hundred. This is so good.'

'I agree with you, on both counts. I've been thinking that I might put in for early retirement.'

'Can you afford it?' Annabelle asked.

'I'm fifty-five, my government pension is secure and you're finally financially independent, and anyway I probably only have twenty good years left before you'll have to push me around in my wheelchair and listen to my complaining about the weather or the price of beer.'

'You're not decrepit yet and just because I'm working doesn't mean I won't need some help to buy an apartment. So maybe in a few years?' said Annabelle.

Just as David bit into his third fig, his mobile phone bleeped.

TEST

He grabbed the phone and stood.

'Who is it?' Annabelle asked.

'Just the office. I'm going to have to call in,' he told her, trying to appear calm.

He never thought he would use Nautilus. Walking between the fruit trees of his orchard, he pretended to have a conversation with London. What he couldn't imagine was why on earth he had sent himself this message. There was no major conflict on the radar. What could have happened to invoke the Protocol? The answer lay in London.

'I have to go back to London tomorrow,' he told Annabelle. 'There's a flap on at the office and it's all hands to the pumps. You're welcome to stay on here – there's no need for your holiday to be cut short too.' He moved to his room to pack.

~

He landed at Heathrow at noon on the 29th of August, just thirteen days before the attacks. He took a cab to Harrods and picked up his message. The consequences of what was about to happen in less than two weeks made his legs weak. He slid down the wall of the cramped space, massaging his head with one hand as he digested the details.

'Oh my God,' he said to no one but himself. Why did he have so little time? The message said it was the aftermath of the attacks that invoked the Protocol rather than the attacks themselves. Did America nuke

Afghanistan, Pakistan? Did the superpowers start a war? His mission now was to prevent the attacks and the subsequent conflict. All the same, he wished his future self had acted a bit more quickly. He needed more time.

He re-read the message three times and decided to go for a walk in the park opposite Harrods, as that always cleared his head and enabled him to think straight.

He wondered how to tell the world's best intelligence agencies that an attack was about to happen in six countries simultaneously, and that they had absolutely no clue, without bringing attention to himself or Nautilus.

The message told him to focus on the Americans, and he agreed with the suggestion. *With my contacts in MI6 and MI5, I should be able to handle the London attack easily*, he thought.

The French should not be too difficult; it would be possible to get something to Interpol. The Aussies could be dealt with via the Foreign Office. The Chinese and Russians would be difficult, but they had the lowest death toll. The key was the Americans.

The attack was on their home soil, so he focused on the FBI. A plan was beginning to formulate in his mind.

He went to his office, to research the names that he'd been given on the known combatants list. He was shocked to discover that most of the terrorists who were targeting the UK, France and the US were on various watchlists and had been travelling between the US, Europe and Afghanistan, Pakistan, even Saudi Arabia for over a year, some for several years.

He confirmed that six of the US-based terrorists had recently trained as commercial pilots at American flight schools. How had the FBI missed this?

To protect his identity, he passed snippets of intel to various agencies, including MI5, the Russian FSB, the Chinese MSS, the CIA and Interpol, but this wouldn't be sufficient. There were too many moving parts; he was going to need help. An old friend of Lydia's, Carla Fernandez, worked at the London HQ of Interpol. Even though they had only met on a few occasions since his wife's funeral, she had always been kind, and he sensed there was a fondness towards him. He was not convinced that she would help, but he had to try.

CHAPTER 44

London

September 4th, 2001

The flight school intel had been easy to verify, and David decided to use this as his primary tool for the Americans. He had the six names of the perpetrators who would bomb the Houses of Parliament in London and obtained the details on all the sale or rentals of any large vessels or barges in the past three months.

David had an old schoolfriend, Andrew Burrows, who was an MI5 officer. He called him and agreed to meet up for a drink at the Coach and Horses pub off New Bond Street at five o'clock.

The 200-year-old Mock Tudor public house was heaving with tired shoppers and office workers cradling their beers and gin and tonics. The pub was perfect for the conversation he was about to have. Finding a spot at the corner of the historic, oak bar, he had a direct view to the only entrance. His friend walked through the door precisely on time, just as David had expected.

David ordered two pints of cold lager.

'Cheers,' they both said at the same time.

'Look, Andrew, this isn't entirely a social visit. As you know, I'm off the main desks now, they've got me doing recruitment and training.'

'Jolly interesting all the same, I'm sure,' Andrew replied, taking a pull on his ice-cold beer. 'What's up?'

'I was completing some research on terrorist cells that have operated in the UK and the Middle East as part of a training exercise that I was setting up, comparing recruitment campaigns, training schools, within organisations such as the Taliban, Al Qaeda and so forth.'

'Interesting.'

'I came across a bunch of names, here in London, that we suspect may have been recruited by Islamic extremists. I had an agent placed on them for a while, but all they turned up was an interest in boats, taking multiple river trips up and down the Thames, photographing the Houses of Parliament and Big Ben. As you can imagine, my chief cut the cost of the exercise, saying that I was chasing tourists.'

'I have to say, David, I think your boss has a point,' said Andrew.

'I've got an uneasy feeling about this. I've collected all the intel here – could you look? If I'm wrong, I owe you. But I don't think I am.'

'I'll look at it in the morning, but don't get your hopes up. We're all suffering the same budget cuts,' said Andrew.

David's next appointment was with his wife's friend from Interpol.

Carla was in her late forties but looked ten years younger. Red hair with deep brown eyes and a slender, athletic body you couldn't fail to notice. She had been born in Majorca and worked for Spanish Intelligence, currently on secondment to Interpol at Gray's Inn, located in the City of London.

They met for dinner at her favourite Spanish restaurant, Fino on Charlotte Street. David had arrived early, so was pleased that his guest was punctual. She looked amazing, wearing leather pants and a cropped white silk blouse, accentuating her athletic arms. As she approached the table, David wasn't the only guest in the restaurant to gaze at her.

'Hola, David, cómo estás?' she said, kissing him on both cheeks, then giving him a long hug.

'Fine, thank you. You look beautiful as always,' said David.

'How's Annabelle? A pity she couldn't join us, no?' she said, ignoring the compliment.

'She's fine. I had to come back early from Spain, so I told her to stay and enjoy the sunshine,' he said.

'I don't blame her. London is beautiful, but so cold, David. Do you want me to order?' she asked.

'You're the expert.'

The waiter arrived, and without looking at the menu Carla ordered in Spanish – prawn tapas, Iberian jamon, Manchego cheese and some olives to start.

'You prefer Rioja, if I remember correctly?'

'Thank you,' David replied.

'Muga, por favor,' she said to the waiter before turning back to David. 'This sudden return to your cold country has something to do with our date?'

'Directly to the point as usual, Carla. I've come into some intel regarding an attack from Al Qaeda from a source that I trust completely, but I can't reveal their identity even to my own section.'

'Tricky, no?'

David knew he was taking a big risk involving Carla. He poured two glasses of water and pushed Carla's towards her.

'Tricky is correct. I need to get this information to several national agencies, but I can't have it traced back to me. I'll understand if you say no, but would you be willing to assist me?'

The waiter returned and served the delicious food and poured the wine. Carla was thoughtful, turning the glass in her hand, the halogen light above their table piercing through the ruby liquid and casting a mauve shadow onto the crisp white tablecloth. Looking directly into David's eyes, she took a sip of her wine.

'Why can't we follow procedures and send it through the channels?' she asked.

'If there was any other way, I would. The first problem is time – we only have one week before the planned attacks. The second problem is that if I go through my superiors, they'll force me to give up my source, which I can't do.'

Carla swirled the red wine around in her glass, breathing in the aromatic fumes, all the time searching David's face. She placed the glass on the table and leant forward slightly on her chair.

'You ask a lot of an old friend, David, but I'll help you, and protect you. I owe that much to Lydia.' She smiled, picked up a prawn and popped it into her mouth.

David quietly explained what he knew about the six target cities and the method of the attacks, Carla's eyes getting wider the more he spoke.

'I can handle the English-speaking targets, Sydney, London and of course the US, but I need your help in Moscow, Paris and with the Chinese.'

'If I didn't know you better, I'd say you're a crazy man. Are you confident in your source?' she said. 'Surely Al Qaeda doesn't have this sort of funding and planning capability? And if it does, how come none of the agencies have any chatter about this? It sounds too extreme, but if you're right – the Americans alone would want to destroy the Islamic world.'

'I struggled with it myself, but the consequences are too high. We must get the information to the relevant agencies as fast as we can.'

He reached inside his briefcase next to his chair and pulled out a brown manila envelope, handing it to Carla.

'Here's all the intel I have for your three targets. Let's meet at my apartment tomorrow night at 8pm for a debrief. And thank you for trusting me.'

With Carla's assistance on three of the national targets, and Andrew working on London, he felt that he could finally breathe. But the clock was ticking, and the deadline was looming ever closer.

He took a Black Cab and returned home to concentrate on his plans for foiling the attackers in the US and Australia.

The Australian intel was relatively easy to send. Australia had a similar system to the UK: ASIS, the Australian Secret Intelligence Service, was charged with obtaining overseas intelligence, and ASIO, the Australian Security Intelligence Organisation, worked with intelligence from within Australia.

He had the names of the attackers and the timing of the boat strike on the Sydney Opera House. Utilising his MI6 database, he found case officers at both ASIS and ASIO. Now all he needed was a credible way to deliver the information without it being traced back to him.

He went to a mosque in North London dressed as a believer and prayed with the congregation. Leaving the mosque after prayers, he went to a nearby internet cafe and sent the anonymous message to the two intelligence officers based in Sydney. He told the Australians that he was a true Muslim and supported many beliefs held by Al Qaeda but couldn't condone violence of this nature.

Within ten minutes of pressing send, he had walked past at least five CCTV cameras, knowing that the Australians would ask their British allies for footage once they had tracked down the origin of the message. He entered a large Primark shop, leaving twenty minutes later dressed like any other Western shopper, wearing jeans, a T-shirt and a baseball cap. His task achieved for the day, he returned to his office at MI6 headquarters, near Vauxhall Bridge.

The Australian approach was not going to work with the Americans. They received hundreds of threats every day from all over the world, and on top of this they were incredibly confident in their abilities, to the point of arrogance. They would likely construe the intel as fantasy, a hoax.

He logged in to his computer terminal, searching for promising candidates at the CIA, the FBI, even someone at the Federal Aviation Administration, anyone who might be able to help. Several hours later, he was satisfied that he had found enough contacts and left for home, and his rendezvous with Carla.

At 8pm, she pressed the intercom to his apartment. Buzzing her up, he left the door ajar while he poured two glasses of wine.

'I think I've had some success today, with the French,' she said. 'I checked the names you gave me against flight schools in France but came up blank. I did find them on flight manifests between Paris, Washington, Afghanistan and more recently Pakistan. The biggest thing is that I found one of them, Khalid Sayyaf, a Saudi national, had undertaken commercial flight training in South Florida at the Pan Am Flight Academy. I also contacted a colleague at Interpol in Paris, who has put Khalid on a watch list and will let me know when they find him.'

'Did you stress the importance of the timetable? This will need active follow-up – we only have six days left.'

'We need to be patient,' Carla said. 'The Russian FSB and the Chinese MSS don't have to worry about due process, warrants and probable cause. So I'm thinking to give them both one name from the cells in Moscow and Hong Kong plus the location of the target. My thought is that the subjects will be picked up very quickly and tortured to provide all the details of the respective attacks and the location of their fellow terrorists. Most people can only survive active torture for a few hours, at most twenty-four, so the timetable should work. What do you think?' she concluded.

'Remind me not to cross you in the future, but yes, I think it will work.'

David updated Carla on his activities and shared his plans regarding the Americans.

'Are you hungry?' he asked. 'I cooked some pasta earlier, not my best, but it should be okay.'

'Yes, I'm starving, let's take a break.'

David opened a second bottle of wine, pouring a glass for each of them. As he served her food, she stroked his arm, sending tingles through his body.

'Thank you, David,' she said, retrieving her hand.

They continued working late into the night, checking and rechecking their plans. After many hours, Carla yawned; they were both exhausted.

'Do you mind if I stay here? It's very late,' she asked.

'Of course, you can have Belle's room,' he said innocently.

'I don't think that will be necessary. We're probably going to end up in jail, or worse. So, I think I should get to know you better.'

David was unsure – of course he found her attractive, any man would, but he knew this would not be one of his casual flings.

'We've both had a lot of wine, Carla – are you sure that it's such a good idea?'

'No, probably not,' she teased.

She stood up from the sofa where they were sitting and unzipped her dress, stepping out of it, leaving it crumpled on the floor. Her body was perfectly tanned, but he couldn't take his eyes off her luxurious lingerie. She held out her hands and signalled him to join her.

'Is that what you wear to the office these days?'

'No, this is something that I've wanted for some time, but out of respect for the memory of Lydia I resisted. But time has passed, and you have never remarried. Seeing you again, in this situation, I think we deserve to be happy. I know she would want you to enjoy your life, to love again. She would be happy with this.'

He was taken by surprise, the mention of his wife causing a niggle of doubt, but Carla was impossible to resist. He held her hand and walked into his bedroom, kicking off his shoes and discarding his clothes as he went. Carla lay on the bed, her toned legs wrapping around his naked body. They kissed hungrily, the excitement sending his heart racing, his chest pumping up and down, in rhythm with his own thrusts inside the beautiful woman who was staring up at his face, her large eyes dilating.

'Slowly, David, take your time. I want to enjoy you. I want you to enjoy me.'

She locked her legs around his back and pulled him further inside her and held him there, giving him time to catch his breath, enabling their lovemaking to last longer. Carla was totally in charge, he the willing victim. She pushed him over onto his back and straddled him, placing her hands on his chest, moving rhythmically, slowly increasing the pace. She moaned out loud, thrusting faster and faster, which was too much for David and he came inside her, much to her enjoyment.

The couple continued to talk and kiss each other long into the night until finally they fell asleep. They had made love. This was intimate, and David began to feel guilty for the pleasure that he had not felt since his wife.

~

David woke with a small headache from the previous night's drinking, but he felt energised. The attention and passion that he'd received from Carla was surprising and made him feel confident and excited. But the woman was gone. He checked his watch, 8am. He put on some fresh coffee while he took a hot shower.

The steaming hot water and caffeine brought the mission back to the front of his mind. Today was Thursday: only five more days before the attack. The timetable was daunting, and he began to regret the wine from the night before. He swallowed some aspirin and got down to business.

Working from his home with his laptop, he set up a dummy email address from the Pan Am Flight Academy and made himself an instructor with a false name. Using these credentials, he sent information on three of the terrorists who had trained there.

Mohamed Atta, Marwan al-Shehhi and Ziad Jarrah were destined to fly three of the planes into the US targets. A fourth potential pilot, Zacarias Moussaoui, had also trained at the flight school, only more recently and at a different centre, in Minneapolis. All these men had entered the US in mid-2000 through San Diego. A further terrorist pilot, Hani Hanjour, a Saudi national, had trained at an Arizona flight school and received his commercial licence from the FAA in the late 1990s, returning to the US under a student visa in December 2000, again through San Diego.

The intel was sent to the FBI and the CIA at the relevant field offices, and for good measure he sent it to the FAA as well, using appropriate fake email addresses from both the Florida and Arizona schools. The five-hour time difference between London and the US east coast was frustrating and he chastised himself for wasting a day. He should have sent the message last night when the Americans were still at work. He had to be more focused; there was no time for selfish activities, however pleasant they might be.

To his surprise, he received a response later that day from an FBI field officer with supervisor rank at the Minneapolis office. They thanked the fake flight instructor for the information and committed to investigate the matter, informing other security services of the perceived threat.

He also got a reply from the CIA at Langley, which was less surprising. Again, he was thanked for the information, but this time the CIA officer said he would refer it to the relevant domestic agencies, effectively passing the buck.

The Americans were not taking him seriously enough and there was so little time. David re-evaluated his plan and considered making radical changes, but then was interrupted by contact from his two helpers, Andrew and Carla.

He met Carla at Hyde Park at the bridge crossing the Serpentine Boating Lake.

'I have news,' Carla said. 'The French secret service was contacted by my colleague at Interpol. They've captured our first suspect, Khalid al Hazmi. He's not talking, but they've recovered documents from his apartment containing training manuals and flight schedules departing from Paris. They also discovered combat knives and a lot of cash. The better news is that they were also contacted by the FBI about Zacarias Moussaoui, who was born in France and who they consider a person of interest. I can only assume he's one of your American suspects.'

'What about the Russians and the Chinese?'

'I sent one name to my contact at the FSB in Moscow. It's been acknowledged, but I have no update whatsoever. Similarly with the Chinese, I sent a name for them to investigate. I've had no acknowledgement at all, so I also sent it to the counterterrorism unit at police headquarters in Hong Kong for good measure.'

'Good idea. I've covered the other targets as best I can for now. But the weekend is going to be so frustrating. Despite the presence of weekend duty officers, it is highly unlikely that we'll receive any feedback until Monday. There must be something I've missed, but I can't put my finger on it. All we can do is wait. Can we meet up on Monday?' he said.

Carla looked disappointed. 'I was hoping that we might spend the weekend together,' she said.

'That would be lovely ... I just didn't want to presume,' David said clumsily. 'And I've got a meeting with an MI5 agent tonight. He is helping me with the London threat.'

David considered whether spending time with Carla would be too distracting from the project. On the one hand, it absolutely would be, but on the other, he really didn't expect to receive much feedback, especially from the Americans, so the thought of spending some quality time with a beautiful woman might just be what he needed. It would also give them some time to talk properly, to learn about each other's lives more.

'Why don't we meet at Harrods tomorrow for lunch? I can pick up some supplies and try to impress you with my culinary skills over the weekend. We can't stray too far from our computers, though, in case we hear something.'

'Sounds perfect. You're the only person I can talk to about this crazy thing that we're doing. You understand, no?'

He leant towards her and kissed her firmly on the lips. 'Twelve?'

'See you tomorrow,' she said and walked off over the bridge.

Later that day, he went to see Andrew at the Coach and Horses.

The Friday-afternoon throng were well into their third and fourth drinks, customers two deep at the bar and causing a racket with their boisterous conversations. The shoppers were long gone, their Black Cabs whisking them away to Kensington and Chelsea, while the office dwellers were settled in for the night, drowning the stresses of the week.

David and Andrew sought their own refuge on the street, where the noise was bearable and they could enjoy some fresh air.

Andrew had ordered them pints of lager and was clearly eager to tell David his news.

'I don't know how you did it, old boy, but your information has scored a bullseye, and the proverbial feather in the cap for yours truly.'

'Do tell,' said David eagerly.

'At first, the section commander was not too keen to commit resources to the case, but I managed to get forty-eight hours of surveillance out of him. On the targets themselves, there was nothing too exciting. They lived in separate addresses, attended different mosques, separate cafes – nothing. Just when I was about to give up, we followed the one they called Massoud down to St Katharine Docks, where he rented an old Thames barge for £3000, which he paid for in cash.' Andrew paused to take a long drink from his pint. 'This was enough to get the old man's attention and a warrant. We raided all the target locations, and they were a goldmine: bomb-making material, tidal charts, weapons and, the pièce de résistance, photos of the Thames wall and structure right under the terrace restaurant of the Houses of Parliament. Exactly where you said it would be.'

'And the terrorists?'

'All currently at Her Majesty's pleasure, helping with enquiries. I have to say, David, your gut is pure gold. We'd have some serious egg on our face if we'd missed this one. Whereas it's drinks all round and a promotion for jolly old Andrew. Thanks to you. Are you sure you don't want to be involved in this success? It seems extremely selfish to take all the credit.'

'I don't want any fuss. Just glad we got the bastards.'

Andrew wanted to celebrate, and the two old friends swapped stories over several more drinks. By the time they were ordering double whiskies, David knew it was time to go and said his goodbyes.

At home, he reviewed the work of the day. On the face of it, two of the targets had been neutralised – London and Paris. It had been a successful day, and he was going to spend the next two days in the company of the beautiful Carla. With that pleasant thought, he fell asleep, fully clothed.

~

David and Carla met for lunch at the Garden Terrace restaurant on the top floor of Harrods with stunning views over Knightsbridge.

David brought Carla up to speed with the London success, but he was far from relaxed, not helped by a thumping headache courtesy of far too many drinks the previous night. And the new day had delivered nothing from the remaining target countries. The worry was written across his face.

'Despite all the technology,' Carla said, 'all the resources, the billions of dollars invested in our business, the weekend still gets in the way, especially when it comes to filing reports.'

David thought how ironic it was that just six floors below from where they were having their pleasant lunch sat Nautilus. He had harnessed its power and was desperately trying to alert the intelligence community to the impending threat, but had he left it too late? Time was running out and disaster loomed.

After lunch, they perused the food halls, thankful that they had full stomachs and could resist the temptations on offer. He made the necessary purchases for a seafood stir-fry, and the couple walked across the park back to his apartment, hopeful he might have messages in his inbox.

There were no messages, but he did have a visitor: Annabelle.

'Hola, Annabelle, so good to see you,' said Carla, breaking the ice.

'What are you doing here?' Annabelle said, surprised.

'Carla and I have been working on a project,' David said awkwardly. 'We've also been seeing each other, socially.'

'I can see that,' said Annabelle, staring directly at the Loewe overnight bag at Carla's feet. 'I take it you're staying the weekend, so I'll get out of your hair and catch the train to Oxford.'

She bent to get her bag, but Carla placed her hand on top of Annabelle's.

'Don't leave. Your father has promised me a wonderful meal tonight. Why don't we all enjoy ourselves?'

'I would love to stay for dinner, and please don't take this the wrong way, but I really must go,' Annabelle said, picking up her bag. She kissed them both on the cheek before leaving the apartment.

David moved to chase after her.

'Leave her, David – this is new for her, she just needs a little time,' Carla said. 'And I should go as well. Call me tomorrow if anything turns up. Otherwise, see you Monday.'

David wanted to object, annoyed with his daughter's abruptness and the cooling effect it had seemed to have on Carla. He had every right to happiness. It didn't mean that he'd forgotten about his wife; he would never forget.

'Don't worry, cariño, we'll work it out, just not tonight,' Carla said warmly before kissing him goodnight, picking up her bag and leaving.

David unpacked the shopping, alone. He poured himself a red wine; he needed the 'hair of the dog' to ease his hangover. Halfway through the first glass, he was feeling considerably better physically. Emotionally, however, he was not so good. In the middle of a global crisis, he was starting his first serious relationship since his wife and had already introduced the concept to his daughter.

'What are you thinking of!' he said out loud. He had to focus on the project. He was a professional; in a few days it would be over, one way or the other. His thoughts clarifying in his mind, he poured the remains of his wine bottle down the sink.

Time to get his game face on.

~

As Carla had predicted, there were no messages until the early hours of Monday, with Hong Kong and Australia being seven and nine hours ahead of London. The Australians had made four arrests and were chasing down the remaining two suspects. David could tick off another country as neutralised. Carla returned from work and brought news that the Russians and the Hong Kong police had acknowledged the intel with thanks but provided no further details. New York and Boston were five hours behind London. There was nothing more David and Carla could do except wait.

The air was cold and damp as they stepped out of his apartment block, the autumn sun lacking the strength to warm them at such an early hour. David led the way towards his favourite French cafe, on Bathurst Street near the park.

'Are you okay?' said David.

'If we pull this off, there will be some serious questions to be answered. Interpol will want to know how I got this intel. Do you want to talk to me about your source?'

David was tempted: Carla had proven herself intelligent, resourceful and, importantly, trustworthy. It would be a relief to share the burden of Nautilus. But Joan had been very clear: Nautilus was powerful, and in the wrong hands lethal. The guardianship must be protected by the family, and even then, only when ready. So he resisted his desire to share.

'It would only put you in danger. The only way to protect you is for you not to know,' he told her.

The coffee and the fresh air had the desired effect, and the two returned to David's apartment hopeful of news. And they got it. An email to David.

From: h.price@fbi.gov
To: David.Munrow@panamflightschool.com
Date: 10 September 2001
Re: Intel received
Dear Sir,
Following your flight school intel, received 6th September 2001 FBI agents have arrested and detained a suspect Zacarias Moussaoui of French and Moroccan dissent. Have received corroboratory evidence from the DGSE in Paris.

We are awaiting both criminal and FISA warrants to proceed with our investigation.

Will keep you advised and thanks for the heads-up.
Harry Price
Special Agent Tel: +1–202–555–1467

'Bollocks!' David exclaimed.

'The FBI have arrested a suspect – you should be thrilled,' Carla said.

David paced nervously around the room. 'There's no time for warrants! They have to arrest these bastards, now! I'm going to have to up the ante.'

David pulled a burner phone from his briefcase and rang Agent Price's number, which was answered immediately. 'Price here.'

'This is Nick Phillips, a senior operative at MI6, London'.

'And how do I know this?'

'You received intel regarding a terrorist threat and have detained a French national, Zacarias Moussaoui.'

'How do you know this, sir?'

'Not important, Price. What is important is that I have a well-positioned CI within Al Qaeda who informs me that you have multiple, mainly Saudi nationals intending to hijack four passenger aircraft and fly them into targets in New York and Washington. Write this down. Their names are as follows: Mohamed Atta. Marwan al-Shehhi. Ziad Jarrah. And Hani Hanjour. These are the four most important. They have all received flight training and intend to take over the following flights. Are you writing, Price?'

'It better not be a waste of ink,' he replied.

'American Airlines Flight 11 out of Boston. United Airlines Flight 175, also Boston. American Airlines Flight 77 out of Dulles. And United Airlines Flight 93 from Newark. You have twenty-four hours, Price. There's no time for verification or warrants, just catch these arseholes. Act now, Agent Price.'

David hung up the phone and immediately destroyed the SIM card.

Carla was stunned. 'Holy fuck, David. I didn't know the extent of your intel. This CI of yours must be very high ranking, I see why you're being so cautious. You're playing a dangerous game. You could be under threat, if not from your own organisation, certainly from Al Qaeda.'

David sat down next to Carla on his couch. 'I'm sorry I dragged you into this and caused you so much trouble.'

'I can handle myself. Is there anything more we can do?'

David looked at the kitchen clock. 'Pray.'

CHAPTER 45

London

September 11th, 2001

At 1.40pm, Carla and David sat in front of the TV in his apartment, tense and on edge, anxious to see if any of their efforts were going to be successful.

At 1.49pm – 8.49am, New York time – they found their answer, with the CNN banner reading WORLD TRADE CENTER DISASTER across their television, smoke billowing out of the North Tower. David hung his head, cradling it in his hands, gutted.

His words, 'Oh my God,' were echoed by millions of people glued to their TVs at home, in bars and in shops around the world. Everyone would remember where they were when they found out the news.

'I failed,' he said. He stood and paced, unable to calm himself, unable to comprehend what had gone wrong. Why hadn't it worked?

Fourteen minutes later, he witnessed United Airlines Flight 175 from Boston flying into the South Tower, piloted by Marwan al-Shehhi from Saudi Arabia, who had taken control of the plane shortly after take-off with four additional members of Al Qaeda, killing the American pilots and crew with box cutters and knives. The passengers were petrified, but the plane was flying steady, and they assumed that the hijacking would end like many others, on the tarmac with negotiation. Suddenly the plane took a steep turn, dived towards the World Trade Center and exploded into the South Tower.

'For God's sake! I should have sacrificed myself, gone straight to the Director of the CIA and demanded that he listen to me!' David sunk on the couch, devastated. 'Those poor people!'

'Everything was meant to be coordinated, right?' Carla said, trying to calm him. 'There are no images from Hong Kong, or Moscow. You've saved London, Paris and Sydney. It is contained to one country. At least there's that.'

Half an hour later, the situation took a turn for the worse when American Airlines Flight 77 from Dulles crashed into the Pentagon.

'The FBI and CIA have done nothing with my intel! Bloody nothing! Now we're going to see the White House go up in flames.'

~

Agent Price was desperate. His calls and actions had failed. Three planes had already hit their target, and he was determined to change the trajectory of the fourth. There was nothing he could do with his agency, the CIA or the military for that matter , but he could try to contact the plane.

After five failed attempts, he got through via the network operator. The man on the other end of the line was clearly stressed.

'Hello, who is this?' said the passenger.

'This is Agent Nick Price from the FBI.'

'Do you know what is happening up here?' said the distraught man.

'I do,' said Price. 'There's no easy way to say this, but three other planes have been hijacked and crashed into their targets. I believe the terrorists onboard your plane intend to crash into the White House or Capitol building. Do you understand?'

'You're not telling me anything that we haven't already figured out,

Price. In fact, me, some passengers and crew are getting ready to attack these fuckers,' he said defiantly.

'Okay, godspeed, Mr …?'

'Lasky, Brad Lasky.'

'Brad.'

'Yes, sir?'

'What you and your fellow passengers are about to do will never be forgotten. I will make sure of it,' said Price.

'Okay. And Nick?'

'Yes?'

'Can you do me a favour and tell my wife and kids that I love them and will wait for them in heaven?'

'Sure thing, Brad,' said Price, struggling to keep his feelings out of his voice.

'Okay, Nick, time to fuck things up!'

The line went dead, and Price imagined the scenes going on inside the jetliner, his emotions torn between deep sorrow at the waste of life and the incredible pride he felt for the bravery and selflessness of ordinary people making such an honourable decision.

At 10.03am local time, United Airlines Flight 93, flown by a twenty-three-year-old Lebanese man called Ziad Jarrah, crashed. Jarrah's intention was to fly the Boeing 757 from Newark to Washington and crash into the White House, the symbol of American power around the world.

Onboard the aircraft, the group of passengers who'd decided to act had attacked the three terrorists guarding the cockpit, forcing their way onto the flight deck and causing the plane to crash into a field in Stonycreek, Pennsylvania. This killed the hijackers and themselves, a selfless act that saved countless lives.

David knew there were no more terrorist-controlled flights left in America, but couldn't stop watching the terrible images on his TV screen.

Two thousand, nine hundred and ninety-seven people died that day, including 343 incredibly brave firefighters and seventy-one law enforcement officers.

This was exactly what Osama bin Laden and his co-conspirators had planned. They were disappointed not to have had successful attacks across the other countries, but failures were bound to happen with such a large campaign. The primary target was America and they had succeeded, a massive blow against the West and a huge victory for Al Qaeda, which was now a household name across the world.

Believing the Americans weak, bin Laden told his supporters that he expected the Americans to withdraw from the region as they had done in Lebanon and Somalia. However, he had made a massive miscalculation. The Americans were in shock, as was the rest of the world, but the people were angry and empathised with the USA. The sentiment was best summed up by the headline of the French paper *Le Monde*: 'We are all Americans now.'

CHAPTER 46

London

October 2001

David was devastated that he'd used Nautilus without preventing the attack on the United States, questioning himself as to whether he had done the right thing. He couldn't get the images of people jumping from the Twin Towers out of his head; he felt he'd failed them. He had also exposed Carla and himself to scrutiny, and potentially put Nautilus at risk.

They'd taken precautions in disseminating the intel, but David couldn't avoid his friend Andrew at MI5. David was going to need a source.

He was in luck.

An Uzbek militant leader, Juma Khan Namangani, was killed by a US strike at the fall of Mazar-i-Sharif in the Balkh Province in northern Afghanistan. Namangani was perfect. He was the commander of the 055 Brigade, a senior member of Al Qaeda, but was well known for his criticism of bin Laden's plans to attack the West. Unlike bin Laden, he believed this would provoke the Americans to invade his country and end their existence. He was proved right, and it cost him his life. David decided to create a cover story of how they met, which of course they never had.

Andrew took David for coffee.

'Our victory with the Thames terrorists was not an isolated event,'

Andrew said. 'The brass are questioning me about my sources. We need to go see the chief.' He picked at the rim of his coffee cup, waiting nervously for David to reply.

'Tell your superiors I was your source. I came to you as it was a threat within the UK and therefore MI5 jurisdiction and we had very little time. If they want to question me, they can go through the channels,' David replied, doing his best to appear calm and confident.

~

When David returned home, Carla was waiting for him outside his apartment. He could tell instantly by her posture and her stern expression that she was annoyed. He opened the door for her and let her in.

'Do you know who I had lunch with today?' she said.

'Contrary to your belief, we don't have every foreign intelligence officer followed. So, surprise me.' This flippancy made her even more agitated.

'Ivan Semenov.'

'The deputy director of the FSB? What did he want? To recruit you?'

'To thank me personally for the intel – he was very grateful for the name we gave him. They captured the entire cell before they reached their target. He took great delight in telling me that, following a vigorous interrogation, they were all executed. He was particularly interested in my source, especially in light of the New York attacks. I told him I couldn't possibly divulge that, which was the answer he was expecting, and then he promptly invited me to Moscow to watch *Swan Lake* performed by the Bolshoi, which I politely declined.'

'Are you asking me to divulge my source?'

'Of course not, but it would be good to know something.'

David took a deep breath. If he could convince Carla, he was sure he'd be able to handle the chief of MI5. David was getting more and more concerned that his employer would start a surveillance operation, with him as the target. He would have to avoid any visits to Nautilus for a while; he simply couldn't risk it.

David had learnt that to create a successful lie, it was best to include as much truth as possible.

'His codename was Nautilus,' David said. 'He was a brigade commander in Al Qaeda in the north of Afghanistan. I met him ten years ago, when I was his interrogator during Desert Storm. Recently, he was at odds with bin Laden's plans to launch attacks against the West, fearing the consequences and reprisals that would inevitably take place. He put his love for his country above his loyalty to Al Qaeda and reached out to me with the plans. Although short on time, he believed Allah's will would prevail.'

'*Was* a commander?'

'Two weeks ago, shortly after sending me the intel, he was at the wrong end of a US missile strike against his command post.'

'What was his real name?'

'I suppose it can't hurt to tell you now,' said David. 'Juma Khan Namangani, a ruthless man, but incredibly brave to defy bin Laden.'

Carla seemed satisfied. With her anger gone, she poured two glasses of wine. She and David sat on the couch beside each other, her hand on his shoulder.

'Why Nautilus?' she said.

'Maybe because I like Jules Verne? It's just a name.'

David resolved never to tell her the secret of Nautilus; she would be protected from that burden. Nautilus's power would remain solely with him, until it was time to hand over the guardianship. The thought of Annabelle having to go through the stress and pain that came with the control of Nautilus made him shudder – he would delay that day as long as he could.

But when that time came, it could go to only one person.

PART 4

CHAPTER 47

Annabelle's Story

Annabelle was born on the 6th of June 1978, the thirty-fourth anniversary of D-Day, a day that she studied and celebrated while remaining blissfully unaware of its personal significance to her and her family. This would continue until her fortieth birthday.

Her early life had been extremely joyous, with her being fussed over by doting parents and completely spoilt by her grandparents from Scotland and her grandfather in Spain. This vanished when she was six years old. Losing her mother left a void in her life and her heart broken in a way that would never completely heal.

Growing up in Scotland with her paternal grandparents, and attending school there, gave her a good solid grounding. Her father would visit when he could, but the most exciting holidays were when he took her to see her Spanish family. Late-night fiestas, long, cool drinks and romantic walks along the beach with the locals completed her adolescence.

She continued to suffer immense loss in her young life, though. When she was eighteen, her Scottish grandparents, David and Claire, passed away within six months of each other, both peacefully. Her grandparents had spent more time with her than her own parents, which made their deaths unbearable. She felt that her heart would never recover and that the world was cruel to inflict so much loss and grief upon her. Not wanting her sorrow to consume her, she knew she needed to focus on something new, something serious.

The young and frivolous Annabelle had died with those she loved, replaced by a more studious young lady. She graduated with a first class honours degree in biochemistry at Oxford. After a further three years of study, she become Dr Annabelle McIntosh following the completion of her PhD in viral medicine.

By the time of 9/11, she was twenty-three years old and working in a research lab at AstraZeneca in Oxford.

Around the same time, her father seemed to withdraw into himself. She couldn't quite place it, but he seemed angrier with the world.

The Middle East became a priority for the West, and despite his age, when David asked to go back to active service, his request was approved, given his vast experience of the region and his acquired knowledge of Arabic. He was sent to Iraq and once again teamed up with an SAS unit, who were supporting the US marines in their search for weapons of mass destruction held by Saddam Hussein. Her father's tours lasted for six months at a time, which meant once again he was absent from her life. When he was home, they would spend time together in Oxford and London depending on her workload. He would also travel to Spain, splitting his time between Madrid and his home in Mijas, but always with Carla.

It was over a year since her outburst when she discovered that Carla was seeing her father. It had taken a long time for her to accept that he was in love with someone who wasn't her mother. Of course, her father had dated since the death of his wife, but never anything serious, never someone like Carla. But she made him happy, and for that Annabelle was grateful.

In April 2003, the invasion of Iraq was in full flow. Air strikes had battered Baghdad, and US and coalition forces were attacking the city. They faced strong resistance from Saddam Hussein's Republican Guard, but it was short-lived. The US 'shock and awe' tactic was overwhelming, and within three weeks Baghdad fell, the Iraqi leader in hiding.

Over the next eight months, David helped hunt down the man the Americans labelled HVT1 or High Value Target Number One. There were twelve failed operations conducted in search of Saddam, with over 300 interrogations, many conducted by David with US special operations Task Force 121.

David and then Task Force 121 interrogated a former presidential driver, who led them to a high-ranking comrade of Saddam, Omar al-Musslit. After two weeks of intensive questioning involving forty members of his family, Omar eventually revealed the location of Saddam's hiding place in his hometown of Tikrit.

As this was happening, Annabelle was working late at the lab, dealing with a new threat.

A deadly coronavirus had emerged in the Guangdong region of China and spread to neighbouring Asian countries, producing a form of pneumonia named severe acute respiratory syndrome, or SARS. The virus spread to other countries, including the US; mask wearing and Asian travel bans were put in place to prevent a worldwide pandemic. Within six months, the World Health Organization declared that the virus was contained, and travel restrictions were lifted. SARS affected twenty-nine countries, with over 8000 reported cases and 774 deaths.

Terror and destruction never seemed far away from Annabelle and her family.

On the 11th of March 2004, Al Qaeda carried out a bombing campaign in Spain. A series of ten bombs exploded simultaneously across four trains in the early-morning rush hour at Madrid's Atocha station. The explosions left 191 dead and more than 1800 injured. Carla was recalled to her office in Madrid at the Centro Nacional de Inteligencia.

She called David to let him know that she would be needed in Spain for at least a month and was pleased when he offered to come over and keep her company.

When David saw the aftermath of the explosion, he felt a conflict. On one side, this was a contained event with a relatively small death toll, but on the other, every death would be devastating to someone – a wife, son, brother, father, daughter, friend. He had the power to prevent that sorrow. Why shouldn't he save every life? He felt a conflict with the Protocol set by his father and was tempted to ignore it.

But he could hear Joan's voice in his head: 'Nautilus is a last resort and only to be used to avoid a global conflict. However painful a tragedy may be, it is forbidden to expose the existence of Nautilus for anything less.'

~

Al Qaeda's power and ambitions were growing. London was to be next.

On a beautiful summer's day in July 2005, David was tempted to walk to his appointment to enjoy the London parks in full flower. There really wasn't a more beautiful place to be, he thought, than England in summertime. But much to his annoyance, he was late for his meeting in the city, so he took the Underground and joined the throng of workers and tourists in the packed carriages, the only air conditioning a few slit windows.

Respite from the heat came at every station of the Circle Line as the train stopped, its sliding doors opening, the patient English crowd waiting on the platform to allow the exiting passengers space before they shuffled forward, cramming in more and more people until the warning bell sounded and the doors closed.

At Edgware Road Station, a passenger caught David's eye and he tensed. The youth was wearing a backpack and was most likely from Pakistan.

David stared at the young man, who averted his gaze and shifted further, closer to the doors. At the next station, he alighted to the platform and David relaxed, chastising himself for his prejudice against a stereotype.

Two minutes later, his senses were on full alert as he noticed that far from leaving the train, the youth had merely swapped carriages, possibly seeking a less crowded carriage, but now the man was staring at David, sweat visibly falling from his brow, the backpack clutched in his hands. The tube train was travelling at speed as David evaluated his target. Was the young man just a nervous tourist? He decided to change carriages at the next station and question him.

Then he saw it: the man shifted his weight onto his left leg and his tracksuit jacket opened ever so slightly. But David clearly saw the multicoloured wires. The terrorist followed David's gaze and realised his error. Scared and confused, he reached inside the pack and pulled out a trigger. David's training kicked in and he pressed the emergency stop button on the train – anyone standing was thrown to the floor as the braking system rapidly decelerated the train.

'Bomb! Everyone, on the floor!' David shouted.

As the train stopped, he reached up to the open connecting door to see what had happened to the bomber.

As he peered through the door, he realised he was too late – the bomber was looking directly at him as he screamed his victory cry and detonated the bomb vest, the impact of the blast tearing the carriages apart.

~

Two days later, David woke in a private room at St Mary's Hospital, near his home in Paddington. With him were the two women who loved him most, Annabelle and Carla.

'Welcome back to the world,' said Annabelle as she leant over his injured body and kissed him on his forehead. 'We thought we'd lost you. The doctor said you lost a lot of blood but you're strong and will make a full recovery.'

He looked at his heavily bandaged hands.

'How many?' he asked.

'Two on the left, one on the right,' Carla said.

David tried to use the palms of his hands to sit up in bed, but the pressure on his mangled hands was too painful. Annabelle and Carla grabbed an arm each and they pulled him up together.

'You're going to need a little help for a while,' Annabelle said gently.

Carla reached for the oxygen mask next to his bed and slipped it over his nose and mouth.

'You inhaled a lot of smoke. Rest now,' said Carla.

David defiantly yanked the mask from his face. 'How many died? I need to know.'

Carla patiently replaced the mask, giving him a stern look.

'We're not sure yet. There were four bombs,' Annabelle said. 'Two more on trains like yours, and a bus. There are hundreds of injured victims scattered across the London hospitals. One survivor said you stopped the train and got everyone on the floor. You saved his life and many others. If the explosion had happened at a station, there would have been hundreds more dead. They are calling you a hero.'

David ignored the comment. 'Do you think it was a coincidence that the bomber was on your train, or revenge?' Carla said.

'Revenge? For what?' Annabelle asked.

'Nothing,' David said. 'I've been active in the war against terror, but I was just in the wrong place at the wrong time.'

Annabelle went to the table next to David's bed and picked out three cards from the flowers that had been sent to him.

'According to the people that sent these, you were exactly at the right place at the right time. I'm very proud of you, Dad.' Annabelle kissed him on his cheek. 'I think we should let you rest. Carla, I'll take you to a nice pub I know – we can come back later.'

'What about me?' David complained, but all he got was blown kisses. He slid down the bed. *All I have to do is get myself blown up to make my two girls get on. Well, whatever it takes!* he thought, and drifted off to sleep.

~

David left the hospital ten days later. His active service days were well and truly over, and he was confined to a desk.

A week before his sixtieth birthday, he was invited to Buckingham Palace. The Queen bestowed upon him a knighthood, not just for his courageous act during the bombing, but for countless others he had performed over his long career, known only to Her Majesty and the higher echelons of MI6.

For saving so many lives during the 7/7 bombing, he attained an unwelcome minor celebrity status and received countless invitations to parties or to speak at events, invitations that he mostly ignored. He retired from MI6 wanting nothing more than to slink away to Spain and obscurity, content to focus his attentions on his garden and Carla.

One invite did get his attention, though, in mid-2008: a private viewing of Impressionist artists at the Royal Academy of Arts in Piccadilly. The works on show included Turner, Monet and Sorolla, three of his favourite artists. He invited his daughter to join him. Annabelle was also a fan of Impressionism, although that was where their mutual tastes mostly ended.

She was staring at Sorolla's *Strolling Along the Seashore* when a young man came up beside her.

'Do you like Sorolla?' he asked.

Annabelle turned to study the man. Slender, tall and handsome, with a lovely smile, he was well dressed, and stylishly so. She noticed the brightly coloured material on the inside of his jacket and his brogue shoes polished to perfection – this was clearly a man who spent time on his appearance.

'I do,' she replied. 'I like the way he uses light. It's like the painting is basked in sunshine. You can almost feel the wind and touch the water ...'

'Edward,' he said, offering his hand.

'Annabelle,' she replied, taking it. 'Are you a guest of the exhibition?'

'I'm a lawyer, and our firm is a guest of one of the sponsors.'

'What sort of law do you practise?'

'Commercial law, technology and media companies mainly. You?'

'I work for a pharmaceutical company. Viral research, but don't worry, I washed my hands before coming to the exhibition. I'm here with my father. I should probably go find him. Lovely to have met you, Edward,' she said, turning to leave.

'Excuse me. I know this is awfully forward, but could I give you my card?' he said. 'I would love to continue our conversation. You could just put it in your handbag, making my day feel infinitely better even if you discard it later, hopefully out of my sight.'

Annabelle paused, taking in his manner – intelligent, a hint of humour. Compared to the lab rats that filled her normal day or the intense scientists who could hardly string a sentence together, he was certainly worth further investigation.

'Thank you, Edward. I promise I wouldn't be so cruel.'

Allowing a few days to pass so as not to appear too keen, she called Edward.

'Edward Morris,' he answered, all business.

'It's Annabelle. You gave me your card at the art gallery last week.'

'Ah yes, lovely that you called, I was certain that you wouldn't. How are you?'

'I'm in Oxford in the lab, thought of you and decided to call.'

'I'm not sure that's a compliment. I hope at least you were working with a cute lab rat,' he said.

Realising her error, Annabelle recovered quickly. 'Very cute, the cutest,' she said with a laugh.

'That's okay then. Are you free on Friday evening by any chance?'

'I might be,' she replied. 'What do you have in mind?'

'Our firm is having a cocktail party, and I thought we could have dinner afterwards.'

'Yes, that would be lovely. You now have my number – text me the details and I will see you on Friday.'

'Thank you, I'll look forward to it,' said Edward, ending the call.

CHAPTER 48

Spain

July 25th, 2009

Edward and Annabelle lived busy lives, him in London or jetting off around the world with his legal career, her in the lab at Oxford working long hours. They saw each other as often as they could, and over the weeks and months following their first encounter, they got comfortable and, eventually, intimate. They enjoyed, like every new couple, the honeymoon period, where they discovered almost everything about each other, never ran out of conversation at dinner and the sex was wild and fun. Edward had dated lots of women but had never been challenged as much as he was by Annabelle, and he found her intelligence and understanding of the world refreshing as she made him question some of his own beliefs and understandings.

They had a lot in common: art was a given, but also a shared love of travel, hiking and nature, leading to fabulous weekends away in the Scottish mountains or kayaking around the Lake District. Their favourite trips were to Spain, Annabelle's second home.

On Saturday the 25th of July 2009, they were in the picturesque fishing town of Baiona, Galicia, in the north of the country. Edward had booked them into the Parador, a beautifully restored 12th-century castle that overlooked the Atlantic Ocean.

They were walking around the ramparts and watching the sun set on a violent sea, temporarily turned gold as it crashed against the rocks that encircled the historical castle, now a hotel. The sun slowly sank behind the horizon, dropping the temperature, making Annabelle shiver.

'Shall we go in?' she asked.

Edward took off his jacket and wrapped it around her bare shoulders. Holding her there, he said, 'Before we do, I need to ask you something.'

Edward slipped his hand inside the pocket of the jacket that was draped around her shoulders, producing a small turquoise box. 'Will you marry me?' he asked. Unusually nervous.

Annabelle took the box from his hand, carefully undoing the bow and lifting the lid. She stared at the brilliant-cut one-carat diamond ring that sparkled in the remaining light.

'It's beautiful, Ed, gorgeous,' she said, admiring the ring, oblivious to her surroundings.

'I know it's beautiful, but the question?' said Edward impatiently.

'Sorry, yes! Sorry! Yes, yes, I'll be your wife.' She flung her arms around him. Edward pulled her towards him, kissing her, as they both laughed and cried at their own happiness.

Annabelle's life filled with excitement as she planned her wedding. Guest lists had to be prepared encompassing her Spanish, Scottish and English friends. She tried on wedding dresses in London and Madrid, finally choosing a Spanish creation of gold and lilac made by her mother's tailor. This time passed so quickly that it felt as though one day she simply awoke and it was her wedding day.

One hundred and fifty family members and friends congregated on the spectacular grounds of Edward's manor house in Dorset. Beautifully arranged flowers exuded their fragrance, an intoxicating aroma that personified an English country garden in summertime. Annabelle's family from Spain could be heard talking in a continuous babble, much to the shock of the more conservative and stuffy English guests. Annabelle didn't care; she was happy, she was in love and her father was there to take her down the aisle to the exquisitely decorated bridal arch, where her future husband was waiting patiently for her to arrive.

~

'Mum would have loved this,' David said to his daughter during a rare quiet moment where they were alone, producing a tear from her that was quickly wiped away to avoid a make-up disaster.

'I can feel her, you know, not all the time, but when I need her, she is here with me,' Annabelle told him quietly.

'Good, Belle, I'm very proud of you. You know that, right? I love you, sweetheart. Now, c'mon, give your old man a dance.'

The celebrations continued through the night, the Spanish contingent vowing not to abandon the dance floor until sunrise. Finally, family and friends said their farewells to the newlyweds as they were whisked away to their honeymoon and the next chapter of their lives.

After a perfect week in the Maldives, which ended far too soon, they returned to London and settled into married life. The couple had decided early on that they would have children straightaway. Annabelle was slightly disappointed that she wasn't pregnant after their honeymoon: *I certainly tried hard enough*, she thought.

They tried for the next twelve months but with no luck, so they decided to get themselves tested. The results turned out to be inconclusive and unhelpful. A friend of Edward recommended an IVF clinic in Harley Street, and they both agreed to go. The clinic itself was brightly decorated and overseen by a gregarious Greek doctor who seemed to staff his clinic with beautiful young doctors and nurses from all over Europe.

A fertilised egg was embedded in Annabelle's womb and a week later her pregnancy was confirmed. She was so happy to be pregnant. After she had her sixteen-week scan, she began to relax and enjoy the rest of her pregnancy, which thankfully was relatively free of sickness and pain.

On the 25th of October 2012, Annabelle gave birth to a son, Alexander, who was joined by a brother, Justin, eighteen months later. Their family felt complete and Annabelle had never been happier.

~

While Annabelle and Edward had been creating life, the world continued to destroy it. Wars and conflict were followed by death and destruction as sure as night followed day.

Osama bin Laden had been shot in his compound in Pakistan by SEAL Team Six, and his body committed to the sea. Saddam Hussein had been hanged and Colonel Gaddafi assassinated. These leaders of hatred were gone, but others would replace them; the terrorist threat would remain.

Edward's law firm was thriving, thanks to some government contracts he had recently won, much to the relief of his partners. With two energetic children in tow, he was happy to have the extra work, especially as Annabelle had resigned from her position at AstraZeneca to focus on the kids.

The young family lived in Shalford village, four miles from Guildford. They bought a charming four-bedroom house with a large garden, allowing the children to enjoy an outdoor life. They were only thirty miles from London, an hour by train.

Soon, though, Annabelle's brain was becoming numb from watching so much children's TV. She needed a distraction and a new challenge. She decided to enter the world of politics.

Joining the Conservative Party in late 2014, she was chosen to stand for the constituency of Guildford.

David Cameron was the sitting prime minister within a coalition with the Liberal Democrats. Although born to upper-class parents and having attended the elitist Eton College, his brand of economically sound policies was also socially responsible, which gained him strong support throughout the nation. He won the 2015 general election with an unexpected but overall Conservative majority and brought with him the newly elected member for Guildford, Annabelle McIntosh-Morris.

Annabelle felt completely unprepared, having expected to come in a respectable second, allowing her a further five years to plan her political program and her life. As a Member of Parliament and mother of two young children, she would have to juggle to squeeze in a bit of wife too. A daunting prospect, but exhilarating.

Her introduction to politics was intense. With her background in medicine, she was soon noticed by the Secretary of State for Health, Jeremy Hunt, and joined several committees regarding the NHS and social reform.

The Cameron government continued to thrive domestically and overseas. However, in 2016 the Prime Minister, brimming with confidence, said he was going to honour an election manifesto pledge and hold a referendum on whether the UK would remain part of the European Union. The referendum was held on the 23rd of June 2016, the result 52 per cent in favour of leaving the EU and 48 per cent against.

The day after, Cameron resigned as prime minister and was replaced by Theresa May, who, wanting more women in positions of power, promoted Annabelle to junior minister for health.

The work was hard, but she thrived, gaining respect among the party and civil servants alike.

Two years later, she turned forty.

CHAPTER 49

London, Savoy Hotel

June 6th, 2018

Annabelle finished the last of her martini and continued her conversation with her father.

'Okay, so if this machine—'

'Nautilus,' replied David.

'If *Nautilus* can do the things that you say it can, what happened to it? Where is it now? I can't believe we're even having a serious conversation about it. First you tell me that Alan Turing is your father, my grandfather, and that he changed the events of World War II by building a time machine ... What I don't understand is the relevance of me being forty? Why did you wait?'

'Turing was more than just a code breaker. He was a genius, a genius at another level, Belle. Think Einstein, Newton, da Vinci, and at a very young age. But he also recognised that despite his intellect, he was reckless in his twenties. He did not have enough common sense and found it hard to control his emotions. He understood the need for maturity, for wisdom, and despite everything he realised that it only came with age, with time. Turing and Joan agreed only to share the secret with family, and only when the age of forty had been reached. I know this is difficult

239

and you probably think I've gone mad, but the only way to explain it to you properly is to show you.'

'But what's it for? Why would you use it unless you want to win the lottery? You're not hiding a fortune from me, are you?' she joked.

'No, Belle, that's why it's a guarded secret. This machine is powerful, even catastrophic in the wrong hands, which is why we need maturity to fully understand the responsibility that comes with its guardianship. Let's meet in the morning and I'll show you the machine called Nautilus.'

'You sound so dramatic.'

'It's deadly serious, and you must tell no one, not even Edward. You must promise me, Belle.'

'Where do you want to meet?'

'Harrods at 9.30.'

'Don't tell me it's in the dome? I always wondered what was in there.'

'It's not in the dome of Harrods. It's in the basement.'

CHAPTER 50

London, Harrods

June 7th, 2018

David met his daughter on the ground floor of Harrods, and she followed him down the stairs to the safety deposit centre.

'It's very discreet – you'd never know what was down here,' said Annabelle.

'That's the point.'

He gave his password and they proceeded to the door of the secure site that had been rented to Alan Turing over seventy years prior.

Annabelle looked at the antique door and pondered the complex access device. David punched in a code and then took a blood-sugar testing kit from his pocket.

'Give me your thumb,' he said.

'Ow!'

He squeezed it, raising a droplet of blood, and placed her bloodied thumb on a glass screen that had ejected from the locking device. Punching in another set of codes, he repeated the operation on himself. The two glass slides withdrew into the locking mechanism and ten seconds later it lit up green. A series of steel bolts withdrew from the wall, leaving the door free to be pushed open.

'That was melodramatic,' Annabelle said.

'Just necessary,' David said. 'You and I are now the only people in the world who can open this door. You need an access code to release the slides, then a sample of blood, which is profiled for the correct DNA, and then – abracadabra.'

Once inside, he shut and locked the door behind them, turning on the light, illuminating a world that looked a long way from high tech.

'Welcome to Nautilus,' he said. 'It doesn't look like much, but you're looking at the most powerful and dangerous machine in the world.'

Annabelle glanced around the small room, largely unimpressed.

'My old laboratory looked more sinister than this. Are you going to give me the tour?'

'This machine here attached to the Morse code sender is where you enter the messages. You'll have to learn Morse code.'

'I'm not learning anything until you tell me what all this is for,' she replied.

'The message is entered here, and instead of travelling via a telegraphic wire, it goes through this magnetic accelerator, which was designed by Turing. My understanding, as explained to me by Joan, is that the electronic message is broken down into electrons and travels beyond the speed of light, enabling its passage through time. It's then received and reassembled at this machine, which we will call the receiving station, and triggers a message to the sender. This used to be a telegram, but I modified it to a text message to my mobile phone. That reminds me – I need to add your phone number to the contact list and delete mine.'

'Keep going first. I'm still trying to decide whether you've gone mad. It's only because it's you telling me this that I'm still here.'

'It's simple. The message doesn't *go* anywhere, except from here to here, between the two machines. The cleverness, the uniqueness, is that the message is received eight weeks ago.'

'Okay,' said Annabelle, 'let's assume I buy that the machine works and that this is not some science-fiction fantasy. When would you use it? And why can't I win the lottery eight times?'

'Turing set up an honour code, what he called the Protocol. He passed this on to Joan, who passed it on to me. If you can't accept this code, or there is no one to pass it on to, then the machine must be destroyed. And believe me, no one, including Alan, ever *wanted* to use the device, and I hope you never need to.'

'Why pass it on to a civilian? The power you are describing is too much for one person to control. At least you and even Joan had training and were members of the clandestine services. I have no skills for this. This should be passed on to the government or MI6.'

'Turing was very wary of government, even MI6. His reasoning was that individuals run these organisations, and those individuals change and can have a personal agenda that might not always be in the interest of humanity. He therefore became convinved that the most suitable guardian of Nautilus should be family. Over time, I reached the same conclusion. The power that lies within this room is managed and controlled by the family of its creator. I hope with time you will realise that and agree with his wishes and the Protocol.'

'What Protocol? Explain it to me.'

'First rule, Nautilus must never be used for personal gain, so no lottery numbers.'

'There goes the fun part,' interjected Annabelle.

'The next rule is that Nautilus should only be used when it's possible to change the outcome. Time is the most important factor here. You only have eight weeks, so we can't change anything beyond that threshold. Remember, we're not travelling anywhere – the message goes back to an earlier you, eight weeks ago.'

'When would you want to use it?' asked Annabelle, frustrated.

'The next rule is that changing history is a godlike event, so must only be contemplated to change a global horror, or mass destruction.

Wars have been part of the world's history for hundreds of years and will continue to be so. But world wars, millions of lives – these are the events that you should consider.'

'World wars don't begin and end in eight weeks,' complained Annabelle.

'There lies the dilemma. The best way to help you is to show you when Nautilus was used, including by me.'

'You've used it? Changed history? I can't believe it. How can we, you, wander around changing history whenever you feel like it? This is a big deal,' Annabelle said, getting increasingly concerned at what she was hearing. 'So tell me when you actually used this thing,' she said, now scared to hear the answer.

'Let's start with Turing,' replied David. 'I already told you that he changed the outcome of D-Day.'

David explained the details of the D-Day dilemma that Turing had faced and how he changed the outcome of World War II. He showed her the message, the maps, documents, everything. Almost against her own judgement, Annabelle was fascinated.

'Are these documents for real? The D-Day landings were changed?' she said.

Nodding his affirmation, David repacked the documents into the safe and went on with his explanation.

'Your paternal grandmother, Joan, wanted nothing to do with Nautilus and considered its destruction many times. But she promised Alan to preserve the legacy and, out of her deep love for him, respected his wishes. It was Joan who put me in the same position that you face now. I was full of doubt, just as you are, but Nautilus is very real and very dangerous. Its protection is paramount. Joan told me that Alan was paranoid that Churchill had him followed by MI6. It's absolutely vital that no government agency ever gets to know about Nautilus, Belle, especially ours.'

Annabelle's fascination turned to worry.

'I'm not sure about all this. You worked for MI6 and I'm a Member of Parliament. Have you thought that we might be breaking the law?' said Annabelle, certain that they were.

'I always come up with the same answer. If we are saving the world from destruction, then it doesn't matter.'

'When did you decide to use Nautilus?'

'9/11, Belle. I used Nautilus after the attacks by bin Laden.'

'But 9/11 happened! Thousands died.'

David took out another file from the safe and showed her the message he had received. While she read the text, he explained the work he and Carla had done to prevent the attacks.

'So you knew there was going to be multiple targets and multinational retribution, but you don't know exactly what the outcome was going to be, because your own actions changed history, albeit not completely?' said Annabelle.

'That's it. The eight-week window gives you limited time, so you have to send the message with as much time as possible to your earlier self to give the best chance of success.'

'Tricky.'

'That's what Carla said when I told her,' he said.

'Carla knows? You can tell people?'

'Absolutely not. I told Carla that I knew the locations and the date of the attack from a source. She still to this day believes my source was an Al Qaeda commander. You can't tell anyone, not Edward, not your children.'

David omitted to mention that at some point she would have to have the same conversation with her boys, but now was not the time to open that can of worms.

'And especially not your prime minister,' he said. 'No one, Belle.'

He explained every detail to her, showing her all the documents, the maintenance, the back-up generators and finally the security codes and destruction devices that were embedded in the various machines. He informed her that a forced entry would trigger a minor explosion that would destroy Nautilus and incinerate the documents in the safe, leaving nothing but some twisted metal, a bronze Morse code sender and a lot of ashes.

'Lastly is the self-destruction code. If you ever feel that Nautilus is going to be captured or your family put at risk, you can destroy everything here.'

David handed Annabelle a piece of paper, which she read and committed to memory. Then David burnt it with a lighter.

'If you ever receive this message, Belle, come here as quickly as possible and set the timer on the door. Don't worry, the explosives are small and precise – they won't harm the store or anybody that works here,' he concluded.

'This is too much. I need some fresh air to think,' she said, exhausted by the vast amount of material that she had taken in and the consequences of that knowledge.

They left the store and walked up Brompton Road towards Hyde Park Corner. The lunchtime traffic edged along Piccadilly, the sound of taxis and buses mingling with the throaty exhausts from Lamborghinis and Porsches as their owners revved their engines to display their wealth. Conversation was impossible, so they used the underpass to reappear in the tranquillity of St James's Park.

'I think this is very dangerous,' said Annabelle. 'I'm not sure I could bring myself to do it. Perhaps Nautilus should be destroyed.'

'I've considered that, Belle, but on every occasion I come back to the fact that Nautilus has always done good. Hitler may have won the war, and who knows, maybe the Middle East would have been wiped out. I'm at peace with what I did, I saved countless lives. Do you want to give that opportunity up?'

'Maybe,' she said. 'This is such a huge responsibility, and the decisions that you made without being able to discuss with anyone, including your family. It's a big ask, Dad.'

They continued their walk across the bridge towards Westminster, stopping every now and then for the tourists to take their pictures of the beautiful scenery and the pelicans swimming gracefully across the lake.

'I'm seventy-two years old. I will need a decision soon,' David said gently.

'Let me sleep on it,' said Annabelle.

~

David and Annabelle visited Nautilus several times to train her in the machine's applications, maintenance and security. She still did not accept the guardianship, but suggested that she would be able to make a more informed decision if she knew how everything worked and understood the task at hand.

As she grew comfortable with the apparatus, she recognised the moral duty she had to take on, the responsibility of her legacy.

'If you don't want this, I understand,' said David. 'Nautilus could be described as a poisoned chalice.'

'I keep thinking: what if one day our country is threatened or my kids' lives are in danger and I pass up an opportunity to protect them?'

'It's your choice, Belle, and the biggest decision you will ever make in your life,' said David, offering her an out.

Finally, Annabelle agreed, and David changed the phone number to hers. The transition was complete, and he could rest.

CHAPTER 51

London

2019

As a new year was heralded in, the world was uneasy, a political tinderbox. America was at loggerheads with Iran over oil, and a trade war had commenced between Trump's administration and China, resulting in tariffs being imposed by both nations, upsetting the free-market economy and causing ruin and anguish on both sides of the world.

In London, Brexit had the whole country in disarray. Theresa May was failing to reach any kind of compromise with the European negotiating team, leading to a slew of no-confidence votes and ultimately her resignation on the 24th of May. She was replaced by Boris Johnson two months later.

Annabelle felt unsettled, confused and inexperienced in these matters. Colleagues were resigning, 'crossing the floor' and joining the opposition, while the party whips were cajoling MPs and junior ministers such as her to toe the party line and support Boris no matter what. The situation got so bad that the Prime Minister suspended Parliament, giving her an unexpected holiday.

With the children on summer break, Annabelle and Edward decided to leave the political unrest behind and spend the summer at their Dorset residence in the charmingly named village of Puddletown. The sun shone down on the lush green grass, and the local farmers' fields were bursting with ripe wheat and barley: it was the epitome of a picture postcard landscape. They went to the beach, a twenty-minute drive from their house, and unpacked a blanket and their picnic. Annabelle watched her boys paddling in the small waves, building sandcastles a little too close to the water's edge, their creation destroyed by every seventh wave. Unperturbed, they giggled and redoubled their efforts, excavating the sand with their bare hands.

'Look at how happy the kids are. We should stay here forever,' said Edward.

'Don't joke,' said Annabelle. 'I've been wondering about this whole politics business and whether I should stay.'

'Why do you say that?' asked Edward.

'I wasn't completely naive. I expected the games and the backstabbing, but this Brexit disaster has taken it to a whole new level. And look at the kids – look at how much we miss when we're both away, working. What do you think?' she asked.

'Maybe see how Boris handles the Europeans. If anyone can get Brexit over the line, it's Boris. And remember, be careful what you wish for. When you looked after the kids full-time, that also left you unfulfilled. You entered politics for a challenge, intellectual stimulation, and you are very good at it, Belle.'

'I suppose you're right. I'll ride out the year and see how I feel.'

'Let's scoop up the kids and head home for tea. Everything will be okay, you'll see,' said Edward confidently.

~

Soon it was time for the boys to return to their school at Sherborne, while their parents travelled to Guildford, back to their work and politics.

In December, Boris held a snap election. The Conservatives recorded a massive victory and an overall majority. Annabelle had her own personal success, increasing her majority by 6000 votes.

This personal recognition and support allayed her fears of the summer, replacing them with excitement – to be part of a government that now had a mandate to act and the votes to effect change.

On December 20th, the withdrawal agreement from Europe was passed. Britain would exit from the EU.

As the world prepared for their Christmas holidays and family celebrations, life returned to normal.

Annabelle went Christmas shopping at Hamleys on Regent Street. The packed toy store was a hive of activity as time-poor parents battled to find the perfect last-minute gifts for their offspring.

She had received a report earlier in the day regarding a new coronavirus that had appeared in China, in a city called Wuhan. The Chinese were attempting to contain the virus within its borders, and she made a mental note to catch up with the World Health Organization after the holidays. For now, though, she was sure it could wait, and she returned to the more important matter of organising Christmas. This year, they were returning to their Dorset house for the holidays and were entertaining David and Carla as well as Edward's parents.

The fireplaces would be lit, fuelled by chopped pine logs from the wood store in the barn. The children would fetch holly branches and pinecones, decorate them with glitter and string them around the house. Annabelle smiled as she imagined the scene.

~

Christmas was a huge success; everyone tore open their presents and laughed at bad jokes and poorly chosen gifts. The children were spoilt rotten by the grandparents, and the family all declared that they had added five kilos thanks to Edward's cooking and generosity. Annabelle was happy but had noticed that Edward was distracted a little, getting too many phone calls from the office, which appeared to make him angry. He also said that he'd broken some wineglasses; it was most unusual for him to be clumsy. She worried that he was stressed, and when everyone had gone to bed, she raised the subject.

'Ed, is everything okay? Was it too much, having such a full house?' she asked, concern in her voice.

'Everything's fine. I'm just tired from too much cooking and too much wine,' he replied, trying to avoid the conversation.

'The food was fantastic, love, but you always work so hard preparing it. And why is the office bothering you so much during the holidays?' She knew there was something worrying her husband and she was concerned about him.

'Nothing, Belle, just a deal that was meant to close before the break and an anxious client. I'll fix it when I get back to the office.'

'Okay, well, come to bed. Let's see if Santa has any more surprises for you,' she teased, trying to lighten the mood.

CHAPTER 52

London

January 2020

The novel coronavirus, now officially called SARS-CoV-2, or more colloquially Covid, had spread throughout Wuhan and the rest of Hubei Province, which had a population of nearly sixty million people. On the 23rd of January, the Chinese government ordered a hard lockdown of the entire city to stem the spread of infection.

The mood in the West remained relaxed, though, and politicians played down the threat even when cases started to appear in their countries.

Annabelle, however, was not relaxed at all; rather, she was gravely concerned. She had spent the last two weeks talking to colleagues in many different countries, and at the CDC and WHO, researching facts about the nature of the virus, symptoms and likely cures and vaccines. At the end of February, she was summoned to Number 10 Downing Street to present a report she'd prepared on possible strategies to contain the effects of the virus within the UK.

There were still only nine cases in the UK, which created a sense of ease among the politicians. Annabelle's report argued that this was a similar situation to the Spanish flu of 1918, which lasted for several years, infecting 30 per cent of the world's then population of around two billion people and killing between sixty and one hundred million.

'The Prime Minister will be with you shortly,' said the permanent undersecretary to Boris Johnson. Five minutes later, she was ushered to the cabinet meeting room.

This was not going to be a cosy one-on-one chat. Apart from the PM and his civil servant advisers, Rishi Sunak, the Chancellor of the Exchequer, and Dominic Raab, the First Secretary of State, were present, accompanied by several aids.

'Come in, Annabelle, take a seat,' boomed Boris in his usual jovial style. 'Thank you for your hard work in preparing this detailed report, which we have all read. I have to say that you paint a rather gloomy picture of this situation. By your own admission, we have less than a dozen cases, yet you are suggesting that this could spread to millions, tens of millions, comparing it to the Spanish flu! Surely this is an exaggeration. I understand that we need to be vigilant, but you are advocating a national lockdown, which would be an economic disaster.'

'No, Prime Minister, I'm not exaggerating, and yes, I am advocating a lockdown. All the modelling I am seeing is that this virus is going to explode through the population, and if we do not slow it down by isolating the people, the NHS and all the doctors will be overwhelmed and people will die in their millions.'

Rishi Sunak spoke. 'Can I ask, Annabelle, whether you see any alternative to lockdown? What about the principle of herd immunity? I believe Sweden has suggested that they favour this model. You must understand that the economy is fragile and the average household savings is around £10,000. For low-income families, the situation is much worse, as they have nothing. If we deny them access to employment, they will riot on the street.'

'The herd immunity model might work in countries like Sweden, which has a small population and a massive landmass, but if it were adopted here, the rise in case numbers and deaths, especially among the elderly, would be astronomical. According to my sources, there will be no vaccine available for eighteen months at best. If we do not act now, you will have dead bodies on the street,' said Annabelle, desperate to get across her point of view and her recommendations.

'Thank you, everyone,' said the Prime Minister gravely. 'We seem to be in a Catch-22 situation. Neither strategy seems very appealing to me. Annabelle, please contact the WHO. If we are to act, it might be more palatable to the public if a worldwide pandemic was declared. Rishi, you will need to talk to the European Central Bank and the Bank of England. If we do decide on a level of lockdown for any extended period, we're going to need a package of financial assistance. Get the Treasury working on this straightaway.'

'Yes, Prime Minister,' Sunak replied.

'Thank you, everyone,' said the PM, concluding the meeting.

~

Annabelle contacted her colleague at the World Health Organization. A week later, a global pandemic was declared.

On the 23rd of March, Boris Johnson went on national television ordering the entire population to stay at home, to protect themselves and to preserve the NHS for the most seriously ill.

London became a ghost town but was also the largest source of infection. Annabelle and Edward decided to bring the children to their country home in Dorset, taking advantage of the large house and wide-open spaces, but mainly the lack of people. Much to Edward's annoyance, his business trips were cancelled, and to make matters worse Annabelle had to return to London, staying at her father's apartment to do her bit and assist the government in any way she could.

CHAPTER 53

London

April 2020

Covid was a huge opportunity for the pharmaceutical giants – Pfizer, AstraZeneca, Moderna and others. Every possible resource was utilised to finish the vaccine and be first to market so that the successful company could snap up the lion's share of orders from health departments across the world.

Annabelle worked fourteen hours a day, travelling between London and AstraZeneca's head office in Oxford, studying data and talking to the scientists. It appeared that the lockdowns were having a positive effect. By the end of April, Annabelle could advise the Prime Minister – who was himself recovering from the disease – that the peak had been reached. Further declines in May led to a lifting of restrictions in June, allowing people to holiday, albeit within the UK, and return to work.

To celebrate her birthday, Annabelle booked a train to take her to Dorset, to her husband and children. Edward and the boys had so far avoided Covid but barely survived homeschooling, and they were desperate to see Annabelle come home. But before she left, she paid a visit to Harrods, which thankfully was now fully reopened.

Annabelle made several purchases from the decadent but beautifully displayed food counters to spoil her family when she arrived home. And then, before leaving for the station, she went to see Nautilus.

She sat staring at the machine, checking and rechecking all the settings, following all the maintenance procedures. Nautilus was functioning perfectly, almost waiting for a message, but what could she send? Clearly Covid qualified as a global threat to mankind, meeting the required Protocol, allowing Annabelle the freedom to use its phenomenal power.

But what could she possibly send to her eight-week-younger self except statistics, case numbers? There was no vaccine, no secret formula that could be passed on, just a timetable.

Nautilus was impotent against Covid. She removed her hand from the Morse code sender, frustrated and angry. 'I have all this power and I can do nothing, save no one,' she said to herself.

She picked up her groceries and switched off the light.

~

On the train ride home to Dorset, her phone rang. It was her father, who was isolating with Carla in Spain.

'Happy birthday, darling,' he said cheerily.

'How are things in Spain? Are you safe?'

'We're both fine. Are you in London?'

'No, I'm on the train going to Dorset to see Edward and the kids. I need a break, and case numbers have improved. I thought I'd take advantage.'

'That's great to hear,' said her father, relief clearly heard in his voice. 'I was beginning to worry you were spending too much time away from home. I'm proud of you, but you need to find a balance,' he said.

'I'm doing the best I can, but sometimes it's not enough,' she said, frustrated.

'What's bothering you?' he asked.

'I went to Harrods today.'

'Okay, what did you do?' he asked, concerned.

'Nothing. That's the point. It started purely as a shopping trip, but I did stop in to see Nautilus. I was racking my brain to concoct a message that would help with the pandemic, but there's no gem of information, no plan. It's so frustrating.'

'As it should be, unfortunately. We use Nautilus at our peril, Belle, and sometimes we must simply let life follow its path.'

'I have no choice, but be warned – this virus isn't going away. I saw my old professor recently, who was back at AstraZeneca. He showed me modelling that scared me, Dad. He told me over the next twelve months there will be hundreds of millions of infections and millions of deaths, despite a vaccine that he thinks will be available early next year. So please be careful – you're no spring chicken, and this damn disease isn't kind on the old.'

'Don't worry, Belle, I wear a mask everywhere. Carla's even stopped me from going to my local bar.'

'Poor you.'

'Kiss the kids for me, and tell them we can't wait to see them as soon as we can travel.'

~

Annabelle walked through the door of her Dorset home and was jumped on by her two offspring, who hugged her, then squealed with delight when they saw the green and gold bags from Harrods, assuming they contained presents.

'You two, out of them! That's food for your dad to work his magic with.'

'Really? Just food!' they complained.

'The contents of that bag might not be so tasty,' she teased, pointing to a large green and gold bag next to the front door.

Alex and Justin tore open their gifts, paying no attention to the beautiful wrapping paper. They retreated to their bedrooms, allowing Edward to hug her and welcome her home.

'This food is amazing. We haven't seen anything like this for months.'

That night, to celebrate Annabelle's birthday, Edward treated his family to a delicious meal of lobster with butter in a Thai sauce with stir-fried crispy vegetables.

~

For the next ten days, Annabelle relaxed, soaking in the love and affection that only children and family can bring, and for the first time in ages she was happy and content.

She would have to return to the hustle and bustle of London, but she was determined to enjoy every minute in Dorset.

One evening, near the end of her break, her phone rang. It was Carla.

'Hola, Carla, how are you?' she said with a joyful voice.

'Not good, cariño, it's your father. I'm sorry to tell you he has Covid,' Carla replied, her voice clearly worried.

'Is he going to be alright?'

'I don't know. He's at hospital in Marbella.'

'Hospital?' said Annabelle, alarmed.

'They told us to stay at home, that there was no room for him. But I suspected that this was due to his age and, quite frankly, being British. He took a turn for the worse last night, could hardly breathe, so I used a contact and got him a bed. I'm here now, but he's in isolation on oxygen, which is helping a lot.'

'Can I speak with him?'

'Not at the moment.'

'Please, please, call me later if anything changes,' Annabelle said, fear rising inside her. 'And thank you, Carla,' she added before hanging up.

Moving straight into action mode, Annabelle contacted the Spanish health minister and called in a favour. The following day, she received a message from the medical team in Marbella. Her father was very ill, and they couldn't say whether he would recover, but she was allowed to speak to him.

'How bad is it?' she asked her father directly.

'I feel like I have a ton weight on my chest, and I'm coughing and can't stop. I just feel so weak.' He sounded weak too. He sounded, for the first time in her life, vulnerable.

'Just rest. I've got an idea of how to help you.'

David struggled to speak, the effort draining his energy. 'I'm listening,' he managed.

'I want to use Nautilus to warn me and therefore you – I need to try.'

'You can't, not for me,' he said, coughing.

'I have to try. You would've done the same for Mum – you know you would, you told me so. I'm not going to lose you.'

David was too exhausted to reply, but it didn't matter. Annabelle had already hung up.

Straight after ending the phone call, Annabelle started packing her bag, despite Edward's protests.

'What are you going to do, Belle? They're not going to let you go to Spain,' he cried.

'I have to try. I'm going to ask the Prime Minister for permission. I'll call you when I get to London,' she said determinedly.

Seeing he had no hope of persuading her, Edward relented and kissed her. 'Good luck. Let me know how you get on.'

~

Annabelle returned to London with no intention of visiting Downing Street, instead making her way straight to Nautilus. The message was brief, merely informing her earlier self of the date and severity of the illness. There was nothing more that she could add.

CHAPTER 54

Dorset

June 2020

·

Annabelle's phone rang. It was Carla, delivering news that her father had Covid.

Annabelle was stunned. How could this be? She had received the message and given the warning to her father, who had taken extreme measures, to the point where Carla thought he had become completely paranoid.

Annabelle went to London but not to Nautilus. She would convince the PM to allow her to fly to Spain and to seek permission from the Spanish government for her to enter the country. As with most things, there was one set of rules for the masses and another for the rich and powerful. Her trip was approved.

She reached the hospital and was taken immediately to the intensive-care ward, where she changed into protective clothing, including a full head mask and gloves, to visit her father.

'How did this happen? I sent you the warning, we created the isolation plan – what went wrong?'

'Carla,' he said.

'Where is she?'

'Covid ward. Isolation. She was asymptomatic but they tested her yesterday and she is positive. She'll be fine, but they don't want her in the community, infecting anyone else.' He coughed again, causing Annabelle to wince, seeing her father in so much pain. She wanted to tear off the protective clothing and hug him and tell him that everything would be okay, however little she believed it.

'We can try again,' she said. 'I'll warn you about Carla. I could even see about getting you to England.'

'You can't repeat the message. Nautilus's timing mechanism will prevent you.'

'There must be some way around that. I have already broken the Protocol and I would gladly do it again to save you,' she said desperately.

'It won't work, and even if it was possible, I don't want to live apart from Carla. I wouldn't give up a single day – and for what, to catch it again, in the supermarket or petrol station? Nautilus can't help me. You have to accept that.'

For the next two days, Annabelle visited her father and Carla as much as the medical team would allow. In between visits, she considered scenarios to save her father, but none would work, not without his full cooperation and his strength, which he no longer possessed.

Finally, the doctor reported that his situation was getting worse. They were putting him on a ventilator, and he would therefore no longer be able to communicate with her.

She hurried to the ward and donned the protective clothing one more time. Entering his room, she was shocked to see how much he'd deteriorated since the previous night.

'Hello, love,' he managed to say in a rasping whisper.

'Last chance to go to a deserted island,' she said.

'I think I'm past that, sweetheart, and to be honest I've had enough sand in my life.'

'The doctors are transferring you to the ventilation unit later today to help your lungs. You'll feel more comfortable – it will help.'

'Do you remember what your grandparents used to say when we came up from London all bothered and stressed about God knows what?'

'*Dinna fash yersel*,' she said. 'Don't be troubled.'

'That's how I feel. Untroubled. I've lived a great life. I've loved and been loved. I'm proud of you, who you've become. Don't fret for me. If I survive this thing, I'll be grateful. If I don't, I've lived an extraordinary life. You'll want to go back to Nautilus, work out a plan, I know you. But the outcomes will all end up the same, with me here, asking you to stop.'

'Rest, Dad, save your strength and fight,' she whispered through tears.

'I will. Get some rest yourself. I'll see you on the other side.'

Annabelle gripped her father's hand, caressing his withered fingers through her latex gloves, watching him fall asleep.

That night, David's body could fight no more and he died peacefully in his sleep. Annabelle couldn't visit her father after he died: the body had already been moved to the morgue and would later be cremated to prevent further risk of infection. It was brutal and upsetting, but at least she had been able to say goodbye, which she knew was not the case for most families in Spain, or anywhere else in the world for that matter.

Annabelle tried to visit Carla in the hospital but was denied direct access for her own protection. Both women waved and blew kisses to each other through a window. Carla had tears rolling down her face. She wiped away her tears and grabbed a piece of paper and pen, scribbling a message in her grief, turning it to face Annabelle.

They wouldn't let me see him!! Were you there? Did he die alone?

Annabelle sobbed.

She wrote her reply:

I was with him to the end. He died thinking of you xx.

~

At the airport ahead of her flight back to London, Annabelle opened her handbag to find her mobile to call Edward. Inside her handbag, she found an envelope addressed to her; the handwriting was her father's. She carefully opened the envelope and retrieved a single page.

Dear Belle,

I asked a nurse to put this letter in your bag should I no longer be with you.

Remember me for my love of you, my love for your mother, my love for my grandchildren. Tell them who I was, what I stood for and how I'll miss them all terribly. Look after Carla, she'll be alone now, and will need your love.

I love you, Annabelle, my Belle, my beautiful girl. I'm so proud of you, you have been the light in my life, the reason I always came home, the beat of my heart.

Live your life to your fullest, have more joy than regret and believe in yourself.

Like I do.

All my love

Dad xx

When Annabelle touched down at RAF Northolt just outside London, she was tempted to tell the driver to take her directly to Harrods.

But this time she would respect her father's wishes. It was time to let go, to stop trying to manipulate history. She vowed never to visit Nautilus again.

CHAPTER 55

London

July 2020

Annabelle was devastated by the loss of her father. But she had his strength, his courage and his sense of determination, so she returned to work in London, committed to helping save lives, to preventing as many families as she could from experiencing the pain that she'd endured these last weeks since returning from Spain.

Despite the warm summer, Covid case numbers continued to grow, fuelled by the younger generation, who believed that they'd only suffer minor symptoms if they caught the virus, determining that the rules didn't apply to them.

In September 2020, the UK imposed another lockdown to protect the NHS.

In America, cases soared, and it became the first country to record ten million infections.

It was soon joined by India and Brazil, and the following year by the UK, Spain and Italy.

The big pharma companies doubled their efforts, and Annabelle cut the required testing times in the race to get a vaccine to market and save lives.

The UK was the first country to approve the Pfizer vaccine and administered 800,000 doses in December 2020. Further vaccines followed from AstraZeneca and Moderna.

Countries scrambled to get their orders and to start the process of putting shots into the arms of their citizens.

The presence of a vaccine gave hope to the world; however, a large proportion of each population would have to be immunised with at least two doses to have a significant effect against the case numbers. It took a further twelve months before life started to return to a form of new normal. A normal where Covid would mutate into new variants, less deadly but more infectious. A normal where daily deaths would occur without a headline in the papers: case numbers that would have shocked only two years prior now went unreported. A normal where the old and those with low levels of immunisation would continue to contract the disease and die.

Annabelle remained in London, despite Edward's protests. The guilt was present every day she was separated from her family, but there was too much work to do. She had to ensure that the distribution of the vaccines was going as fast as possible.

With the summer closure of Parliament, Annabelle finally returned home to Dorset, to her family and to reignite her relationship with her husband.

Annabelle closed the door and dropped her bags on the floor. Edward was on the phone but hung up upon seeing his wife.

'I'm so glad you're back,' he said, kissing her.

'What an awful year, and it's only halfway through,' she said, exhausted.

'The kids are playing in the garden. Go see them, and after I'll run you a hot bath.'

That night, Annabelle revelled in reading her children a bedtime story, tucking them in bed, being a mum.

When the boys were down, Annabelle and Edward sat talking over a glass of wine.

'You need a break,' Edward said determinedly.

'It's so hard. The vaccine rollout is going well, but it takes so much time, and meanwhile the deaths just keep mounting. It's heartbreaking. I just want to play with the boys, watch old movies on the couch and snuggle up with you.'

'We can handle that. Let's take our wine upstairs and see about reconnecting,' said Edward.

With the restrictions gone, the family could enjoy trips to the beach, the boys playing in the waves while Annabelle unpacked picnics full of delicious morsels lovingly cooked by their dad.

'These little pies are so yummy, Ed,' said Annabelle, pushing another one into her already full mouth.

'How long before you have to go back?'

'Not for another two weeks. The kids will be going back to school. What about you? Are you coming back to London or are you getting too used to working from home?'

'I've been able to get a lot more done here, away from the office distractions, but I do miss the company. And you.'

When they returned to the house, she received a call telling her she was needed in London.

'Oh no,' said Edward. 'I know that look – what now?'

'Parliament has been recalled early in response to the American withdrawal of its military personnel from Afghanistan. I'm so sorry.'

Annabelle promised her family that she would return every weekend before they went back to school. The disappointment seen on her children's faces was getting harder and harder to deal with. Edward was resigned to the situation, putting his arms around his boys' shoulders as their mother left in the taxi.

President Biden had ordered the complete evacuation of all US personnel from Afghanistan and wanted it completed by September, the twentieth anniversary of the 9/11 attacks on New York, which had triggered the first invasion of the country.

As the last planes took off, the Taliban reclaimed the capital city and reimposed their draconian rule.

Russia and China were also starting to flex their muscles, Russia sending troops to the Ukrainian border to complete military exercises and China enacting naval war games in the Pacific islands close to Taiwan, an island its leaders claimed to be part of the bigger China. Australia, the UK and the US formed a pact called AUKUS to allow Australia to build a nuclear submarine fleet to counter Chinese influence in the region.

Annabelle continued to oversee and monitor the UK's vaccine distribution.

She still carried the scar of failing to save her father, every Covid death a reminder of her loss, driving her to work harder to save lives. But immunisation rates increased, providing herd immunity, and new, less lethal variants such as Omicron gave her hope that the worst was behind them.

Tired and lonely, she returned once again to her family for the Christmas holidays. She knew this year would be a challenge, a Christmas without her father.

She told herself to remain cheerful, at least in front of the children, who thankfully had short memories and a happy outlook on life, especially when there were presents involved.

With the travel bans lifted, Annabelle was able to fulfil her promise to her father to take care of Carla. The whole family went to Heathrow to meet her off the plane, the car journey home filled with laughter and stories.

Carla was spoilt, as Edward cooked mouth-watering dinners and desserts and the boys took her for long walks, showing off the village and all their favourite places.

Annabelle was happy to have Carla with them and was even able to talk to her about her father without crying.

The world also seemed ready to move on. The media was tired of

Covid and resorted to the tried and tested headlines of scandal, politics and the royals to sell their papers. The West was focused on rebuilding its economies, controlling inflation and creating jobs.

But President Putin had other plans, moving his troops towards the Ukrainian border, ready to strike.

CHAPTER 56

Ukraine

January 2022

Russia had annexed the Crimean Peninsula in 2014 and since that time had engaged in an unofficial war in the Donbas region of East Ukraine, where pro-Russian separatists were supported by Russian weapons and personnel.

NATO, led by the US and UK, was concerned, putting its own troops on high alert. The UK sent NLAW anti-tank missiles to assist the Ukrainians, and Boris Johnson visited Kyiv and Ukrainian president Volodymyr Zelenskyy, who told him he expected an imminent Russian invasion.

On February 4th, 2022, China and Russia released a joint statement opposing the expansion of NATO and demanded that Ukraine never be allowed to join the organisation. They further opposed the recent AUKUS pact with Australia in the Pacific. The Western allies sent military aid to Ukraine and diplomats to Moscow, while the Russians were sending more troops through Belarus and their Black Sea Fleet to Odessa.

On February 13th, while the Americans were watching the Super Bowl and British diplomats left Kyiv for London, Russian troops started to cross the border in the east, and their tanks, with the permission of the pro-Russian president of Belarus, travelled south to the Ukrainian border, only 230 kilometres from Kyiv.

In London, Annabelle attended an emergency cabinet meeting. There was chaos within the government. Annabelle had worked for two bosses in the last twelve months due to resignations from ministers unhappy with Boris Johnson; they were fleeing the sinking ship, conscious of their own political future, already plotting a leadership challenge.

Annabelle had no such ambitions and consequently now found herself as Secretary of State for Health and a member of cabinet.

On the other side of the world, the Chinese military was being mobilised.

At their underground naval base on Hainan Island, four Shang II–class nuclear attack submarines prepared to sail and move north into the South China Sea. American satellite imagery showed an escalation of forces at the Longtian Airbase, revealing thirty-six Shenyang J-6 fighters, a formidable aircraft based on the Soviet MiG-19, as well as two squadrons of PLA bombers stationed at the base.

Ten days later, Russia invaded Ukraine.

Despite heroic resistance, the speed of the Russian attack had not been seen since the Blitzkrieg of Hitler's Third Reich. Ukrainian forces suffered huge losses. The eastern campaign alone resulted in 40,000 military casualties and a similar number of civilian deaths and injuries.

In the south, the Black Sea Fleet opened fire from the safety of their anchorages outside of the port cities of Mariupol and Odessa. Simultaneously, the Russians launched an air attack on Kherson and Melitopol, pinning down the Ukrainians.

The final pincer movement came from the north. Four hundred T-72 tanks crossed the border and encountered fierce resistance as they approached the capital, Kyiv.

Annabelle and her fellow cabinet members consulted with their

American colleagues and NATO commanders. There was no appetite for sending troops; instead, the West responded with condemnation. Sanctions were imposed against Russian banks, politicians, and businessmen. Neighbouring countries such as Poland, Moldova and Romania accepted over five million refugees from the fighting and war-torn cities. But there was no military intervention, no show of force by NATO, save for the supply of some weapons and loan packages from the US.

~

Not long into the invasion, the PM asked Annabelle to stay behind after a meeting late one afternoon.

'Thank you for remaining. You're one of the few ministers who doesn't seem to want my job,' he said. 'Any reason you haven't thrown your hat in the ring?'

'I'm not ready to have the fate of the world resting on my shoulders. You seem impatient about how things are going in Ukraine – are you unhappy with our response?'

'I am,' said Boris. 'My hands are tied to NATO and our allies. But I detest bullies, always have, and wish there was more that we could do for the Ukrainian people.'

'They need weapons. Let's start with that and see where this goes,' suggested Annabelle.

'We need to tread carefully,' said the PM.

'I understand, but we must not let tyranny prevail unchecked. Freedom must win out,' she insisted, surprised at her own candour in front of the Prime Minister, who smiled and thanked Annabelle for her time.

~

The siege of Kyiv had stalled. Zelenskyy's forces were dug in and determined to hold the city. Russian fatalities increased, and the aged T-72 tanks were being crippled by anti-tank missiles, which were now being supplied to the Ukrainians through Poland.

There was hope that the Russian advance could be halted, giving the Ukrainians time to regroup and reinforce the defence of their country.

But Putin had other ideas.

Three squadrons of Tupolev Tu-160 bombers with Sukhoi Su-34 fighter escorts attacked Kyiv's defences, creating a destructive path. One hundred state-of-the-art Russian T-90 tanks, forming three attack battalions that had been lying in wait, slowly advanced on the city. The Ukrainians had no answer to the T-90s, which rolled into the city supported by five brigades of infantry, comprising almost 5000 men.

But still the Ukrainian soldiers refused to give up, inflicting huge losses on the Russians.

President Zelenskyy consulted with his high command, who unanimously advised their president to fight on. Zelenskyy could see the bravery and courage shown by his generals, but he could also read a butcher's bill, and finally on the 8th of March 2022, less than two weeks since the first occupying troops invaded his country, he surrendered and ordered his troops to lay down their arms.

The victorious Russian president accepted the surrender, stating that the Ukrainian people were liberated and returned to Mother Russia, where they would all live as one nation, as one Soviet Empire.

CHAPTER 57

March 8th, 2022

Russia and China had agreed a secret campaign. If Russia conquered Ukraine without military opposition from NATO, China would invade Taiwan and then send naval battlegroups to Japan and the Coral Sea, threatening Australia.

Following the announcement of Ukraine's surrender, Russia and China announced their pact, warning the West not to interfere with their right to regain territories that they believed to belong to the mother states.

As a minister, Annabelle attended another cabinet crisis meeting.

Taiwan was surrounded by the Chinese Navy, the Chinese Air Force flying sorties within Taiwanese airspace. China delivered their ultimatum: complete surrender within twenty-four hours or invasion. The Taiwanese government prepared for a fight.

The Hungarian prime minister, Viktor Orbán, was a staunch supporter of Putin despite his country being a member of NATO. Upon hearing the news of the Ukrainian surrender, Orbán withdrew Hungary from NATO, pledging his support to Russia and allowing a safe corridor for Russia to move into Western Europe and also attack Romania, Slovakia and ultimately Poland, the jewel that Putin wanted returned to his crown.

The West was facing a dilemma. The actions of Russia and China could not be tolerated, but military action against such powerful adversaries would lead to World War III.

The Americans called an emergency NATO summit, attended by video link by the British prime minister and defence minister. Annabelle was invited to attend as an observer, an act of trust from the PM. She didn't like what she saw or heard from the military commanders. She was scared for the world and even more so for her family.

In Taiwan, as China's deadline was reached, a defiant people and government refused to surrender, mobilising their reserve army of 1.5 million, to support their professional full-time defence force of 200,000 personnel.

China attacked. A typhoon of missiles rained down on Taiwanese military establishments from the Chinese destroyers, submarines and fighter-bombers. The power and sheer volume of the weaponry deployed against the small island of twenty-four million people was apocalyptic, the likes of which had never been seen in modern warfare.

NATO advanced its forces further east to support Poland and its neighbouring member states as Putin advanced into Hungary, like chess pieces moving across the board.

Western leaders still maintained that a diplomatic solution could be found. The price was going to be Taiwan and at least a large slice of Ukraine, but these were considered acceptable costs compared to an all-out global war. Envoys were despatched to Moscow and Beijing. The Western politicians and military advisers gathered in their situation rooms, watching the Battle of Taiwan unfold and looking for any aggression from the Russians against a NATO state.

CHAPTER 58

London

March 10th, 2022

During the crisis, Annabelle stayed at the London apartment she'd inherited from her father. As a cabinet member, she needed instant access to the war rooms, but she also wanted her family close by. The children had been given a special exeat to leave school and join their 'important' mother, so, at her request, Edward and they joined her in the city.

'Mummy, we saw you on TV!' Justin and Alex screamed, beaming, as they burst into the apartment.

Their joy and enthusiasm buoyed her spirits, freeing her mind from the complex world in which she lived, if only temporarily.

The children ran to their bedrooms.

'Thank you for coming back to this circus,' she said, finally managing a hug and kiss for her husband.

'I'm not sure this is the best place to bring the kids,' Edward said, clearly displeased at being ordered to London by his wife.

Annabelle tried to defuse the situation.

'Let's not talk about it until we get you unpacked and the kids to bed.'

'Mum, you should see the new Lego set Dad bought me,' called Alex, charging back into the room. 'The Millennium Falcon. It's amazing. It took me a week to build. Daddy, show Mummy the photo that you took.'

As Edward searched his phone for the image, Justin seized his own moment.

'Mum, did you hear about my soccer match? We won, and I scored a goal, Mummy. Did you get the video?'

Annabelle searched her phone for the video and pressed play. 'Look, Justin, here it is! What a great goal, well done!'

Justin beamed a wide smile at his admiring mother. 'Next week, I'm going to score two!'

After the boys finally wore themselves out and headed off to bed, Edward poured himself and Annabelle a glass of pinot noir as she came up behind him at the kitchen island and wrapped an arm around him, caressing his hair playfully. Edward turned with the two wineglasses. Annabelle kissed him, letting out a moan. He set the glasses down on the island. She kissed him harder.

Edward put a palm on her chest. 'We need to talk first,' he said. 'I'm not falling for this ploy.'

Annabelle chewed his ear, breathing heavily into it. 'Sure you want to talk? The boys will be asleep in two minutes.'

Edward broke the embrace and sat down on the couch, pushing discarded toys to the ground. 'We *need* to talk. I need to understand the risks.'

Annabelle grabbed her wineglass and sat on the other end of the couch, frustrated. 'I'm not sure what I can tell you that you don't already know from watching the news,' she said.

'I see the reports, but where's the line going to be drawn? What would trigger a declaration of war? What's going to put our children's lives at risk?'

'Nothing is set in stone. The pieces are moving fast and in every direction. Putin is high on his success in Ukraine and wants to restore Russia back to the "former glory" of the Soviet Union. Meanwhile, China has seized the opportunity to expand their influence in the South Pacific and claim Taiwan, which was always just a matter of time. When we handed back Hong Kong, we lit that fuse,' Annabelle explained.

'But what's the plan?' Edward said. 'Tell the Chinese they can have Taiwan and a few South Pacific islands as long as they break the pact with Russia?'

'Pretty much. Perhaps you should go into politics. The hope is that we can broker a deal with the Chinese before Putin invades a NATO member state and forces us into World War III.'

'What if the Chinese aren't interested and make a move on Japan or Australia?' Edward sipped his wine, a favourite of his, but there seemed to be no enjoyment in it for him; his face was dour.

'Then we are in real trouble,' Annabelle said. 'The loss of life in a full-scale war between NATO and a Russian-Chinese alliance would be in the millions.'

Edward set his glass down on the coffee table. 'Do you really think the Chinese will let it happen? It would be an economic disaster, especially for them.'

'That's what we're relying on.' She drained her glass and poured herself another.

'Do you think the Western leaders are up to it?' asked Edward.

'The US, UK and NATO are the strongest military force in the world. I can't believe Russia and China want to hit the self-destruct button.'

'I hope you're right,' replied Edward.

'Global destruction wasn't exactly what I had in mind for tonight,' Annabelle said. 'But you may have blown your chances now.' She rose and walked towards their bedroom. Then she looked back, unbuttoning her dress. 'May have.'

CHAPTER 59

London

March 11th, 2022

At 5am, Annabelle's mobile went off. It was the cabinet duty officer informing her that a car was going to arrive shortly and she was required to attend the war rooms at 70 Whitehall.

'What's going on?' asked Edward sleepily. 'What time is it?' He rubbed his eyes.

Annabelle whispered, 'Five o'clock. Go back to sleep. I have been called in. Nothing to worry about.' She kissed his cheek, then fumbled through the apartment in the dark, trying not to wake the children.

Within twenty minutes of the phone call, she was in a black government Jaguar. Although the person on the other end of the phone had given no details, the early hour and the speed at which they were travelling through Central London did nothing to calm the butterflies in her stomach.

At 5.45am, Annabelle entered the meeting room, which had more than the usual contingent of guests, and a more than usually dishevelled Boris Johnson, who was in heated debate with the Chief of the Defence Staff, Admiral Radakin.

Annabelle saw Ben Wallace, the Secretary of State for Defence.

'What's going on?' she asked him urgently.

'You're about to find out – Radakin and the boss are about to speak. It's not good.' The two of them sat and fell silent, and the room followed suit. Around the large nineteenth-century oak table, all eyes were on the PM.

'Ladies and gentlemen, thank you all for getting here so promptly, but I'm afraid I have dire news. I'm saddened to say that our earnest efforts to move towards peace in Eastern Europe have been dealt a deadly blow. Just over two hours ago, Russian forces crossed the borders of two sovereign states. Attacking from the sea and with land forces in the south-east of Ukraine, the Russians have invaded Moldova. More alarmingly, due to their membership of NATO, the peaceful country of Slovakia has been attacked by Russian forces from both Ukraine and Hungary with the assistance of our former ally.'

Annabelle felt a knot in her stomach, hardly believing what she was hearing.

'Admiral Radakin will now brief you with the details of the attacks and our possible responses.'

The chief military man proceeded to present maps and footage captured by spy drones to the collective audience.

'The Moldovans, not being a member state of NATO, surrendered, to avoid any bloodshed for their population and destruction of their towns and cities. Slovakia is a different problem. Its army is minuscule, consisting of less than 20,000 military personnel, mostly based in the capital Bratislava. However, as a member of NATO since 2004, it should be afforded and is demanding protection under Article 5 of the North Atlantic Treaty from the other twenty-nine member countries.'

The Admiral concluded by saying that, in his opinion, Putin was testing NATO's resolve by invading two small territories without any major loss of life, or he wanted to use the attacks as a bargaining chip in peace negotiations.

The PM took over from there.

'As one can understand, it is increasingly more difficult to judge the behaviour and thinking of Mr Putin. I have conversed with the US president and many other NATO leaders, and we are agreed that Slovakia will be given the support they are due. I have further spoken with the supreme commander of NATO forces, General Tod Wolters, who's been given command of US and UK forces in Europe and is currently preparing to support the Slovakian people.

'Ladies and gentlemen, it is my intention, with your blessing and support, to issue an ultimatum to the Russian president that he has twenty-four hours to confirm that he will withdraw from both Slovakia and Moldova or face the fact that Russia and the United Kingdom will be in a state of war. I should add that similar ultimatums are being prepared across the NATO member states.

'I further want to add that no such demands or threats are being made against China unless they attack a member state or declare war on the side of the Russians. There is still a strong view that China, when faced with the number of opposing countries, will abandon Russia and protect its economic interests.'

The Prime Minister received unanimous support from his cabinet, including Annabelle, who was told to return in six hours for an update. Her driver was waiting and took her back to Paddington and her family. She had three missed calls and two texts from Edward. She replied by text: *on my way home.*

'Have you seen the news?' Edward said urgently the moment she opened the door.

'I've been with the Prime Minister, the chief of the armed forces and just about everyone else who has a say. Where are the boys?'

'Playing with some friends in the park. Is Putin really pushing into Western Europe? Is he mad? We'll go to war! What is the PM saying?'

'We must be calm. The Prime Minister is going to address the country in half an hour on the BBC. Yes, Russian forces have crossed the Slovakian border, but so far without bloodshed. But as you know, with Slovakia being a member of NATO, he may as well have marched up Oxford Street. The Prime Minister, the President and all the other NATO countries are issuing Russia an ultimatum, demanding his agreement to withdraw, or face the consequences,' said Annabelle, as calmly as she could. 'So it's war.'

Edward rubbed his chest, sat down and took some deep breaths. 'What are we going to do? What about the kids? We need to get out of London. We can't go to Dorset – we live too close to the Blandford army base, which is sure to be a target – and Guildford is too close to London. We need to get out of the country, but where?' said Edward, panicking.

'Edward, this is only posturing. We aren't about to be attacked by supersonic missiles from Siberia. We'll send troops into Poland, Romania, even into Slovakia itself. This will start as a conventional battle and NATO will have superior air cover from its bases in Germany and Turkey.'

'What if Putin is all in and takes the first strike?'

'He hasn't done that to date. He's used short-range rockets followed by ground forces, albeit at an astonishing speed. He knows we'd retaliate with in-kind force – everything would be destroyed.'

'Are you willing to bet the lives of our children on the choices made by that madman? We need to go.'

'Where? Spain? Australia, perhaps – far away enough for you?' asked Annabelle, showing her frustration.

'Australia is a no, in case the Chinese decide to attack.'

'No European countries, no Australia or Far East. The bloody Falklands, then?' she said, exasperated.

'Canada. Could be safe. We can't keep the kids here. I'll get tickets reserved for Vancouver in the morning. Four tickets. I know what you're going to say, you're a member of the government, you must stay, Queen and country. But the children must go. We must go.'

'You already know I can't leave. And to have you all so far away, I'm not sure I'd be able to cope. This could go on for months, years.' She sat beside him, put a hand on his thigh. He placed a hand on her hand.

'We will never forgive ourselves if the kids were hurt or worse. Maybe disaster will be averted and we'll come back, or you can join us and have a family adventure in the Rockies.'

'There has to be another way to keep us together,' Annabelle said, tears now in her eyes. 'I don't want you to go – what else can I do?'

Edward stood and stared out of the window.

'What are you thinking?' asked Annabelle.

Edward dug his nails into the soft wood of the windowsill, then turned to Annabelle.

'There is one option I can think of. You could take a trip to Harrods and see if your secret machine can help,' he said, staring coldly at her.

CHAPTER 60

London

March 11th, 2022

Annabelle was stunned by the words that came from her husband's mouth, the obvious implications already starting to generate questions in her head.

'What did you say?' she managed to ask.

'You heard me. And before you start throwing accusations at me, remember you've kept this secret from me.'

'How do you know about Nautilus? How long have you known, and what do you know? And who the *hell* told you?'

'First of all, I didn't know it had a name.'

Annabelle's face reddened with her stupid error.

'This goes back to Winston Churchill, so I've been told,' Edward went on.

Annabelle's anger rose, her face hot. 'What the fuck are you talking about, and who are these people?'

'I'll tell you what I know and then you can fill in the gaps. Fair?' said Edward.

'I warn you, Ed, I'm so ... shocked and pissed right now.'

'Let me explain. Two and a bit years ago, I was approached by a guy from MI6.'

'Are you fucking kidding me?' she blurted, fear creeping into her voice.

'It's complicated. Please, Belle, let me finish. He told me that he had some legal work for our firm and invited me to a meeting at Vauxhall Cross. I was intrigued – we've all seen the movies, and who wouldn't want to see inside that building? When I arrived, I was told the meeting couldn't go ahead unless I signed a document confirming my obligations under the *Official Secrets Act*, which concerned me, but I agreed.'

'Who was at the meeting?'

'The agent who approached me, and a superior, no card, no name. They explained to me that during World War II, Alan Turing had developed a machine which they assumed had something to do with deciphering intelligence but was way beyond Enigma. They said that Turing and Churchill had met several times during the war and Churchill was convinced that Turing somehow could interpret intelligence in such a manner that it may have changed the course of the war.'

'Turing was a genius – he probably made lots of machines. Why the focus on this one seventy years later?' she said, realising that they may not know the true power of Nautilus.

'According to the agents, this particular machine may have got Turing killed by a foreign agent. After his death, they searched his house and workplaces and, as you say, found an Aladdin's cave of machines and ideas but nothing that the boffins could pin to Churchill's assertion. To all intents and purposes, that was that. That is, until your father intervened with 9/11.'

'What about 9/11?' Annabelle stammered, floored by Edward knowing this and keeping that knowledge from her. Except she had kept it from him too. But that was different. One involved the government, the other family. 'Dad was their agent. He was a hero.'

'According to the nameless officers of MI6, he may have been an even bigger hero than people know – except, I'm assuming, you.'

'Go on,' she said, still nervous, watching every step that Edward made as he paced around the room, unwilling to sit close to his wife. He stared out the window once more.

'They told me that there were potentially multiple sites targeted by Al Qaeda and that somehow your father scuppered their plans and was fundamental in saving thousands of lives.'

'Because he had sources within the terrorist organisation who fed him the information,' she said, repeating her father's cover story.

'They had your father followed. And eventually it led to a storage room underneath Harrods. The problem they encountered was that the security system was beyond state-of-the-art, which is where I came in.'

Annabelle felt the blood drain from her face. Her mouth was dry.

'What did they want and why didn't you tell me? How could you have these conversations about my family, *your* family, without talking to me? We're meant to trust each other, not keep secrets.'

Edward looked like he was about to object, to accuse his wife of the same thing, but wisely chose not to do so.

'They told me that they wanted to tread carefully. Your father was one of their own and a hero to boot, so they asked me to keep an eye out for any information and to, well, help with a few tests of the security. I should've come to you with this, but they threatened me, Belle, said I would be disbarred if I spoke to anyone about it, even you.'

Annabelle knew how they could be, knew how they could leverage personal lives, careers, marriages against a person. It was like breathing air for MI6.

'What did you give them?' Her anger crept higher.

'I had no choice,' he said. 'They thought the security might work from fingerprint or retinal-scan technology, so I gave them some wineglasses from one of our dinner parties, the ones I said that I broke, and told them where you and your father went for your eye prescriptions. That was it, that's all I did, and it came to nothing, nothing worked, so that was that.'

His shoulders sagged; he was defeated and exhausted.

'There's something you're not telling me. Are you really a lawyer? Is your real name Edward? Are you being paid to be my husband?'

'Stop it, Belle. Of course I'm a lawyer, and no one is paying me to be your husband. I love you and always will. But in the interests of full disclosure: with the stick also came the carrot. As a thank-you, as they put it, they did push some very lucrative work to the firm, all legit and above board, real cases. It helped, Belle – with the practice during Covid. You remember the hours that we all put in just to keep the firm afloat and manage the payroll.'

'The meeting with MI6 – when was that exactly?'

'Just before the election.'

'So just over two years ago, an MI6 agent convinced you, a lawyer, to spy on your family, pass over their fingerprints and then you took their thirty pieces of silver. Is that a fair summary?'

'I was naive, and the whole cloak-and-dagger thing was exciting. The wineglasses, I'll give you, was too far, I'm truly sorry. But they couldn't get past the door. They'd tried for years but they said it was booby-trapped, surmising that a forceful entry would destroy the contents of the room.'

'I don't know what to think. You've been dishonest with me for our entire marriage.'

Edward had had enough and the gloves came off. 'That goes both ways. This Nautilus must be very valuable or dangerous for MI6 to be so interested in it. Why the high-tech security and why the secrecy, your secrecy? Why have you kept it secret from me for our entire marriage?'

'I didn't know of its existence until I was forty, just four years ago. And I'm so tired of it. Ever since Dad died, I've vowed never to visit Nautilus again.'

She joined Edward and looked out the window, watching the sun setting in the distance.

'I'm going to get an early night, alone,' she said. 'And forget those damn reservations to Canada too. You can go on your own if you want, but my children are going nowhere without me.'

~

The next morning, Edward took the boys to a horse-riding class, then returned with coffee and croissants, starting his charm offensive early.

Annabelle, still incensed and brimming with misgivings, finally agreed to take a walk with him in the park.

'Last night,' Edward said, 'one thing I have never understood is how your father got involved with this. Is there a connection between Alan Turing and your dad?'

Annabelle took a deep breath and let out a long sigh.

'After last night, Edward, I don't feel inclined to answer any of your questions,' she said. 'I'm so hurt and will be for some time.' She stopped walking and looked at him. 'However, I have concluded that Nautilus may be able to help in this current crisis and, by doing so, make the world a safer place. If I'm going to do this, I'm going to need your help, and I'll need to tell you the secret of the Protocol. But I warn you, if you divulge anything to anybody, we'll be done, and I'll make your life a living hell. Do you understand?'

'Perfectly,' said Edward. 'I'm ashamed and deeply sorry for how I betrayed you. Us. Our marriage. You have every right to be irate and disappointed and untrusting of me,' he said with sincerity.

They spotted the boys by the lake, trotting their horses between the trees. Alex rose steadily out of his saddle, in sync with his horse. Justin bobbed along and, spotting his parents, gave a wave and a grand smile, nearly falling off his horse in the process.

Annabelle waved back, watching them ride towards Kensington Gardens to continue their lesson.

'It's time I put all my cards on the table,' Annabelle said. 'Dad's biological father was Alan Turing.'

'What?' Edward exclaimed in disbelief. 'You can't be serious. Turing was gay, for starters.'

'He was, but he loved Joan Clarke, and he and Joan, celebrating the end of the war, had one night of passion at the Savoy and Joan became pregnant. Joan decided that Dad would be better off being raised by the McIntoshes in Scotland and they agreed to do it. Turing carried on with his groundbreaking work until his death, which looks likely to have involved foul play. Dad's real mother, Joan, passed the secrets of Nautilus on to him, and he subsequently passed them on to me.'

Edward rubbed his jaw, reflecting. 'That's quite the revelation. You saw proof of this?'

'I did.'

'And you believe it?'

'With absolute certainty.'

'No wonder you're all so bloody clever. But that doesn't explain all the security. And what does the damn thing do? Can it protect the kids?'

'I think it can, but if we use it, we need to protect ourselves, legally. You're going to have to perform some of that lawyer stuff, and I mean watertight. And afterwards, Nautilus needs to be destroyed. If you agree to that and agree to secrecy, I'll explain what Nautilus is capable of.'

She knew that she was taking a risk, that she was breaking the rule of sharing the secret with anyone, breaking the promise she'd made to her father. Even if Edward had not betrayed her, she'd have had misgivings. But she had to think of the boys. She had to put her children first.

Walking back to the apartment, she considered what a terrible job she had done as guardian of Nautilus. First she had broken the Protocol by trying to save her father, now she was about to share all the secrets with her husband and finally she was resolved to destroy the machine.

But not before it could be used to save the world one more time.

CHAPTER 61

London

March 12th, 2022

Edward was astounded by the explanation of Nautilus's capabilities and more than once questioned whether Annabelle was sane. She went on to explain the occasions that Nautilus had been used, from Turing at D-Day to her father at 9/11, even her own attempt to save her father.

Edward was terrified for his family, even more so for Annabelle.

'If the intelligence services knew this, they'd lock you in the Tower until you showed them how to use it. I'm not even sure whether you committed a crime by not telling them.'

'Exactly, Ed. That is why we have to be so careful. We need complete immunity from prosecution before we go any further.'

'I'll draft an agreement between MI6 and ourselves that gives us full immunity from prosecution and complete security from disclosure to anyone outside the Service. But how do we do this?'

'You need to go to MI6 and tell them that you've convinced me to divulge the importance of the machine, and that you think, but don't know, that it may be able to help with the current crisis. But you must stress that I will only do so under the protection of immunity, and on the basis that this stays within the realm of the clandestine services, not to be shared with government.'

After Edward prepared the legal documents, he took a taxi to the Secret Intelligence Service Building at Vauxhall Cross, where he was shown to an interview room and told to wait.

Edward was taken aback when he was met by Andrew Foster, the Chief of MI6.

During their thirty-minute discussion, Edward informed the Chief that he'd confessed to his wife, the Secretary of State for Health, that he'd been asked to spy on her and her father several years ago by the service. He explained that, despite her anger, she was willing to discuss the use of the machine housed in the basement of Harrods but only under strict terms, which he laid out in front of Foster, with his papers.

The Chief agreed to the terms, took out his green pen and signed the immunity papers with the letter C, as was customary.

'I require your actual signature, sir,' Edward insisted.

With the document signed, Edward called his wife.

'How'd it go?' Annabelle asked.

'I'm here, with C,' Edward said.

'You're with the Chief of MI6?'

'That's right, he is seated opposite me as we speak.'

'He signed the papers?'

'Yes. I think you ought to come over. He's anxious to meet with you.'

~

With Annabelle's arrival, Edward noticed a change in the mood of the room. Being a minister, she was afforded all the courtesies that came with her station. The meeting moved to the Chief's office on the top floor, and there was an overall tone of politeness and deference in the way the Chief and his personnel carried out their questioning.

Edward showed his wife the signed immunity papers.

For what she hoped was the last time, Annabelle explained the history of Nautilus, the connection with Turing and how the machine had been used over the last seventy years. Despite the incredible nature of the information she was producing, the head spy just sat at his desk, listening intently, soaking in the information without so much as a raised eyebrow.

When Annabelle was finished, he stared at her directly, making her feel quite uneasy, as if he were scanning her face for any inkling of a lie. Which, of course, he was.

'Minister, if what you have just said is true, and I can't see any reason or profit for you to lie, this ... technology is, quite frankly, invaluable. What are your thoughts on next steps for its use?'

'As I've stated, the maximum window for transmission is eight weeks, so if we were to send a message tomorrow, being March 13th, Nautilus can send it back to myself on January 15th. To get the message to you, I would need some way of contacting you without you thinking I had gone quite mad. You would then have just under six weeks before the Russian invasion, to prepare Ukraine and NATO with the intelligence that we can provide and, I assume, supply them with enough weapons to stop Putin and his army from conquering their country and advancing.'

'I'll assemble a team, but I think perhaps that I should see Nautilus for myself, Minister.'

'You will, but in the past.'

~

The Chief's team prepared detailed intelligence on troop movements and strengths, weaponry, air strikes and detailed locations of all the major battles that took place in the first week of the campaign. While his team was busy with facts and figures, the Chief himself prepared a personal message for Annabelle, instructing her on what to say to him, in the past.

When the Chief received and verified the data in January, he would pass the crucial information to President Zelenskyy and his military commanders, explaining that they had a highly placed mole within the Russian military command. The Ukrainian military would be able to organise their own forces to meet the oncoming invaders at the exact time and place where the main thrusts of the invasion would take place. The Chinese submarine and naval movements would be sent to the CIA, US Navy and Taiwanese military along with a request to reposition the US Pacific Fleet.

The plan was to get advanced defensive weaponry and personnel in sufficient numbers to halt the Russian invasion in its tracks. NATO would amass an impressive show of force on the Russian border and in the South China Sea, particularly near Taiwan. The Chief concluded that, with precision timing at all the strategic locations of the current war, if they could stop the first domino from falling, a global war might be averted.

The team worked long into the night, preparing succinct but crucial data that could be used in the execution of their plan.

~

The next morning, the Chief of MI6 met Annabelle in Hyde Park and they took a stroll around Kensington Gardens. 'It's hard to imagine in such serene surroundings that we're discussing an operation to save the world from destruction,' he said.

'Have you and your team managed to come up with a plan?' Annabelle asked.

'In this folder are a series of messages containing the military targets where we want the Ukrainians to focus their defence. There are further messages that MI6 will pass on to NATO and the Americans and the Taiwanese. I believe we have sufficient detail to move our forces to all the pressure points around the world. Credibility is key, and the first person we need to convince is myself. To that end, I have supplied you with a code word: *Apokaluptein.*'

'To reveal,' said Annabelle.

'Exactly. There are only a handful of assets in the world that have this code word. If you say it to me on January 15th, I will be curious and I will find you,' the Chief instructed.

Annabelle opened the file and scanned the messages that MI6 wished her to send, placing the folder in her bag when she had finished.

'Do you have any questions?' said the Chief.

'No, I understand. It won't be a problem.'

'Then I'll wish you good luck and godspeed,' he said. 'And, Minister ...'

'Yes?' Annabelle said.

'You and your family surprised me today, and I take pride in the fact that I'm rarely surprised.'

With that, they walked their separate ways, Annabelle in the direction of Harrods.

~

Once inside the strongroom, Annabelle sat on the small chair in front of the antique desk that housed the Nautilus machinery. As she prepared the series of messages, she thought of her father, and her biological grandparents, Alan and Joan, all of whom would have sat at this very spot, harbouring the same self-doubts, the fear of the consequences of the actions they were about to take.

But this was not the time for hesitation – she had to act decisively. She read through the papers and intel that had been passed to her by MI6 and began to prepare the message.

The first part of the message told her earlier self to explain to Edward everything about Nautilus and to prepare the immunity document. Subsequent parts gave the detailed intelligence from Foster's team regarding the Ukrainian invasion, the Russo-Chinese pact and the consequences if they failed. The last part provided the contact details and code word for the Chief of MI6.

As Annabelle stared at the message, she reminded herself that she had vowed never to be put in this situation following the death of her father. But here she was. She thought about the countless lives that could be saved, her own children and all the families that would be protected from the horrors of war. If she could avoid a global conflict, she had the potential to save millions. Her responsibility was clear.

'I'm doing the right thing, Dad, I know I am,' she said softly, and started sending the data.

CHAPTER 62

Guildford

January 15th, 2022

Annabelle was woken by her children playing noisily downstairs in their family home, thirty-five miles south of London. She had slept for eight solid hours, for the first time in weeks.

She still hadn't come to terms with the loss of her father and the guilt that she felt for not being able to save him. To distract herself, like many people when they find themselves in this position, she'd thrown herself into her work, and now she was exhausted. That one solid night's sleep was golden.

She could smell the heavenly aroma of bacon, eggs and mushrooms emanating from the kitchen. She wandered along the corridor, listening to Edward wrestle with his ingredients and their demanding children.

'I want pancakes, Daddy,' chirped Justin, excited that everyone was together and smiling.

'Smells amazing,' Annabelle said, making herself a cappuccino. She poured milk into a glass jug to warm in the microwave for the boys' hot chocolate and squeezed her husband's bottom as she passed by. It was going to be a nice day.

'What do you want to do today?' she asked the boys.

'Go for a bike ride,' Alex said.

'Play with my toys in the garden,' Justin said, pushing out his lips.

'I'm glad that we're all in agreement,' Annabelle said. 'We'll go for a bike ride along the river. Justin, you can bring three toys, and we will have lunch at the Jolly Farmer.'

The combination of pub food, crisps and fizzy pop brought the whole family to a consensus, and they finished off their hearty breakfast and prepared for the outing.

It was a beautiful winter's morning. The sun shone low over the horizon, producing very little heat but creating starbursts of light through the cold mist that hovered like a low cloud over the river as the young family travelled along the riverbank. The children rode enthusiastically, amused by seeing their breath in the cold January air. Justin struggled to keep up as Alex showed off his superior bike-handling skills. Despite a few muddy crashes, Justin was unperturbed, riding on without complaint through the long journey. They reached the country pub just before noon. Edward chained the bikes together out front and they all stepped inside, rubbing their frozen hands together.

They were greeted by the aroma of the carvery: roast lamb, beef and turkey with roast potatoes. Next to the huge joints of meat were china bowls brimming with colourful vegetables, Yorkshire puddings and pots of steaming gravy. A large wood fire crackled in the hearth, and they all suddenly felt ravenous from the exercise and the cold. They sat down at a table next to the fire, the warmth generated from the pine logs drying the mud on Justin's jeans.

Annabelle acknowledged a few nods from the locals who recognised her from the TV, but they all kept a polite distance, not wanting to interrupt what was obviously a private family occasion.

As they tucked into their scrumptious lunch, Annabelle's phone chimed. Three faces looked up at her from their dinner plates and smiled as she flipped over the phone to obscure the message. Several other messages arrived during lunch, but after a nudge from her husband, she silenced the device and enjoyed dessert with her family.

With their tummies full, the children complained that it was too cold to cycle back and they'd be sick. Edward was despatched to fetch the Range Rover from home. While he was gone, Annabelle borrowed a set of dominoes from the bar and played with her children. With the boys distracted, she finally reached inside her pocket and read her messages. Several were from work and could easily be ignored, but what caused her heart to race and her hands to sweat was a one-word text from Nautilus.

TEST

Edward rejoined his family but could not miss the look on his wife's face. 'You have to go?' he said, the kids protesting.

'I won't be long. Back by bedtime, promise.'

The text from Nautilus couldn't be ignored. She knew that whatever it signified would need her urgent attention.

~

On the train to London, she pondered what could possibly be waiting for her inside the strongroom at Harrods. She was nervously excited, hoping there was some amazing breakthrough against the fight with Covid that would save millions of people.

The train journey was quick, and within two hours she was in front of Nautilus, deciphering the intel and data that her eight-week-older self had sent her.

It was mind-boggling, the extent of the Russian attacks, the Chinese. The facts that were laid out in front of her were alarming and certainly passed the Protocol test. If Nautilus was to be used, surely it was for something like this: to stop a third world war.

What alarmed her on a personal level was to be told that not only were MI6 aware of Nautilus, but so was her husband, and had been for some time. Clearly an argument that would have happened in two months' time was now going to occur a little earlier. A knot of betrayal and anger was already forming in her stomach, but there was no time for her personal feelings. She had to focus on the mission.

She decided to make her calls from the park, thinking the cold, fresh air would clear her mind.

First, she rang Edward, masking her true feelings as she told him the work was going to take a little longer than expected and that she wanted him to drive up to the London apartment.

'Are you sure that's a good idea, Belle? The kids are settled. Why don't you stay the night in town and come back down in the morning?' said Edward.

'I need your help on a document, so come soon, will you?' said Annabelle, unwilling to have a debate with her husband.

'What document? Can you email it to me?'

'It can wait until you get here. Please, Edward.'

Hearing the urgency in his wife's voice, Edward finally agreed.

The thought of placing the next call made her anxious. She looked at the message one more time and entered the numbers to the personal mobile of the Chief of MI6.

After three rings, the phone was answered.

'Andrew. Annabelle McIntosh-Morris here.'

'Yes, Minister, how can I help you?'

'It's more how I can help you. I have in my possession information which I think you will find incredibly useful regarding the current crisis with the Russian forces amassing on the Ukrainian borders.'

'A little outside of your ministry,' he said, but was ignored by Annabelle.

'I believe that the data I have is of vital importance, to the UK and to NATO.'

'How did you come to acquire this information?'

'It involves some machinery housed in a secure room in Harrods that I believe your department has shown more than a casual interest in for some time. To make sure you fully understand the authenticity of this information and its absolute importance, I offer you a code word: *Apokaluptein*.'

There was silence on the other end of the phone.

'Are you there?' asked Annabelle.

'We should meet,' the Chief said seriously.

'Come to my apartment in Paddington at 7pm. My husband will also be there.'

'I know where it is.'

'Of course you do. Seven sharp, Mr Foster.'

Annabelle ended the call, shaking. She placed the papers in her briefcase and left. Walking back to her apartment through Hyde Park, she thought to herself. Here were all these people, residents, tourists going about their day, oblivious to the fact that within two months they would be at war with some of the mightiest nations in the world. Unless she, Annabelle, stopped it. She quickened her pace.

~

At 6pm, her family arrived safely at their London home.

She sent the boys to play in their room while she and Edward made their dinner.

Edward reached out to kiss his wife, who stepped away.

'What have I done?' Edward said.

'A good question. Let's start with the fact that you have been spying on your wife and her father.'

Edward went pale and quiet. By the look in his eyes, she knew it was the truth. He had failed her.

'Listen carefully to me, Edward. We aren't going to get into this right now, but believe me, we will soon. The machine in my strongroom at

Harrods is called Nautilus and it has the power to supply certain valuable information. I received that information today and in less than one hour Andrew Foster, the Chief of MI6, will arrive here, and I'll explain to the two of you how the machine works and the nature of the information in my possession. Are you following me?'

'Yes, but—'

Annabelle cut him off. 'I don't want to talk to you right now. I don't want to be near you. You have betrayed me in such a way that we may never recover. But what I do need is your skills, so do as you're told and don't talk to me unless I invite you to do so. While I make dinner, you need to draft an immunity document for us both that is airtight, your best work.'

'I need to know what type of information we're talking about.'

'Military information pertaining to Ukraine, Chinese naval intel in the South China Sea, Al Qaeda, NATO defections. Make sure it covers anything regarding my father, our family, the past, and throw in that the agreement itself should be covered by the *Official Secrets Act*. I believe you are familiar with that particular document, having signed it.'

'I'll get it done straightaway,' Edward said, chastened and desperate to regain her trust.

By the time the Chief pressed the buzzer, the children had been fed and were reading in their beds.

Annabelle opened the door and greeted the Chief. Taking his coat, she directed him to join her and her husband at the dining-room table.

'First of all,' Annabelle said, 'I'm aware that MI6 coerced my husband to monitor me and my family regarding the equipment housed in my strongroom at Harrods. I assume that you have scanned the room and have seen that it holds certain communication devices, some of which are modern in nature, such as the mobile phone, and others that date back to World War II.'

The Chief nodded to her, confirming that what she was saying was true.

'In light of this, I will only continue this conversation if you sign these agreements,' she said, placing two copies of the immunity agreement on the table.

'Edward, fetch some whisky while the Chief reads and signs the agreements, would you? I think we would all benefit from a stiff drink.'

The Chief signed the copies, returning one to Edward.

'Thank you, I will continue. I think it best that I remain uninterrupted, if I may?' she said, her voice strong, level and commanding.

'Certainly, Minister, please continue,' said the Chief, eager to find out what she knew.

'Alan Turing was my paternal grandfather. He built all the machines in the room and devised a method to send a message to himself. The main machine, which he named Nautilus, can send that message back in time – eight weeks back, to be precise.'

Edward refreshed the whiskies and Annabelle took a sip.

'That's impossible,' the Chief said, straining to believe a word of what he was hearing.

'Correct – and that is the only natural reaction. It's the reaction I had when I was told by my father, and it was the reaction that he had when visited by Joan Clarke, only at that meeting he also had to deal with finding out that she was his mother and Alan Turing his father. Quite a day for the old man, let me tell you.'

Annabelle swallowed the rest of her whisky in one go.

'I can't offer you definitive proof that what I'm saying is true, as this information has come into my possession from myself, eight weeks in the future. But ask yourself: how do I know about your interrogation of my room, my husband's past transgressions? And, most importantly, how do I know your code word? I can tell you it's because you gave it to me, in eight weeks' time from now.'

'All very intriguing, Minister, but you mentioned on the phone that you had information regarding the Russians?' The Chief was still sceptical, but was intrigued to discover if she had any reliable intel.

'I do.'

Annabelle retrieved her briefcase and pulled out the long message she had deciphered earlier that afternoon.

'This message explains precisely when and where the Russians will attack Ukraine, together with troop strengths and military hardware. The information on the number of T-90 tanks they have in active service I'm sure you will find interesting. It also alludes to a pact between Russia and China. Putin's army will take Ukraine quickly, Hungary will resign from NATO and Russian forces will attack certain neighbours, namely Moldova and Slovakia. If this aggression goes unopposed, China will strike Taiwan and seek further targets in the Pacific. You have coordinates, submarine and naval movements, air strikes. It's all there. This information was prepared by your own department so that I could deliver it to you as I'm now doing, to enable you to prevent World War III. Do you see your style in here, a sort of professional signature to the work?'

Foster took a quick drink, also finishing his single malt at a go, then shook his head. The reality that Annabelle was telling the truth was starting to hit him. 'Incredible. Yet undeniable. It's hard to believe this could happen in the next eight weeks and that we have less than six weeks until the planned invasion. I would like to take this back with me tonight. I also need to see Nautilus. Can we meet at Harrods at 6am tomorrow?'

'I don't think they open so early.'

'They will open for us,' he said confidently.

He collected the documents together. At the door, he turned and said, 'Minister, if this intel is accurate, you have done your country an amazing service.'

Once he'd left, Edward poured two more large whiskies.

'I can't believe what you've just said. Why haven't you told me? How did you keep this secret?' he said.

'I withheld information from you for your protection. What I didn't do was supply details about you and your family to MI6.' Annabelle picked up her whisky glass and went to bed alone.

CHAPTER 63

London, Harrods

January 16th, 2022

Standing in front of the old steel door with the head of MI6, Annabelle nervously tapped in her code, retrieved the blood-testing kit from her handbag, punctured her thumb and squeezed blood onto the slide. She pressed another button and the slide receded into the locking mechanism. Five seconds later, the mechanism turned green and the door opened.

'DNA?' the Chief asked.

'Yes,' replied Annabelle, 'my father's modification.' She moved into the room.

'He always was a clever man, and a great agent.'

'This was his legacy to me, and I just hope that the information I've provided you will help, and live up to his standards.'

Annabelle showed the Chief the equipment, explaining the functions of each piece. She also shared her father's notes regarding 9/11 and, the coup de grâce, documentation and maps from Alan Turing himself relating to the D-Day landings, and what could have been.

At the end of the tour, the Chief spoke. 'In all my years in the intelligence service, I've never encountered anything that can compare to the importance of what you've shown me in this room. Nautilus must be protected at all costs. You and your family have performed an incredible job, keeping it secret for so long, but it's too dangerous to leave it here, in the basement of a department store.' He couldn't hide his desperation to get control of the amazing apparatus.

'We will discuss that when we don't have the fate of the modern world on our shoulders. What I want to know now is do you believe me and are you going to act?'

'I do and I am. I was relatively certain of the authenticity of the intel last night, but now, seeing this, your father's notes, it explains a lot about some suspicions we had about him at the time of the New York attacks. I can see now how brave he was. And you, Minister, he would be so proud of what you have achieved today. I can't guarantee we will totally avert disaster, but I'll get this information into the right hands and let's see if we can't slow Mr Putin down.'

'You must, Andrew. I have broken every rule, a sacred Protocol that I swore I would uphold. If you can prevent this escalation, it will have been worth it. I will reconcile my behaviour with the saving of life. Alan Turing built this machine as a counter to Oppenheimer's atomic bomb. Where one sector of the scientific community resolved to create weapons of ever-increasing power, hoping that mutual destruction would protect the world from their use, Alan created the power to prevent death, to balance destruction with peace.'

'I will do my best, Minister,' said the Chief, turning to leave the room.

CHAPTER 64

London

February, 2022

For the weeks that followed, Annabelle was absorbed with the intelligence briefings that were made to cabinet. The Minister for Defence presented the current situation faced by Ukraine. Annabelle and her fellow ministers sat transfixed by the large screen showing the positions of Putin's troops and military hardware. The Black Sea Fleet was assembled in its Crimean port; Russian armoured battalions in Belarus were primed to attack Kyiv.

Annabelle knew that the invasion could not be stopped. But her intel was being used, and that gave her hope. The data provided to NATO was being attributed to an MI6 agent inside Moscow. Only Annabelle and the Chief knew this to be untrue.

The Ukrainian Army consisted of over 250,000 men and women, and they were waiting for the Russians in strength and at the correct strategic locations to defend their country. The US had given incredible support to the Eastern European nation, with over $10 billion of military aid. President Zelenskyy's army now had access to 5000 Javelin anti-tank missiles, which, when added to their domestic Stuhna-P missile system and 1000 NLAW missiles from the UK, gave them some serious fire-power to deal with Russia's formidable motorised divisions.

In addition to the hardware, the allies supplied reconnaissance intel from NATO-controlled satellites and UAV drones. There were also thousands of volunteers from friendly nations, men and women who did not wear insignia but were highly trained operatives and could handle themselves in a fight.

MI6 sent a copy of all the intel to NATO headquarters, and General Tod Wolters moved troops further east. The US 5th Army relocated from its German barracks to Poland. Two F-35 squadrons landed in the UK, and a further squadron was sent to Estonia, none of which went unnoticed by the Russian high command, or the Chinese.

In East Asia, the US 7th Fleet, encompassing the *Ronald Reagan* aircraft-carrier battlegroup, sailed from Tokyo Bay towards the South China Sea, past Taiwan, contending that they were taking part in planned war games with the island nation. The Chinese were furious to see such firepower protecting Taiwan.

Putin, though, was unperturbed by this show of strength by NATO and its allies. At 6am on the 24th of February, the Russians invaded Ukraine.

It was a three-pronged attack. From the north, crossing the Belarusian border, came Putin's tank divisions. Further locations along the eastern border were bombarded with artillery, then advanced upon by ground forces joining the Russian separatists in the Donbas region. In the south, from their Crimean base and heavily supported by the Russian Navy, ground and amphibious forces moved in on the cities of Mariupol and Kherson, which were also subjected to a barrage of deadly ordnance.

The attacks came from exactly the positions outlined in the intel. The defensive actions from the Ukrainians shocked the Russian attackers. The precision strikes from the Javelins wreaked havoc among the columns of invading tanks.

Within the first two weeks of the war, the Russian military plan was expected to have delivered a mighty blow, and victory. It was true that vast amounts of territory in the east were taken, linked to Crimea. The southern port of Odessa was occupied by Russian forces, and Kyiv, though not taken, was surrounded. But the harsh reality was that the Ukrainian military forces were everywhere they needed to be.

The missile systems around Kyiv had created a fortress. Hundreds of Russian tanks had been destroyed; crucially, over sixty of the superior T-90s had been disabled or captured. In the east, artillery was highly active against the cities, but the Russian infantry advance was slow. Images of tank columns parked miles from the front line were beamed around the world, giving hope and strength to the defenders, causing punishment and recriminations within Putin's military leadership, who had promised him a swift victory.

Despite having nearly 150,000 Russian troops deployed, the invasion wasn't going well, and was certainly not going fast. Russian fighter-bombers sought out the missile batteries, but the Ukrainians kept moving. Even in the air, a determined and motivated Ukrainian air force consisting of only one hundred fighters were keeping the Russian pilots busy, often shooting down twice as many planes as they lost.

Putin resorted to sending cruise missiles from the safety of Russian airspace, causing considerable damage, especially to infrastructure, power stations and the energy network. The Ukrainians, without a protective missile system such as the US Patriot, suffered horrendous damage to their cities and civilian population.

Weeks turned into months, and the Special Military Operation, so named by President Putin, was starting to look decidedly *not* special. His troops were demoralised, economic sanctions were causing hardship in the motherland and his supporters were being attacked by Western government agencies, with billions of dollars of assets seized or confiscated.

The plan concocted by the MI6 team and sent by Annabelle was working, although still she was worried about the Chinese.

The Chinese had retaliated with their own battlegroup in the South China Sea. Taiwan was once again threatened by naval warships breaching territorial waters and multiple incursions from Chinese fighters flying over the island.

But there were no announcements of a pact, Hungary remained in NATO and the Ukrainian war appeared to be in a military stalemate.

The war was by no means over, with the Russians still taking territory, but it was being fought at a much slower pace. The defenders were well equipped and highly motivated, which contrasted greatly with the Russian troops, many of whom were doubting the validity of the invasion.

Annabelle was extremely pleased, and equally so the Chief of MI6, who invited her to join him at his club, at 13 Great Scotland Yard. The sun was shining, so she decided to walk and enjoy the crisp, cold air. She passed several private gardens, their manicured lawns and beautifully tended flowerbeds showing the first signs of spring. Bright-yellow daffodils had burst through the black earth, their petals opening to absorb the sunshine. Annabelle smiled to herself; perhaps it was a sign, she thought.

She had broken the Protocol for the second time in her life; she had not only put Nautilus in grave danger, but also her family. But she had saved life, executed the power of Nautilus for good. On balance, she thought that Alan, Joan and her father would understand, and be happy with her actions.

The Chief was waiting for his guest and escorted her to a private dining room where they would not be overheard.

'I've ordered a bottle of Veuve Clicquot to celebrate,' he said.

He poured two glasses.

'Cheers to Russians stuck in the mud,' said Annabelle, holding her glass aloft.

'Long may they stay there,' he replied.

Over their lunch, Foster conveyed to Annabelle the latest position.

'Although we can't say where this war will end, I think we can say that the position proposed by the messages from Nautilus has changed its course completely. Are you sure you don't want to take some credit? With the state of your party, you could become its next leader, even prime minister.'

'I've spent enough time away from my family. I rather feel I may give up politics altogether – travel a little with my children or go back to research.'

'A great loss to the country, but it does emphasise another reason why I wanted to talk to you. I think it would be in the best interests of the country, and indeed your own family, that Nautilus comes under our control.

'I wouldn't let its capability be known. I would be the only person who would know of its existence, and only when I leave the Service would its presence be known, and then only to my successor. As you can imagine, when this office changes hands we have a few secrets to pass on, that only we hold.

'I was hoping that you would agree to meeting me at Harrods, at your convenience, of course, to allow for the safe transportation of Nautilus to one of our secure facilities. I would also require your help in cataloguing all the notes and procedures for its maintenance and continued use, which of course would only happen in dire need, in situations of national importance such as the one that we find ourselves in today,' he concluded.

Annabelle sipped her champagne. 'I knew this was coming, your – what shall we call it? Request? But I'm afraid I will have to decline,' she said. 'It's not possible to comply with your demand.'

'Why the devil not?' he said, unable to contain his anger.

'When I got all that information back in January, it contained an additional message. It's part of what we call the Turing Protocol.'

'What on earth is that?'

'A code. It establishes how Nautilus is to be used. It may not be used for personal gain, for example. And the guardian must only use Nautilus at a time of global distress, which we have just accomplished. I think it is also fair to say that those who came before me adhered strictly to the code, despite extreme danger and without seeking personal glory.'

The Chief was clearly concerned that he was losing control of the conversation and, more importantly, of his goal: possession of Nautilus. Then he smiled, topping up Annabelle's champagne before replying to her comments.

'We can both agree that during these past two months, we have made quite a formidable team,' he said, 'and, may I say I only have the utmost respect for your intelligence and professionalism. All that I'm proposing is that we relocate Nautilus to a more suitable location. You will remain its guardian, but if you will allow, jointly share the responsibility with me, and of course have access to our extensive resources.'

Annabelle took a sip of her champagne while formulating her response.

'It's a great offer, Andrew, but I need to explain the final rule of the Protocol. The guardian is instructed that if they receive a particular code, they must destroy Nautilus and all the documentation. The code confirms that Nautilus has been compromised or potentially captured by friend or foe.'

'What is this code? Did you receive it?' he said, testy once more.

Annabelle picked up her handbag from the floor. Opening her purse, she retrieved a piece of paper and slid it across the table to her companion, while draining her glass.

Foster unfolded the small note, puzzlement on his face.

'HH? What does this mean, Minister?'

'Heil bloody Hitler,' she replied.

ACKNOWLEDGEMENTS

I would firstly like to thank my agent, Shane Salerno, owner of The Story Factory and reader of my first draft. Despite its rawness, you believed in my novel and helped me to reshape it. You have supported me unshakably, including signing multiple deals and taking my late-night calls on a Sunday. I thank you immensely.

Thank you to my editors at Affirm Press: Cate Blake, Kevin O'Brien and David Golding. David, your copyediting skills were phenomenal.

To Dan Ruffino and Ian Chapman at Simon & Schuster: I am lucky to have such friendship and belief.

To Keiran Rogers at Affirm Press – sales director, fly-fishing coach and friend. Thank you for your continued support and for tying my trout flies.

Thanks also to the lovely authors who have given their time to review my book and said such wonderful things: Don Winslow, Trent Dalton, Fiona McIntosh, Dervla McTiernan, Megan Rogers, TJ Newman, Candice Fox, Christian White and Chris Hammer.

Of course, every writer would struggle immensely without their family's support, but this is felt even more so with a debut. The self-doubt always presents. To Esther, my wife: I took you from your beautiful Spain to the cold and damp of London and the Isle of Man, only for you to fall in love with both. The Australian venture added more distance and time from your family and friends, but you have continued to support me in every way.

To my mum, who raised me to be fiercely independent, and to my four children. Lucas and Holly, you both make me so proud of the adults you have become. And Alejandro and Nico, you have so much life left to explore and I cherish watching you grow into the best versions of yourselves.

Finally, to friendship. It is so important for a happy life. Thank you to all my friends for your continued love, and for turning up to the many parties in Spain, London and Brisbane.

NOTE ON HISTORICAL DETAILS

Although this work is fiction, there is much that is real, and it has been the manipulation of history that has made this book so much fun to write.

Events set in our timeline are mainly true but I have also invented or changed reality to suit my story. The same applies to the characters of this novel. Alan Turing is, of course, very real and is a person who I have the utmost respect for. The way he was treated by society and the authorities was a travesty. His death robbed the world of such genius that it is hard to imagine the advances in technology that would have occurred should he have lived. It is true that his relationship with Joan Clarke was romantic. However, I have used artistic licence with the extent of their intimacy and with major aspects of their lives – and those of other characters – solely for the purposes of entertainment. I very much hope that you enjoy reading it.

I encourage you if you find yourself in London to stroll through the myriad of parks, which are so beautiful and calming. The safety deposit centre at Harrods is real, along with the tunnels. Sadly, the bank no longer exists. The war rooms are a hidden gem for any tourist and, of course, the museum at Bletchley Park.

Spain is special at any time of the year: rich in history and culinary delights and the home of so many friends.

While doing my research for this book, I read from many resources but would like to acknowledge in particular: *Alan Turing: The Enigma* by Andrew Hodges, published by Vintage Books. Also, *Chronicle of War: 1914 to the Present*, written by Tim Hill, and *The Definitive Pictorial Chronicle of World War II*, written by Eric Good, both published by Transatlantic Press. Finally, *The Enigma Story*, written by Dermot Turing, published by Arcturus.